Jessica could j dark gaze on her.

Reluctantly her own gaze lifted to his. All of a sudden a tiny shiver of warning scurried up her spine.

His proprietary gaze continued to move over her greedily, making her body tingle with memories she'd long ago suppressed. He was looking at her the way she remembered him looking at her. Jessica knew what he was thinking. She'd always known.

"You look hungry."

"Starving." His eyes never left her mouth. "But, actually, what I'd really like is to clean up. Where should I...?"

Jessica started. The question brought up a whole new set of problems. Where would he stay? What did he expect from her? Surely he didn't expect to just waltz back in and pick up where they'd left off five years ago.

But if he was really suffering from amnesia, then that was exactly what he *would* expect....

Dear Reader,

Once again, we're proud to bring you a lineup of irresistible books, something we seem to specialize in here at Intimate Moments. Start off your month with award-winning author Kathleen Eagle's newest American Hero title, *Defender*. In Gideon Defender you'll find a hero you'll never forget. This is one of those books that is bound to end up on "keeper" shelves all across the country.

Linda Turner completes her miniseries "The Wild West" with sister Kat's story, a sensuous treat for readers everywhere. Award-winner Dee Holmes once again demonstrates her skill at weaving together suspense and romance in *Watched*, while Amanda Stevens puts a clever twist on the ever-popular amnesia plotline in *Fade to Black*. We have another Spellbound title for you this month, a time-travel romance from Merline Lovelace called *Somewhere in Time*. Finally, welcome new writer Lydia Burke, who debuts with *The Devil and Jessie Webster*.

Coming soon—more great reading from some of the best authors in the business, including Linda Howard, whose long-awaited *Loving Evangeline* will be coming your way in December.

As always—enjoy!

Leslie J. Wainger
Senior Editor and Editorial Coordinator

Please address questions and book requests to:
Silhouette Reader Service
U.S.: 3010 Walden Ave., P.O. Box 1325, Buffalo, NY 14269
Canadian: P.O. Box 609, Fort Erie, Ont. L2A 5X3

FADE
TO BLACK

Amanda
Stevens

INTIMATE™MOMENTS®

Published by Silhouette Books

America's Publisher of Contemporary Romance

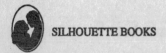 SILHOUETTE BOOKS

ISBN 0-373-07592-8

FADE TO BLACK

Copyright © 1994 by Marilyn Medlock Amann

Books by Amanda Stevens

Silhouette Intimate Moments

Killing Moon #159
The Dreaming #199
Obsessed! #488
Fade to Black #592

Silhouette Shadows

The Seventh Night #14
The Perfect Kiss #24

Silhouette Desire

Love Is a Stranger #647
Angels Don't Cry #758

AMANDA STEVENS

knew at an early age that she wanted to be a writer and began her first novel at the age of thirteen. With the encouragement of one of her English instructors at a local college, Amanda wrote and sold her first romance—to Silhouette Intimate Moments—in 1985. She lives in Houston, Texas, with her husband, Steven, and their twins, Lucas and Leanne.

Prologue

"And if it's a boy, I think we should name him Max."

"You know I hate that name," Jessica Kincaid complained as she pressed down a loose corner of the circus-motif wallpaper in the newly redecorated nursery. "Besides, what makes you so sure it's a boy?"

"Well, Maxine then," Pierce teased her, stretching to paste the last of the glittering stars to the ceiling. Suddenly the ladder he stood on teetered, and Pierce grabbed for a handhold. His arms flailed wide as the ladder toppled and crashed to the floor. Jessica cried out in alarm, but as usual Pierce landed on his feet.

Jessica's hand went to her heart. "Are you all right?"

"Right as rain, sweetheart." Pierce bent to drop a light kiss on the top of her head. "Don't you know by now I have nine lives?"

"By my count, you're getting dangerously close to the last one," Jessica remarked dryly, referring to her husband's penchant for adventure and excitement. Whether it was snow skiing or parasailing, driving a car or riding a motorcycle, nothing ever seemed quite fast enough for Pierce Kincaid. He seemed to relish living on the edge, and he often left Jessica breathless in more ways than one.

Why he had ever been attracted to someone as shy and hopelessly introverted as she, Jessica still couldn't understand, but their marriage had already survived two wonderful years. Not only survived, but flourished. And now with the baby on the way, everything in her life seemed like a dream come true. A dream she prayed would never end.

She reached up and caressed Pierce's cheek with her fingertips. "I wouldn't be able to bear it if anything ever happened to you. You're my whole life, Pierce. I love you so much."

He touched the teardrop on her cheek in wonder. "What's this?" he asked gently. "Why the tears?"

"Hormones," she whispered, but it was more than that. Sometimes when Jessica looked at Pierce, she still couldn't believe how happy they were. Sometimes in the dead of night, with Pierce sleeping peacefully beside her, she would wake up, certain that something would happen to take it all away from her. Just like it had when she was a little girl.

Sensing her need, Pierce took her in his arms. "I'll always be here, Jesse. For you and the baby. We're a real family now. Nothing can change that."

He kissed her again, then turned and, in typical fashion, quickly changed the mood and the subject. But he kept one arm protectively around her shoulders. "I think a celebration is definitely in order here. We've finally remodeled one room in this monstrosity we optimistically call a house, business is picking up at the shop, and Max here will be making his debut in another couple of months. So what do you say, my love? Dinner and dancing tonight? A movie? Or shall we turn in early and celebrate in bed? And I might add that I'm particularly fond of the third choice." His dark eyes teased her as his head lowered to kiss her again, but the phone in the hallway rang, interrupting them. He nuzzled her neck. "Hold that thought," he murmured, then turned and left the room.

Moments later when he came back, his smile was missing. The glint in his eyes had disappeared. It wasn't the first time Jessica had noticed his troubled look, but he would never let on to her that anything was wrong. In spite of what he'd said earlier, she couldn't help wondering if he might be having problems with the business.

"Pierce, is something wrong?" she asked anxiously, touching his arm.

His expression instantly altered as he smiled down at her. "Everything's fine. Now, where were we?" He reached for her, pulling her into his arms and holding her close, as if he could somehow protect her from the outside world. Or, from whatever might be troubling him. "Have you decided what you're in the mood for tonight?"

"Actually..." Jessica trailed off, trying to shake the dark premonition stealing over her. Her own expression turned coy as she skimmed one finger down the front of his shirt. "I have this irresistible urge for..."

Pierce's voice deepened. "For what? For once, tell me exactly what you want, Jesse."

"I want...some ice cream," she admitted. "I'm dying for butter pecan ice cream."

He groaned. "That's all?"

"Well . . . for starters."

"In that case, I'd better get to the store." He paused at the door and looked back, lifting his brows suggestively. "Need anything else? Whipped cream? Jell-O?"

"I'm seven months pregnant, Pierce," Jessica reminded him, but the look he gave her had her heart racing just the same.

"And sexier than ever," he added with a wink. "I'll be back in a flash."

By Jessica's calculations, it should have taken Pierce no more than ten minutes to walk to the store, no more than ten minutes inside, no more than ten minutes to get back home.

When he'd been gone an hour, she started to worry.

When he'd been gone two hours, she drove to the store and looked for him, but no one remembered seeing him.

When he'd been gone three hours, she called her brother, Jay Greene, who was a naval officer at the Pentagon in nearby Washington, D.C.

When Pierce had been gone four hours, she called the area hospitals while Jay searched the streets.

At midnight, when he'd been gone ten hours, Jessica sat in the darkened nursery, hugging a teddy bear to her chest as she rocked back and forth, her dry eyes burning with grief. A star had fallen from the ceiling and lay shimmering on the floor near her feet.

It seemed like an omen to Jessica, that fallen star. Like a symbol of all her lost dreams, her hopeless prayers, her unshed tears.

Because Pierce Kincaid, her beloved husband, had vanished in broad daylight without a trace.

Chapter 1

Five years later...

Where in the world was he?

Jessica glanced at her watch for the umpteenth time as she gave the chocolate batter the requisite fifty stirs. Sundays were the only full days she had to spend with her son, and she'd promised him this morning they'd make brownies together. She'd been out of eggs, though, so she'd sent Max next door to borrow one from her best friend, Sharon McReynolds.

"That was your first mistake," she muttered. Sharon's daughter, Allie, had just acquired a new kitten, a white fluff ball named Snowflake, that attracted five-year-old Max like metal to a magnet.

Jessica grimaced, envisioning the conversation that would ensue with her son as soon as he returned. "Allie's not even as old as I am, Mom, and she has a pet. Why can't I have one?"

Jessica knew the routine by heart because they'd been through it every afternoon for the past four days, ever since Sharon had taken Allie to the animal shelter to pick out a kitten. Explaining to Max that Allie's mom didn't work outside the home and, therefore, had more time than Jessica did to help take care of a pet did no good.

She knew Max already felt cheated because he had to go to the baby-sitter's after morning kindergarten while Allie got to go home and spend the afternoon with her mom. Jessica knew Max thought it also unfair that Allie had a daddy to take her to the zoo on Saturday mornings and work on special projects with her on Sunday afternoons.

Allie had a real family, with a mother *and* a father. Max didn't.

Jessica suspected her son's penchant for superheroes was his own way of trying to make up for the lack of a male role model in his life. Superman and all the other comic-book characters that Max loved and tried to emulate were substitutes for the father he'd never had.

Sometimes Max pretended that his own father was a superhero, off fighting bad guys. That's why he couldn't be here with them now. In spite of the fact that Jessica had told Max his father was dead, she knew that deep down, her son had never really believed it.

Sighing deeply, Jessica wiped a stray lock of hair from her forehead with the back of her hand as she stared out the window, trying to catch a glimpse of Max's red cape as he came through the hedge. Wiping her hands on a dish towel, she reached for the phone just as she heard the screen door on the back porch slam shut. Without turning, Jessica picked up the spoon and began stirring the brownie mix again.

"What took you so long, sweetie?" she asked over her shoulder, trying to hide her impatience. She knew full well what Max's explanation would be.

"You'll never believe what happened."

The deep, masculine voice that responded shocked Jessica to the core. A chill shot up her spine. She whirled to see a tall, dark stranger emptying a bag of groceries into her freezer.

Scream! she commanded. But to Jessica's horror, not a sound escaped her throat.

Run! she ordered, but her feet remained rooted to the floor.

The man stood with his back to her, but even in her terror, Jessica saw that he was tall and lean with dark, unkempt hair. The blue jeans he wore looked old and threadbare, and the cotton shirt was shredded at the hem, as if it had been caught on something sharp.

"It was the weirdest thing, Jesse." He closed the freezer door and opened the refrigerator. "Have you ever arrived somewhere without knowing how you got there? I mean, I left the house, and the next thing I know I'm in front of the ice-cream freezer at Crandall's, and I have no idea how I got there." He chuckled softly as he shook his head. "Anyway, once I finally found the ice cream, I remembered we were out of milk, and then I saw the grapes, and one thing led to another. I forgot the whipped cream, though."

He folded the sack and turned, smiling.

Jessica's knees threatened to buckle. "Dear God." Her hand flew to her mouth. It couldn't be! It couldn't be possible! She clutched the counter for support as she stared at the man, at the darkly handsome face that seemed so familiar and yet so strange.

The brown eyes stared back at her in confusion. "What the devil's the matter with you? You look like you've just seen a ghost."

"You *are* a ghost," Jessica whispered in horror. "You must be."

He started toward her, but she shrank away, her hands still frantically gripping the edge of the counter. "Don't touch me," she pleaded. Then he seemed to look at her, really look at her, for the first time, and he stopped dead in his tracks, as if he'd just been struck by lightning.

For one breathless moment, they eyed each other in utter disbelief.

"Jesse?" His voice was a hushed question. The confusion in his eyes deepened to horror as he continued to stare at her. His gaze roamed over her long black hair, scrutinized her face, studied her slender figure. Then lingered on her flat stomach. "What...what's going on here? Your hair...your face...dear God, the baby...." His voice trailed off as he scrubbed his eyes with his hands. "I must be dreaming," he muttered.

Jessica cowered away from the apparition before her, denied the vision that stood not four feet away. It couldn't be him. It wasn't possible. Not after five years. *Five years!*

She'd long ago resigned herself to the possibility that her husband had met some tragic death because the other alternative—that Pierce had simply tired of their life together and walked away—would have been, in many ways, harder for her to accept. She'd had so many losses in her life. So many abandonments.

But if Pierce had died all those years ago, there was absolutely no explanation for the specter that stood before her now. No *earthly* explanation.

Jessica had the slightly hysterical notion that if she reached out and touched him, her hand would pass right through him. A shiver crawled up her spine as the hair on the back of her neck stood on end. Almost reluctantly she let her gaze move over him.

Whether ghost or man, something about him was different, she realized. He looked older and leaner and...hurt. There were lines on his face she didn't remember, but the scars were the worst. Pierce's face had been so handsome, so perfect. This man was a dark, frightening stranger.

That's it! she thought suddenly. This man *was* a stranger. A stranger who was a dead ringer for Pierce. A new wave of fear washed over her as she stared at him. She began edging toward the door.

"Who are you?" she demanded, but her voice trembled with terror.

He looked at her incredulously. "For God's sake, stop it. You're scaring the hell out of me, Jesse. Is this some kind of sick joke? How can you look so different?" He paused, letting his gaze roam over her again as his eyes clouded in confusion. "My God, I hardly recognize you, but how can that be? How the hell can that be? I've only been gone half an hour."

Jessica could feel the color draining from her face. "Half an hour? My husband has been missing for five years," she whispered.

"Five years?" He gaped at her in horror. "What are you talking about?"

Jessica put trembling hands to her face. "Who *are* you?"

"You know who I am."

"Please tell me your name," she begged. "I have to hear you say it."

Slowly he crossed the tile floor toward her. The knees of his jeans were ripped and his ragged tennis shoes were muddy. A long, jagged scar creased his right forearm, drawing Jessica's gaze for a second longer before she lifted her eyes to his.

The brown eyes were shuttered now, completely unreadable. She didn't know him. He was a complete stranger to her.

He said slowly, "My name is Pierce Kincaid. Now kindly tell me who the hell you are. And where is my wife?"

A stunned hush fell over the room.

It was the kind of silence that always follows some mind-boggling revelation. But why that should be, Pierce couldn't imagine. Why his appearance in his own home should shock anyone was beyond him, but he had the oddest feeling that he'd walked into the last few minutes of a movie, and though the climax was exciting, he had no idea what the hell was going on.

The woman standing before him—face ashen, eyes wide with shock—looked like Jesse, except...different. Her hair was the color of Jesse's, but instead of the short bob of curls with which he was so familiar, it cascaded down the woman's back in gleaming, luscious waves. The wide silver eyes, fringed with thick black lashes, were colder and harder than his wife's. And where Jesse's figure was thin, almost frail-looking, this woman's body was gently rounded with womanly curves.

Pierce felt something stir within him, and he frowned in disgust. He hadn't so much as looked at another woman since he and Jesse were married, and yet this stranger elicited a response from him that seemed disturbingly familiar.

Who was she? A relative? That would explain the overwhelming resemblance. He'd never met any of Jesse's family except for her brother. She rarely talked about her, but Pierce knew Jesse had a sister somewhere. Maybe the woman had simply shown up at their doorstep while he'd been out.

He tried to temper his own shock with a tentative smile. "Are you Jesse's sister?" he asked as he took another step toward her. The woman flinched away, but the coldness in her eyes warmed for a moment with a flash of anger. Doggedly he held out his hand to her. "I'm Jessica's husband."

He watched the last shred of fear fade away from her eyes as a sort of horrified realization dawned in those magnetic gray depths. With an almost visible struggle for control, she pulled herself up straight. She faced him squarely, her eyes dropping to his outstretched hand, then returning to meet his gaze. "Why, you arrogant son of a bitch. What kind of fool do you think I am?"

Her hand swept upward so quickly it seemed to surprise them both. It connected with his cheek, and the stinging sensation triggered an automatic reaction from Pierce. He grabbed her, shoved her up against the edge of the counter and pinned her arms behind her back with one hand while his other hand fastened around her throat.

For one heart-pounding moment, brown eyes stared into gray.

Her face swam before his eyes, a hazy image from a dark dream. Pierce was no stranger to fear. He knew what it looked like, what it smelled like, what it felt like. He could see fear in her eyes again. Could feel her flesh tremble beneath his fingers. For one brief moment, it gave him an almost perverse sense of gratification to be the one to inflict it.

Then the mists cleared, and the face before him was once again a sweet, lovely, familiar face—a face far removed from the blackness, from the explosion of pain behind his eyes. As abruptly as he'd seized her, Pierce released her. He backed away, shocked and sickened by his own reaction.

"My God—" His hands moved to his eyes, as if he could rub away the searing pain in his head. *Black it out,* he mentally instructed himself. *Fade to black.*

The pain subsided, but his stomach still roiled in sickening waves. What the hell was the matter with him? He could easily have hurt her, and he didn't even understand why. He was beginning to think he didn't understand anything. The whole scene seemed so disjointed, like a nightmare fragmented into bits and pieces he couldn't seem to fit together in any way that made sense.

"I don't know why I did that," he mumbled.

She didn't say a word, just stood there looking at him like an animal trapped in a corner. He wished she'd say something, do something to help him understand, to help him put the puzzle together. "Can you . . . just tell me your name?" he asked with a desperate edge to his voice.

Her fingers were at her throat, massaging the vicious red mark left by his hand. She moistened her lips with the tip of her tongue, "I think you already know," she said, as the quiver in her voice shook Pierce anew. He felt his muscles tighten with awareness, with anticipation, as if preparing for a situation fraught with danger.

Their gazes clung for one electric moment, and then she whispered into the silence, "I'm Jesse."

Jessica thought for a moment he would collapse. He staggered backward, supporting himself against the counter much as she'd done earlier. Her own knees were shaking so badly she could hardly stand. The sound of her heartbeat seemed to echo through the silence.

Pierce had come back. Somehow, some way, her husband had found his way back to her. But why had he left? Where had he been? And, dear God, why was he here now after all this time? The questions exploded in her head, mirroring the confusion and shock in Pierce's brown eyes.

She closed her eyes, trying to shut him out, but the man standing before her drew her gaze against her will. He looked at once so dear and familiar, and yet so strange and frightening. His once handsome face was haggard and deeply lined. His body, once powerful and athletic, had thinned to gauntness. A narrow white scar sliced the left side of his face, marring what had once been a perfect jawline.

She reached a trembling hand up to touch it. "What happened to you?" she whispered. "Where in God's name have you been?"

He recoiled from her touch, and Jessica instantly drew her hand back, nursing it against her heart as if to hide the bitterness of his rejection. His brown eyes were bleak, distant now. The eyes of a stranger.

"I don't know," he said numbly.

"You don't know what happened to you?" She knew her voice sounded disbelieving, but Jessica couldn't help it. The whole situation was unbelievable. Incredible, but terrifyingly real. "You don't know where you've been for five years? Were you in an accident? Is that how you got those scars?"

Pierce put an unsteady hand to his temple. "I have no idea what you're talking about," he said.

"Are you saying . . . you don't remember *anything?*"

He shook his head. "I don't know. I remember leaving here to go get ice cream. The next thing I know, I'm standing in front of the freezer in the store. I get the ice cream, I walk back here, and in the space of half an hour, everything has changed. It's like . . . a nightmare. Am I going crazy, Jesse?"

At that moment, Jessica wasn't completely sure of her own sanity. Her heart was beating against her chest so quickly and so hard that for a second she thought she might actually pass out. She took a deep breath, trying to calm herself. "You walked out that door five years ago," she said shakily, "and until you walked back in a few minutes ago, I hadn't seen or heard from you in all that time. I thought you were dead."

If he noticed the faint note of betrayal in her voice, he chose to ignore it, concentrating instead on her words. "*Five years?* That's impossible!"

"Look at me," she said desperately. "You said yourself I look different. I *am* different. I'm five years older."

His proprietary gaze raked over her, stirring something in Jessica she thought had long since died. She struggled to keep her expression calm, composed, but her mind reeled in confusion. The dark gaze probed her face, making her only too aware of the changes five years had wrought in her appearance.

"If what you say is true, then that must mean—" he trailed off as his gaze dropped to her flat stomach once again "—that must mean . . . you've had the baby."

In the last few minutes, Jessica's emotions had run the gamut—terror, shock, disbelief, anger and maybe even a glimmer of joy. But the emotion she felt now overwhelmed all the others. The fierce protectiveness for her child settled around her like an impenetrable shield.

Max was *hers*. She'd given birth to him all alone. She'd raised him single-handedly. She'd made the sacrifices, she'd worked the endless hours to provide for a child she loved more than life itself. No one would take that away from her. Max was the one thing in her life she had ever been able to count on.

She opened her mouth—to say what, she was never quite sure—but suddenly the back door slammed, and both of them jumped. In unison, Jessica and Pierce whirled toward the kitchen doorway where five-year-old Max, clad in jeans, a T-shirt and a shiny red Superman cape, stood staring up at them.

The dark hair, the huge brown eyes, the stubborn set of his jaw and chin—all were identical to the stranger who stared back at him.

The very air quivered with emotion. Max's solemn little eyes took the stranger's measure and seemed to find him lacking. His gaze shifted to Jessica then back to Pierce. He squinted his eyes. "Who are you, mister?" he demanded suspiciously.

Jessica's own gaze was locked on Pierce's white face. She could see a muscle throb in his cheek, saw emotion after emotion sweep across his features. There was no mistaking Max's identity. He looked exactly like his father. Pierce took a tentative step toward him.

The slight movement roused Jessica. She made an involuntary sound of protest which drew both pairs of male eyes. She knelt and opened her arms, and Max flew across the room to her. She hugged him tightly against her as both of them stared up at Pierce.

"My God," he said woodenly as he gazed at mother and son across the room, "I don't even know if I'm dead or alive."

He didn't wait for a response but turned and walked through the swinging door of the kitchen. Jessica wanted to go after him but found that her heart was suddenly pulling her in two different directions as Max's little arms caught around her neck and held on for dear life.

"That man's scary, Mom," he whispered, clinging to her. "Is he going to hurt us?"

"No, darling, he won't hurt us," Jessica soothed, hugging him. But even as she gave voice to her denial, she could feel the tender flesh of her neck where Pierce's hand—a real, flesh-and-blood hand—had pressed.

A warning pounded in her brain. *He's a stranger,* she thought. The man somewhere in her house was not the Pierce she had known and loved. Wherever he had been, whatever he'd gone through in the past five years had changed him. She only had to look into those haunted eyes to know that.

Maybe she'd never known him, she thought with a jolt. She'd shared her life with him, shared his bed, but had she ever really known him?

She thought now, as she'd done for those five years, of all the times he'd been away during their marriage. So many of the trips had been unexpected it seemed now in retrospect. Sometimes when he'd been gone, she hadn't heard from him for days at a time, but the answer to that had seemed very plausible. Many of the remote areas he traveled to in Europe and Asia, looking for treasures for The Lost Attic, his antique shop, didn't have easily accessible telephones. In fact, Jessica had been to some of those off-the-beaten-track places with him.

Back then, it had never occurred to her to question Pierce's absences, the lack of phone calls. She'd simply accepted it. But maybe she should have questioned Pierce. Maybe she wouldn't have gone through the hell she'd gone through the past five years if she'd taken the time to know Pierce Kincaid a little better.

She'd believed what she'd wanted to believe, she realized now, because she'd wanted a home and family so badly. Someone to love her.

Jessica untangled Max's arms from her neck and stood. "Come on, honey. Let's go back over to Sharon's house. You'd like to play with Allie and Snowflake for a little while longer, wouldn't you?"

Max stared up at her with rounded brown eyes. "Are you coming back here?"

"Yes."

"To talk to him?"

"Yes."

Max clung to her hand. "I want to stay with you, Mom. I don't think I like him. I don't want him to hurt you."

She bent and smoothed the dark hair from his forehead. "You don't have to worry about me, Max. I'll be fine. Now, come on. I'll walk you over."

As she and Max stepped outside, Jessica thought how normal everything looked, how perfectly ordinary a spring morning it was. The blue morning glory blossoms that climbed the trellis walls of the summerhouse were opened wide to the early sun. A mild breeze rippled through the trees, stirring the scent of roses and mimosa, and somewhere down the street a lawn mower droned.

Everything was the same, and yet nothing was. Five years ago, when Pierce disappeared, Jessica had thought her life was over. For the first few months, all she'd hoped and prayed for was that he would one day come back to her. As long as no trace of him was found, she couldn't let go of the hope that he was still alive.

But the first time she'd held her tiny son in her arms, the realization had finally hit her. Pierce wasn't coming back. She'd counted on him for everything, depended on him to take care of her, but he was gone. Suddenly she had no one to rely on but herself.

Max had given her life new purpose. Not only had she been both mother and father to her son, but she'd taken over Pierce's antique business, learned everything about it there was to learn, and it had continued to grow into a thriving concern.

She'd accomplished a lot in the past five years, but those accomplishments had demanded restitution. She'd changed, so much so that sometimes when she stared at her reflection in the mirror, she hardly recognized herself. There wasn't a trace of the old, dependent Jesse. She didn't need anyone anymore. Certainly not a man who had walked out on her five years ago. For whatever reason.

Her hand tightened on Max's. She felt his fingers squeeze hers back in response, and Jessica's heart melted with love. She would do anything, anything to protect her little boy.

Together they slipped through the opening in the thick hedge that divided the two properties. Sharon sat on the back porch steps, watching Allie and Snowflake romp in the shady grass beneath an elm tree.

"I knew you couldn't keep Max away," Sharon called gaily. "Might as well come have a cup of coffee while the two of them torment poor Snowflake up a tree."

"Max, come watch!" Allie squealed as she enticed the kitten with a ball of twine. Her squeaky laughter peeled across the yard, an irresistible invitation, but still Max hung back, hugging his mother's leg.

"Go play, Max," Jessica urged.

He looked up at her. "I want to stay with you," he insisted.

Sharon reached over and ruffled his hair. "What's the matter, Superman? How come so shy all of a sudden?"

"There's a strange man at our house," Max announced solemnly, as if that explained everything.

Sharon's cornflower eyes widened as she lifted her gaze to Jessica's. One brow lifted. "How interesting."

Jessica could see the curiosity in her friend's eyes, but didn't bother to explain. How could she, when she didn't understand it herself? "Can Max stay over here for a little while, Sharon? It's really important."

"Well, of course. You know he's always welcome." She turned to Max and grinned. "Allie's been trying to teach Snowflake a new trick. I think she could use a few pointers from Superman."

That did it. Sharon knew exactly how to appeal to Max's male pride. He took off toward Allie and the kitten, his red cape billowing in the wind.

Sharon returned her curious gaze to Jessica. "You want to tell me what's going on?"

Jessica sighed. "I'm not even sure *I* know. I just need some time to deal with . . . a problem."

Sharon shrugged. "You know where to find me if you need me," she said, and Jessica knew her friend wouldn't pry any further. Sharon had learned a long time ago that Jessica wouldn't talk about anything until she was ready.

Jessica turned back toward her house, stopping for a moment to take one last look at her son. Sharon had joined the kids, and all three of them were shrieking with laughter as the kitten rolled and tumbled and became hopelessly entangled with string.

As Jessica stood watching them, she had to fight the overwhelming urge to join them, to try to return her world to the nice, sane place it had been that morning when she'd gotten out of bed. But there in her friend's backyard, with the sound of children's laughter filling the air and the scent of spring flowers drifting on the breeze, the realization hit her full force.

Her world would never be the same again.

"Pierce?" Jessica called tentatively, feeling the strangeness of the name on her tongue. She felt a ripple of anxiety in the pit of her stomach, as if saying his name provided irrefutable proof that the stranger in her house was indeed her dead husband.

Jessica shoved open the swinging door to the dining room and stepped through, then went on into the living room. The room had been completely renovated nearly three years ago. The dark paneling Jessica had always hated had been replaced by Sheetrock painted a cool robin's-egg blue and decorated with Allenburg watercolors she'd acquired through the shop.

Light from the French doors gleamed on the hardwood floors and highlighted the thick Aubusson rug she'd splurged on just last month. A grouping of chintz-covered sofas and oversize chairs flanked the brick fireplace, and the carved oak mantel held dozens of photos of Max, all lovingly displayed in antique pewter frames.

The pictures looked rearranged, Jessica thought, as if someone had picked them up one by one and hadn't bothered returning them to their original positions. Her eyes moved to the curved staircase, upward to the sunny landing and beyond. Her bedroom was at the top of the stairs, a huge suite which took up most of the second floor except for Max's bedroom. The third floor contained only a converted attic, which Jessica was in the process of turning into a game room.

The hair at the back of her neck prickled with unease. Somewhere in this house a stranger roamed, looking at her things, touching them, laying claim to them.

When Pierce had left, the only room that had been remodeled in the fifty-plus-year-old Georgian-style house had been the nursery. That same room had long since been transformed to accommodate a growing boy's tastes and interests. Was Pierce in there now?

The thought unsettled Jessica more than she cared to admit. Her eyes lit on the phone, and suddenly she wondered if she should call the police, her brother, *someone* to help her deal with this situation.

She closed her eyes and rested her head against the wall. No one could help her. No one could even comprehend what she was feeling at this moment. Even she didn't understand. Because in spite of her fear, in spite of her questions and her doubts, one small part of her heart still rejoiced.

Pierce was alive!

The miracle she'd prayed for for so long had finally happened. She should be down on her knees giving thanks, except for one small detail. Jessica had given up believing in miracles a long time ago. Resolutely she opened her eyes and started toward the stairs, halting when she noticed the powder-room door off the foyer stood open.

"Pierce?" There was no answer, but still she crossed the hardwood floor and entered the small washroom, assuring herself that everything was intact. And then her eyes fastened on the mirror, saw her reflection, and she knew. Pierce wasn't in there, but he had been. He'd gazed into that same mirror, saw his reflection, and he'd learned the awful truth about himself.

Jessica backed out of the bathroom, frantic now to find him.

"Pierce!" She called his name as she stood in the hallway. Colored light filtered through the leaded diamond panes in the front door and spilled onto the polished planks of the floor. The wavering, jewellike shadows drew Jessica's gaze downward, then toward the source. The front door was closed, but the dead bolt had been drawn back, and now it was Jessica who had to face the truth.

Pierce Kincaid had walked out on her one more time.

Chapter 2

A little while later, Jessica sat on the window seat in the dining room and watched the street for her brother's car. How long had it been since she'd cried? she wondered. Not since Max had been born. Not since she'd decided that never again would she depend on anyone but herself. Not since she'd vowed that she would never love again because everyone she'd ever loved had left her.

Except Max.

She drew up her knees and wrapped her arms around them, hugging them close. It was an instinctive response to her pain and confusion. For the first few days in every foster home she'd ever been assigned to, Jessica had similarly retreated into herself, had hugged herself tightly as though recalling the feel of her mother's arms around her. Finally, though, after so many homes she'd lost count, she could no longer remember her mother's face, much less the warmth of her arms.

The orphanage had been better because at least there she'd had Jay. The two of them had clung to each other those first few months after their older sister, Janet, had left them there. Their mother had died, their father had disappeared, and eighteen-year-old Janet hadn't wanted to be saddled with two kids, so one cold December morning, she'd dropped Jessica and Jay at the state-run orphanage in Richmond.

After a year, twelve-year-old Jay had gotten lucky. He'd been adopted by an aging couple in Washington, D.C., who had always wanted a son and realized they were too old to begin raising an infant.

Jessica hadn't been so fortunate. She'd been plain and skinny with unruly hair and eyes far too big and too sad for her ten-year-old face. She'd been shy and sickly and had never developed much of a personality. No one had wanted such an unattractive child.

After Jay left, Jessica had been sent to one foster home after another. She'd bonded fairly well with the first couple, but when the man's job had forced them to move out of state, Jessica had been emotionally ripped apart again. After that, she kept herself aloof, sustaining herself on sparse letters from her brother and on the even sparser memories of her mother.

And then, years later, she'd met Pierce. It was the summer she'd graduated business school and moved to Edgewood, a suburb of D.C., to be close to Jay. Jessica had always sworn it was fate that caused her to answer the ad Jay showed her in a neighborhood newspaper about a book-keeping position at an antique store not far from her new address. Fate, and perhaps a touch of desperation. She didn't expect the job to pay much, but she'd been making the rounds at employment agencies for weeks with no luck.

Pierce Kincaid, the proprietor of The Lost Attic, had taken one look at her frail body, her faded blue dress, her scuffed shoes, and hired her on the spot.

Pity, she'd accused him later.

Love at first sight, he'd countered.

Jessica still remembered the exact moment when she first laid eyes on him. His assistant was about to turn her away when Pierce walked out of his office and changed her life with one heart-stealing smile.

"I'm Pierce Kincaid," he said, dismissing the assistant with a curt nod of his head. "Welcome to The Lost Attic. What can I do for you?"

Jessica's first thought was that he was the most handsome man she'd ever seen. He had longish dark hair that curled at the nape, and dark, penetrating eyes fringed with thick lashes. He was casually dressed in jeans, a white T-shirt and a gray sport coat, and as he leaned against the counter, he gave her another smile, one that managed to look both mysterious and openly inviting.

"I—I've come about the job," Jessica stammered, her poise completely shattered by his attention.

"Wonderful. How soon would you be able to start?"

His enthusiasm caught her off guard. "Now. Immediately."

"As in today?"

"*Today?* But I—"

"You said immediately," he reminded her, a subtle gleam in his eyes. "I'm rarely here, you see, and I need someone I can depend on to handle things while I'm away. My previous bookkeeper up and quit without notice. Financial statements are due, tax payments are late, the bank is screaming about overdrafts, and I'm due in Copenhagen tomorrow morning. Frankly, I'm desperate. So can you start today, Ms.... ?"

"Greene. Jessica Greene. And yes I can," she added quickly, before he could change his mind.

He grinned. "Great. Let me show you your office then."

"But don't you even want to see my résumé?" She'd worked so hard on it, had even splurged on a rental typewriter.

He shook his head. "I know a good thing when I see it."

Nonplussed, Jessica gazed around the shop, admiring the treasures. "You have a wonderful store," she murmured.

"Do you know anything about antiques?"

"No. But I know a lot about bookkeeping."

He smiled, and Jessica felt a tingle all the way to her toes. "That's fine. I tell you what, Jessica. You teach me enough bookkeeping so that I know my way around a ledger, and I'll teach you everything I know about antiques. And then some. How does that sound?"

It sounded wonderful. Too good to be true, in fact. Within days, Jessica had settled into the routine of her new job. When she'd been working for Pierce for three months, true to his word, he began teaching her about antiques.

"This is a Lowell," he'd say as he showed her an exquisite glass sculpture. "See the marking on the bottom? Lowells aren't as famous as Steubens, of course, but the designs are original and highly detailed. Andrew Lowell died so young, there aren't many of his pieces around and most of the ones that are documented are in private collections. But I found this in a little shop on the outskirts of Paris. The owner didn't realize what he had."

Jessica was like a sponge. She drank in every word Pierce uttered, exclaimed over the beauty of each and every piece he brought back from his treasure hunts. She loved being surrounded by beautiful things with fascinating histories, possibly because her own past was so dismal. She adored having Pierce spend hours talking to her, devoting his time solely to her. She'd never had so much attention before.

When she'd been working for him for six months, he gave her a raise and added responsibilities. He began leaving her in charge when he went on his regular jaunts overseas. When he returned, he'd tell her intriguing stories about the places he'd been to and the people he'd met as they pored over his findings.

"Pop quiz today, Jessica. Tell me how we can be certain this is an authentic Allenburg watercolor?" he would ask, a teasing glint in his dark eyes as he and Jessica unwrapped the paintings.

With a magnifying glass, Jessica would locate the tiny hidden water lily which identified the artist's work, and Pierce would smile his approval. "Excellent. Perhaps you deserve a reward," he would say, with that mysterious, sexy smile that always sent her heart racing. And then he'd take her out to lunch at some little out-of-the-way place, which would have both excellent service and scrumptious food. And for the rest of the day, Jessica would feel special and pampered.

When she'd been with Pierce a year, he began taking her on buying trips with him occasionally. Slowly but surely, under Pierce's expert tutelage, Jessica began to blossom, to come out of her self-imposed exile. And slowly but surely she was falling madly, passionately, desperately in love with her boss.

When she'd been with Pierce fifteen months, he asked her to marry him. They were in Paris, and at first Jessica convinced herself that the romantic ambiance of the city of light, the effusive flow of champagne at the Cochon d'or had made Pierce impulsive.

"If I were impulsive," he explained, staring at her over the flickering candle on their discreetly located table, "I would have proposed to you the first time I laid eyes on you. Because I knew even then that you and I were meant to be, Jesse. You knew it, too, didn't you?"

"Yes," she whispered. "I knew it."

"Then say you'll marry me," he demanded, his eyes glowing with triumph.

"I'll marry you," she said, and then he lifted her hand and slipped a beautiful antique diamond and garnet ring onto her finger.

"You won't regret it. I'll make you so happy you'll forget all about the past."

"I already have," she vowed.

Weeks later, they were married and settled into their home in a lovely neighborhood only a few miles from the shop. Edgewood, located a few miles from Langley, Virginia, and across the river from Washington, D.C., was home to a lot of government and military employees. Though not as pricey as Georgetown or Alexandria, it still boasted many of the same attractions: tree-shaded sidewalks, cobblestone streets, elegant old Federal and Georgian homes, as well as a close proximity to the nation's capital.

Jessica loved her job at the shop, but she gladly gave it up to concentrate on remodeling and redecorating their home. She had no higher aspiration than to be the perfect wife and mother. She loved Pierce dearly, needed him desperately.

How could she have known back then that the one person she held most dear, loved more than life itself, would eventually leave her just like all the others had?

Jessica rested her forehead against her knees as she closed her eyes, trying to push away the memories. Why? she asked herself over and over.

Why had Pierce left her?

And why had he come back?

How could he not remember five years of his life? And yet that was exactly what he'd told her. What had been five years of grief and loneliness, struggle and frustration for Jessica had only been a mere thirty minutes in time to him. What could have happened to him?

He'd been hurt. She could tell that by the scars on his face and arm. It made her shudder to think what he might have gone through. There was only a shadow remaining of the man she'd known, loved, adored. But was that shadow merely a mirage? Was there anything left of the man from her past?

At that moment, Jessica wasn't sure she could handle the truth—whatever it turned out to be.

Pierce walked the streets. By force of sheer will, his tired legs carried him farther and farther away from that house. From his home. From his wife. From his son.

The image of those huge dark eyes in that solemn little face brought stinging tears to his own eyes. He rubbed the back of his hand across them, trying to erase the vision as he wiped away the moisture. He had a son. Dear god, a five-year-old boy he didn't even know.

And Jesse. Sweet, lovely, fragile Jesse. She seemed so cold, so hard, so suspicious. But five years had elapsed, she'd said. Five years! How could that be? How the hell could that be? Pierce asked himself desperately.

Just a moment in time for him had been five years of limbo for her. One glance in the mirror had told him she wasn't lying—not that Jesse ever would. Not his Jesse, he thought as his fingers moved to touch the scar on his face.

But the woman back there, the cold-eyed, beautiful stranger was not his wife. He felt something of the loss and betrayal now that she must have felt so long ago when he hadn't come back, and he despaired for them both.

A car horn blasted in his ear, and Pierce jumped back from the curb, startled to alertness. The driver shook his fist at him as the car zoomed through the intersection.

Pierce paid him scant attention. Automatically he waited for the traffic light to change, then walked aimlessly across the street. A bright red Coca-Cola sign flashed in the morning sun over a corner café, reminding him rather urgently that he was hungry. He couldn't remember the last time he'd eaten. He couldn't remember anything, in fact, beyond two hours ago.

That wasn't exactly true, he realized. Ever since he'd seen Jesse's shocked face, he'd been experiencing certain... impressions. Impressions of darkness and pain, of wandering around hopelessly lost but knowing all the while there was some place he should be, had to be. That certainty had driven him relentlessly through the mists until, almost as if he'd awakened from a long, deep sleep, he'd found himself at the grocery store and everything had clicked back into place.

For Pierce, the world had stopped for five years, then started back up again in exactly the same place. But why? And how?

He gazed at the scar on his left arm. What the hell had happened to him?

Checking his pockets, he pulled out the bills and change he'd gotten back from the twenty he'd used at the grocery store earlier. He had no idea where the money had come from. Someone must have given it to him....

Suddenly the street noises faded. His surroundings disappeared. For just a flash of time, Pierce was back on an island, standing on the beach, staring at the sky. A bird soared high overhead, silhouetted in the brilliant sunlight. It was an image that instantly brought back feelings of anger and betrayal. A nagging premonition of danger. And then a man's voice at his shoulder. "You'll need money. Here's all I can spare. Go home now. Find your family and protect them."

The vision vanished, leaving Pierce with a pounding headache in the warm morning sunshine.

Find your family and protect them.

Against what? Against whom?

For a moment, Pierce fought an almost overpowering urge to turn around, to go back home and make sure Jesse and his son were okay. But they'd managed just fine for five years without him. How could he help them now? How could he protect them from something he couldn't even remember?

Wearily he put his hands to his temples, massaging away the pain as the memories and the feelings began to evaporate in the sunshine.

His stomach rumbled again—a demand for fuel—and Pierce knew that whatever had to be faced would best be done by getting back his strength. Besides, Jesse needed some space, and he needed time to figure out what to do.

He opened the glass door of the café and stepped inside. As disreputable as the place seemed to be, his appearance still garnered a few curious looks. He chose a table in the back and carefully studied the one-page menu. The meager selections tempted his appetite beyond reason, making him wonder again just how long it had been since he'd eaten. He chose a club sandwich, then checked his money again after the waitress had taken his order.

The bells over the door chimed, and Pierce's head swung around, his gaze immediately scrutinizing the man who had just walked in. He was tall and thin with light brown hair and a thick mustache. He took a seat at the counter, and Pierce studied the man's back for a full thirty seconds, not understanding his own wariness.

Did he know that man?

Caution. It was a deeply ingrained command, an almost instinctive behavior. Pierce's gaze scoured the room, then came back to his own hands resting on the chipped Formica tabletop. They were trembling—from fatigue and hunger as well as emotion—but what caught his attention now was the raw, broken skin across his knuckles. He studied his hands as though they belonged to a stranger. They were scarred and dirty, the nails broken. Disgusted, he rose from his seat and located the men's room nearby.

Trying to avoid his reflection in the mirror, Pierce scrubbed his hands with hot water and soap. The raw places on his knuckles stung, but he ignored the pain, automatically blacking it out. When his hands were as clean as he could get them, he filled the basin with cold water and plunged his face into it, hoping the icy shock would restore his memory.

Why was it he could remember Jesse and their life together so clearly, so vividly, and not anything about the immediate past? He could remember his childhood, his parents and the sterile, loveless home he'd grown up in. He remembered college at Georgetown and even friends he hadn't seen or heard from in years. He could remember traveling in Europe and Asia before he'd met Jesse, and the secret he'd deliberately kept from her, the side of himself he'd never told her about.

Guilt welled inside him as he thought about the evasions and half truths he'd told her for years. She'd innocently accepted each and every one without question.

Except for the past five years, the memories were all coming back to him now, pouring through his mind so fast he felt a little dizzy.

For years, before he'd met Jesse, Pierce had been a specialized agent for a very elite agency that operated within the

CIA. Very few operatives even had knowledge of the group whose specialty was deep cover. Pierce had been recruited out of college because he had a certain reputation for living on the edge and because of the antique business he'd inherited from his parents. It gave him the perfect excuse to travel around the world without arousing questions. His real identity had become a deep cover for him, the very best kind because no one ever suspected.

Not even Jesse.

He gazed at his reflection in the mirror. He'd never told her even after they'd married—not just because of the oath he'd sworn to uphold—but because he'd always thought the less she knew the safer she'd be. It had been his duty to protect her.

It still was.

The washroom door swung open, and Pierce whipped his head around, his hand reaching for a weapon he knew instinctively he hadn't had in years. The man who'd been sitting at the bar now stepped inside the room. He gave Pierce barely a glance as he headed for a basin and began washing his hands. Quickly Pierce drained the sink, then combed his fingers through his damp hair, trying without much success to look a little more presentable.

The man was studying him in the mirror. Pierce turned and their gazes met. He searched the man's face for some sign of recognition. Something other than the niggle of suspicion was worrying him.

"Nice day, isn't it?" the man asked pleasantly as he dried his hands on a paper towel.

"It'll probably rain this afternoon," Pierce replied automatically, not exactly sure where the response had come from.

Somehow the answer seemed expected. Something flashed in the man's blue eyes, and then he smiled slightly, his mustache tilting at one corner. "One thing's for sure. You can never predict the weather this time of year. Be a fool to try." Then he turned, tossed the paper towel in the trash bin and exited the washroom.

Shaken by the encounter and having no idea why, Pierce waited a few seconds, then followed the man out. The stranger was seated at the counter again and didn't look around. But Pierce's appetite was gone. He tossed some bills onto the table and hurried through the café door.

Outside, the sun blinded him. Pierce leaned against the building's redbrick facade as the full realization of his plight hit him square in the face. He'd just spent the last of his money, he was still hungry, and he had absolutely nowhere to go.

Wiping a streak of sweat from his temple, he pushed himself away from the building and started walking down the street.

"Now, let me get this straight," Jay Greene said as he sat across the kitchen table from Jessica. "You're telling me that Pierce Kincaid—a man who disappeared five years ago—strolled through your back door this morning as if he'd only been gone half an hour?"

Jessica nodded weakly. "He even brought me the ice cream I'd sent him out to get that day, right down to the correct flavor."

"And you have no idea where he is now?"

"I took Max next door, and when I came back, he was gone. That was this morning, Jay. He looked so tired, so... ill. I can't help but think of him out there wandering the streets. It'll be dark soon—" The look on Jay's face stopped her.

"I wouldn't get carried away with the pity just yet, Jesse. This whole memory thing seems a little too convenient for me."

"You think he's lying?" Her voice sounded anxious, shaky.

"Wouldn't be the first time a husband just up and took off. Think about it."

She had thought about it. Endlessly. "But... we were so happy," Jessica protested. "We were both excited about the baby. The shop was doing great, we'd just bought this house—"

"And maybe he woke up one morning and decided he couldn't handle the responsibilities anymore. It happens, and Pierce Kincaid was always a bit footloose, if you ask me. You said yourself he ran the business in a haphazard fashion, and frankly he never struck me as the family-man type.

"Now, out of the blue, he appears on your doorstep, just when you've gotten your own life in order. Look at this place, Jesse. It's worth a small fortune, and so is the shop. When he tired of whatever the hell he was doing, why wouldn't he want to come back here?"

Jessica stared absently out the window. Jay wasn't telling her anything she hadn't thought of herself, but it still wasn't easy to hear. It wasn't easy to think that Pierce might have walked out on her. That he had lied about his feelings for her.

She had been so sure. So sure their love had been real.

A breeze lifted the hem of the pale blue curtains as it carried in the evening scents—honeysuckle, clover and roses. Years ago, after long days at the shop, she and Pierce would sit on the back porch and sip wine while they watched the first stars twinkle out. Twilight had always been a special time of day for them, a time when the cares of the day melted away into the coming darkness.

Had none of that meant as much to him as it had to her?

As if echoing her thoughts, Jay covered her hand with his and asked softly, "How do you feel about him now, Jesse? What was it like seeing him again?"

She sighed. "I'm not sure. I know you're right. I do have to be careful, but you didn't see him. I think he must have been in some sort of accident. He has all these scars. Do you think—could he have been kidnapped five years ago? Held all this time?"

"With no ransom note?" Her brother looked skeptical. "It's possible. Hell, anything's possible. But victims who're kidnapped either in a robbery or for sport usually turn up dead. Five years is a long time to hold someone captive."

"I know," Jessica agreed, her tone bleak. "I just keep asking myself where he could have been all this time. What could have happened to him?"

"Did he have any identification on him?"

Jessica shrugged. "I don't know. I didn't ask to see it. I didn't need to."

"You're that sure it was him?" Jay's icy gray eyes scrutinized her face.

"It *was* him. It was Pierce."

Jay swept his hand through his brown hair, setting it on end. He shook his head. "Damn, what a mess. You know I'll do what I can, but I couldn't find out anything about him five years ago. It was as if he disappeared off the face of the earth. We may not have any better luck now."

"I just want you to find him," she whispered desperately. "Whatever he's done, wherever he's been—he needs help."

"*Your* help?"

Jessica hesitated for a moment, biting her lip. "He's still my husband."

"Technically," her brother agreed grimly. "All right, I'll see what I can do." He took out a pen and pad and began jotting down notes. "Give me a general physical description of how he looked, what he was wearing and all that. And how about a cup of coffee? This looks to be a long night," he said with a sigh.

Jessica rose from the table and reached for a cup, but the barking of a neighbor's dog stilled her movements. A shadow swept across the open window, so swiftly she thought at first she'd imagined it. Then came a scraping noise on the back porch, as if someone had bumped into a chair.

Jessica's gaze flew to Jay's, her heart hammering in her chest. He lifted a finger to his lips, silencing her. Slowly he reached for the light switch just as the sound of the back-door buzzer ripped through the quiet. Jessica gasped and Jay cursed softly as both their gazes fastened on the dark silhouette outside her kitchen door.

Chapter 3

At Jay's nod, Jessica rose and went to answer the back door. Heart still pounding, she turned the knob and drew back the door. Pierce stood on the porch, his pale, gaunt features highlighted by the light from the open doorway. If possible, he looked even more weary than he had that morning.

For the longest moment, he and Jessica stared at one another. Neither of them spoke, but the tension crackled between them like a live wire in an electrical storm.

Then his hands slipped into the front pockets of his jeans and he shrugged, a gesture that was at once familiar and dear. The ghost of a smile touched his lips. "I seemed to have lost my key," he said wryly.

They both seemed to waver with indecision. Then with a little gasping sob, Jessica took a step toward him as Pierce moved toward her. His arms went around her and held her tightly as she clung to him, her eyes squeezed shut against the intense emotions spiraling through her.

Pierce was alive!

For a moment, everything else vanished from Jessica's mind. She just wanted to hold him, assure herself that this was no dream. He buried his face in her hair, and she could feel his arms trembling as they held her, could feel his heart beating against hers. One hand came up and brushed through her tangled curls.

"I'm sorry," he whispered raggedly. "Maybe I shouldn't have come back here, but...I had to. I had to see you again, to make sure you were all right...."

"It's okay," she said, her voice cracking with deep emotion. She could feel the leanness of his body against her, the sharply defined ridges of his ribs through the ragged shirt. Pierce had once been so virile and muscular. To see him now made Jessica's heart ache with sorrow.

But even now, when he'd been through God knows what, she could still sense remnants of strength in his arms, a hint of the same confidence she had always admired so much. Pierce was not a man who would be taken down without a fight.

That thought struck her with cold reality. Was that why he had all the scars? Had he been fighting for his life all this time? *Dear God...*

As if sensing her thoughts, she felt his posture stiffen. She lifted her head and saw that he was staring over her shoulder, his dark eyes wary once more.

"Hello, Jay," he said with a thin smile. "Aren't you out of uniform?"

Jessica had forgotten all about her brother. Awkwardness now settled over the room like a funeral pall. She tried to pull away from Pierce, but his arms held her for a fraction longer, as if staking his claim before letting her go.

"I didn't think this was an official visit," Jay said. But even without his uniform, he stood military straight, his cool gaze taking Pierce's measure without blinking.

Jessica backed away, her gaze darting from Pierce to Jay. Her brother's expression must have been identical to the one she'd worn that morning. The mixture of suspicion, disbelief, anger and even touches of fear echoed in Jay's gray eyes.

It seemed a million years before either of them spoke again. Jessica's heart raced with tension as she stared up at Pierce, once again taking in the haggard features, the scar.

Pierce smiled. "You haven't changed a bit."

"Not where my responsibilities are concerned," Jay agreed. "Shall we all sit down? Jesse, can you get us some coffee?"

The command finally motivated her. Jessica headed toward the coffeepot, relieved to have something to do. She could feel Pierce's dark eyes on her, following her every movement. Reluctantly her own gaze lifted to meet his. Something flashed between them—a memory? A feeling? Jessica wasn't sure. But all of a sudden, she felt a tiny shiver of warning scurry up her spine.

Pierce's proprietary gaze moved over her, greedily, familiarly, making her body tingle with memories she'd long ago suppressed. He was looking at her the way she remembered him looking at her. The brown eyes were narrowed slightly, the long, thick lashes hooding his expression, but Jessica knew what he was thinking. She'd always known.

She said the first thing that came to her mind. "You look hungry."

"Starving." His eyes never left her mouth.

Her face flamed at the inadvertent—or not so inadvertent—innuendo. Nervously she wiped her moist palms on a paper towel as she moved past him toward the refrigerator.

"Actually, what I'd really like to do is get cleaned up," Pierce said. He started toward the kitchen door, then checked himself as he looked back at her. "Is that all right?"

"Of course."

He hesitated, his gaze unreadable. "Where?"

That jolted her. Where, indeed? She'd long since removed his belongings from her bedroom, except for a few mementos she couldn't bring herself to part with. The idea of him once again occupying that room was distinctly uncomfortable.

The question of where he should shower brought up a whole new set of problems for Jessica. Where would he stay? Where would he sleep? What did he expect from her? They were still legally married, but five years was a long time. Even if he had no memory of their separation, the reality of those long, lonely years still breathed a life of their own inside Jessica's heart. Surely he didn't expect just to waltz back in and pick up where they'd left off five years ago.

But if he was really suffering from amnesia, then that's exactly what he would expect. His feelings hadn't changed—even if hers had.

Her gaze lifted again, and Pierce's eyes trapped her with a look she thought seemed slightly reproachful, as if he'd read her exact thoughts. She blushed again and said almost defiantly, "Sometime ago, I moved all your things into the guest room downstairs. You'll find fresh towels in the bathroom. Everything you need. . . ."

Her voice trailed off at his look. Not everything, he seemed to be communicating. Then he turned and disappeared through the swinging door to the dining room.

Silence quivered in the air for a long moment, then Jay said, "Well, I'll be damned. I wouldn't have believed it if I hadn't seen it with my own eyes."

With shaking fingers, Jessica pulled the makings of a sandwich from the refrigerator and placed each item carefully on the counter. "So...what do you think?" she asked, not daring to meet her brother's eyes. He'd already seen more than she would have wanted him to. Her reaction when she'd first seen Pierce at the door had been purely spontaneous, an overreaction to the tumultuous emotions racing through her. She hadn't stopped to think about what she was doing, about the wrong signals she might be sending to Pierce.

Now she did stop to think, and she regretted the embrace because it had instantly created a bond between them, an intimacy that was far more than she could deal with right now. She was glad Pierce was alive. More than glad. Joyful. Thankful. They'd conceived a son together. But the years apart had been longer than the years they'd had together. There was no way they could ever go back to what they'd once had.

She hoped to God Pierce understood that.

Jay got up and carried his cup across the room to the coffeepot. He poured himself a fresh cup, took a tentative sip, and grimaced. "Damn, Jesse, I wish you'd learn to make a decent cup of coffee."

"My mind was elsewhere, okay?" she snapped.

"Hey, don't bite *my* head off. I'm an innocent bystander in all this."

"Sorry." She dropped down at the kitchen table and propped her chin in her hand. "What am I supposed to do?" she asked in desperation. "I don't even know him anymore, and he doesn't know me. I don't know where he's been, what he's done, why he's back. I'm not even the same person he left five years ago. I've grown up. I've taken charge of my life. I don't—''

"Need him anymore?" Jay nodded. "I'm sure he'll find that out soon enough, if he sticks around."

"What do you mean *if?*" Jessica raked impatient fingers through her hair as she stared at her brother. "You think he's going to leave me... leave again?"

Jay shrugged as he brought his coffee to the table and sat down again. "Let's just say I'm trying to keep an open mind. Wherever he's been, he's had trouble. You only have to look at him to know that much. What I can't help wondering is what kind. And if he's bringing it back here with him."

Jessica's silver gaze rested on Jay's stern countenance. "Meaning he could be on the run?"

Her brother merely shrugged as he lifted the cup to his lips. But his gray eyes were darkened with worry. "Max is next door with Sharon, right?"

His tone was a little too casual. Jessica found herself shivering with an eerie premonition as she nodded. "She called earlier and asked if he could stay the night. Under the circumstances, I thought it was a good idea."

"So do I."

Their gazes met again, and Jessica saw her own uneasiness mirrored in Jay's eyes. But before either of them could speak, the kitchen door swung inward and Pierce stepped into the room.

Jessica's gaze instantly collided with his. He looked better, she had to admit. Much better. His dark hair, still glistening with dampness, had been carefully combed and the days-old growth of beard had been scraped away, accentuating even more dramatically the white scar down his cheek, the deep creases around his eyes and mouth.

The jeans he'd put on were old and worn, a pair he used to favor for puttering around the house. But even though they were frayed at the hem and shiny at the knees, they were far better than the disreputable pair he'd discarded. They hung loosely on his gaunt frame, reminding Jessica of how snugly they had once fitted him, how sexy he'd always looked in them.

He wore a blue cotton shirt—sleeves rolled up, tail out— that triggered yet another memory for Jessica. He'd worn a blue shirt the day he'd disappeared. Had he remembered that, too, or was his selection an ironic coincidence?

He returned her appraisal, the deep brown eyes warm and seeking as they moved slowly over her face and then downward. Her own jeans fitted a little *too* snugly. She'd always been pencil thin, but after Max was born, she'd filled out and had never been able to drop the extra ten pounds. Actually, she'd always been happy with the added weight, but now she found herself wondering what Pierce thought.

The sudden warmth spiraling through her veins shocked her. And scared her. It had been a long time since she'd felt sexual desire. Not since Pierce had left. Sex with him had been wonderful because it was with *him*. But before she'd met him and after he'd left, abstinence had never been a problem for her.

Pierce had always teased her that she was like a car engine on a frosty morning. She had to be warmed up properly to get the best mileage. Jessica's cheeks heated at the memory.

Finally breaking eye contact, she jumped up from the table and busily began assembling his sandwich. Pierce sat down at the table across from Jay, and the two men eyed each other stonily, reminding Jessica that, to her despair, they'd never been the best of friends. She placed the plate in front of Pierce, and their hands touched briefly before Jessica drew hers back.

"What would you like to drink?" she asked in a brisk tone.

"It's been a long time since I've had a beer," he suggested with a smile that sent a new wave of awareness washing over her.

"How would you know that?" Jay asked quietly. "I thought you lost your memory."

Pierce's head swiveled so that his eyes met Jessica's. "It's just an impression, not a memory. I think I've done without a lot of things."

The bottle almost slipped from Jessica's fingers. Hands shaking, she poured the beer into a mug and set it beside Pierce's plate, careful this time to avoid his touch. She sat down at the table and watched him attack the sandwich.

His appetite seemed ravenous, though she could tell he tried to curb his urgency. The sandwich disappeared in seconds.

"Would you like another one?" she asked softly, her heart feeling as if it would break in two.

The idea of seconds seemed to shock him for a moment. Then he said, "If you're sure it wouldn't be too much trouble."

It took Jessica a long time to make the second sandwich. She stood at the counter, her back to the men as she tried to gather her shattered poise. But as soon as she wiped away the silent tears from her face, a new batch would take their place. Instinctively she knew she wouldn't let him see her pity. That was the worst thing she could do to a man like Pierce.

At last, sniffing as unobtrusively as she could, Jessica placed the sandwich on the table and said hurriedly, "If you'll excuse me for a moment, I, uh, have something to do in the other room."

She all but fled the kitchen, leaving dead silence in her wake.

After a few seconds, Pierce picked up the other sandwich and began eating. Jay reached into the inside pocket of his jacket and withdrew a pack of cigarettes and lit up, leisurely blowing a thin stream of smoke skyward.

"I thought you'd quit," Pierce said as he eyed his brother-in-law curiously.

"I've quit several times since you left. If I hadn't already started again this last time, I'm sure I would have after tonight."

Pierce's brows arched. "I'm glad I don't have to take the responsibility then."

Jay blew a trail of smoke from the corner of his mouth as he spoke. "What about your other responsibilities? You as anxious to dismiss those?"

"Meaning?"

"Jessica and Max. You left them high and dry five years ago. If it wasn't for Jesse's grit and determination, I'm not sure what they would have done."

"You don't have to remind me of my responsibilities to my wife and son. I'll take care of them from now on."

Jay crushed his cigarette in his saucer as he stared at Pierce. "You still don't get it, do you? They don't need you to take care of them. Jesse's managed just fine without you. More than fine. The business you left behind is booming, thanks to her. This house is worth a small fortune, and Max, well, Max won't even know you, will he?"

It was a reality Pierce had been trying to come to terms with since he'd stared into those wide, accusing eyes this morning. Max. How strange that Jessica had named him that after she'd fought him so hard about it. It gave Pierce a small thrill of happiness to know that even after he'd left, Jessica had still wanted to please him.

"Look." Jay folded his arms on the table and leaned toward Pierce. "Let's cut through the crap, shall we? This memory business may work with Jesse, but it won't wash with me. I can recognize a man in trouble when I see one, and I'd say you, my friend, are definitely in trouble. You don't have to tell me what, you don't have to tell me how or when or who. All you have to tell me, Kincaid, is *why?* Why did you come back here?"

"This is my home."

"*Was* your home."

Brown eyes challenged gray. It gratified Pierce to see Jay glance away first. He'd always thought his brother-in-law a little too cocky, a little too self-possessed. Pierce could spot a phony when he saw one, but he'd never had the heart to tell Jesse just how one-sided her sibling devotion was.

"This is my home," he said, feeling the warmth of anger stealing over him. "I don't have to justify myself to you. I may owe Jesse an explanation, one I don't have at the moment, but let's get one thing straight. I don't owe you a damned thing."

The air buzzed with tension. Jay's gray eyes glinted with steely anger as he half rose from his seat. The unspoken challenge lay in the air between them like a gauntlet thrown to the ground. Slowly Pierce stood up.

"What's going on in here?"

Both male heads whipped around to find Jessica standing in the doorway, watching them with an expression that wavered between curiosity and disgust. Her assessing gaze went from one to the other as she did her own summation of the situation.

Jay spoke first. "I need to be shoving off, Jessica. But I don't want to leave until I know everything's all right here."

Her expression softened as she smiled at her brother. "I'm okay. Thanks for coming over."

Jay's gaze returned to Pierce. "Can I drop you somewhere?" he asked bluntly.

The question struck Pierce like a physical blow. He was being asked to leave his own home. For one black moment, it was all he could do to curb the sudden rage hurtling through him. He turned to face Jessica who still hovered in the doorway. He tilted a brow in question.

Her gaze burned into Pierce's until his heart started to pound. What was she thinking? he wondered. Did she still feel anything at all for him? It was impossible to think that for him only a moment ago they had been in love, happy, and now she might feel nothing at all for him except pity.

God help him, he could stand anything but that.

Jessica took a deep breath and released it as if she was gathering her courage for what she needed to say. Pierce's own breath seemed suspended somewhere in his throat.

"This is your home, too, Pierce," she said finally. "I can't ask you to leave. Not when. . . ." Her voice trailed off as she gazed at him, the gray of her eyes turning to mist. Pierce knew how he must look to her, and it made him cringe.

"Go on," he said evenly.

Her gaze dropped. "Not when you obviously need a place to stay."

"Jessica, for God's sake, what do you think you're doing?" Jay objected. "He can't stay here. What about Max?"

"What about Max?" Pierce said in a deadly quiet voice that seemed to hold both brother and sister in thrall.

"My God, man, you have to know what this will do to him. He's only five years old."

"I'll take care of Max," Jessica said, and the firm note of resolve in her voice surprised Pierce. Once she would have turned to him to make such an important decision.

Five years, he thought again. Five years of his life gone in the blink of an eye. How much more was lost to him than just that time?

"I hope to hell you know what you're doing," Jay muttered angrily as he pushed past them both and strode out of the kitchen.

Jessica chewed her bottom lip, a nervous habit Pierce remembered so well. It heartened him to know that at least some things hadn't changed.

"I'll be right back," she said, then turned and hurried after her brother. Pierce hesitated a moment, then pushed through the door, too, distracted once again by all the changes Jesse had carried out on the house. Changes they had once planned to work on together.

Had she done all this by herself? he wondered as he walked through the formal dining room. The decor was elegant, but somehow the room left him cold. It was almost too perfect, he thought, remembering the house he'd grown up in. There was no life in it. No warmth. No love. It was a room that matched the hard chill in Jessica's eyes.

He walked through to the living room and looked around. He liked this room better. The pictures of Max in here added a homey touch that somehow soothed him.

Jessica had walked her brother to the door, and now they both stood in the foyer, their furtive whispers attesting to the nature of their conversation.

Pierce crossed the hardwood floor to the fireplace and picked up one of the pictures of Max he'd studied so intently that morning. A baseball cap angled over the boy's forehead as his brown eyes squinted into the sun. There was a rip in his shorts and a scab on one scrawny knee.

Pierce's heart melted. He'd loved the baby Jesse had been carrying, and now he loved this little boy with an intensity that astounded him.

Jessica stood at the end of the sofa and watched Pierce. He didn't look up, and she realized he hadn't heard her come in. She watched him trace a finger gently along the photo, and the look of fierce possessiveness that came over his face shocked her. Her heart skidded with warning as her own defenses rose in reaction.

Pierce glanced up, and the expression in his eyes confirmed her deepest fears. When he spoke, his voice gave rise to new ones. Jessica trembled with dread as his gaze continued to hold hers.

"Where is he, Jessica? Where's my son?"

Chapter 4

Jessica tried to keep her voice controlled. She didn't want to give away her fear, didn't want to appear weak or vulnerable even to Pierce. Especially to Pierce. "Max isn't here," she said, glancing away.

"Where is he?"

"He's somewhere . . . safe."

"Safe? That's a strange term to use."

Her eyes challenged him. "Is it?"

He lifted his brow, and the scar twisted it, giving him an almost sinister appearance. "Are you implying that I'm a threat to our son? Or to you?"

Jessica hesitated, then said, "You barely resemble the man I knew back then. You've obviously been hurt. Maybe you're even in some sort of trouble. God knows what might have happened to you since you left. You've been gone for five years, Pierce. *Five years.* I don't even know who you are anymore," she finished in a whisper.

His voice lowered. "I'm your husband."

"Technically," she said, borrowing Jay's term. Jessica took a deep breath and let it out, trying to calm her pounding heart. She walked over to the window and stared out into the darkness. "Can you even begin to imagine what this is like for me? All those years you were gone and not one word, not one clue, and now suddenly here you are, acting like nothing's happened. Acting like you think...everything should be the same between us. It's not. It's not the same." She turned and faced him. "It'll never be the same again."

His eyes close briefly. "Don't say that."

"Why not? It's the truth. I don't want to hurt you, but the sooner we face it, the better off we'll both be."

"My God, Jesse." He spread his hands in appeal. "You're acting like you think I left because I wanted to. And given your background, I guess I can understand that. My... disappearance—whatever you want to call it—must have seemed like the ultimate betrayal to you. You must have felt as though I had deserted you, too."

"You can't know how I felt," she said, crossing her arms.

"No, I guess I can't," he agreed. "But one thing I do know. I didn't leave you because I wanted to."

Her chin lifted a fraction. "Then why did you leave me?"

"I've already told you," he said helplessly. "I don't know what happened."

"You have no idea?"

Pierce hesitated, as if searching for the right words. "I have no memory of the past five years," he finally said.

"It's incredible," she whispered. "So hard to believe."

"Yes, it is," he agreed. "It's even hard for me to believe. So I guess I have to ask you, Jesse, given the circumstances, where does this leave us? Where do we go from here?"

Jessica made a futile gesture with her hand. "I don't know. I think the first thing you should do is see a doctor, but beyond that…I just don't know…." Her words trailed off as she glanced away. She couldn't bear to look at him any longer. Couldn't bear to see what the past five years had done to him. To her. "You need a place to stay for the time being. I won't ask you to leave, Pierce. I…can't."

"Is it just pity you feel for me, then? I know how I look to you," he said, with a derisive smile. "As you said, I'm hardly the man I once was."

"That's not what I said," she flared out. "It has nothing to do with the way you look. At least not in the way you mean. It has everything to do with where you've been these past five years. What you've been doing. Why you left me in the first place."

Her anger deepened as she forced herself to meet his dark gaze. Her voice grew shaky with emotion as she spread her hands in supplication. "Can't you understand? Maybe you didn't leave because you wanted to, but that doesn't change the fact that you *did* leave me. I thought you were *dead*. All these years, I've mourned you, and now I find out it was all for nothing. It was all a lie."

"You sound disappointed, Jesse."

His observation startled her. Made her feel just a trifle uneasy about herself. *Was* she disappointed? Or was she just feeling hurt and confused? Angry and betrayed and… wronged. "I feel a lot of things," she admitted. "Not the least of which is fear."

"I would never hurt you."

"You already have," she said. "You have no idea."

"But not intentionally. Never intentionally." Pierce took a step toward her, but stopped when she flinched away. "You have to believe that, Jesse. I don't know what happened five years ago. I don't know where I've been, what I've done, why I couldn't come back to you. I wish to God I did."

He raised his hand to massage his right temple. His eyes closed for a moment as though he were experiencing excruciating pain. "It's something I have to figure out. I have all these bits and pieces of memories floating around inside my head, and somehow I have to fit them all together again. I know none of this makes any sense to you right now. To me, either. But the one thing I do know is that I never stopped loving you."

"How can you possibly know that?" she demanded. "If you have no memory of the past five years, how can you be so sure there wasn't someone else?"

He lifted his gaze to hers. "Because there could never be anyone else. At least . . . not for me."

It took Jessica a few seconds to register the note of accusation in his tone. The brown of his eyes deepened almost to black. His gaze was intense, probing, his voice a little too calm. Jessica felt a chill of apprehension as he said slowly, "Perhaps that should have been my first question. I'm almost afraid to ask it, though."

Jessica glanced away guiltily.

"With good reason, it would seem. Is there someone else?" he persisted.

She hesitated, then shook her head. "No."

"You don't sound too sure."

"There isn't anyone else," she repeated angrily. She tossed back her hair and eyed him defiantly. "But there could have been. And who would have blamed me? You were gone all that time. I didn't know if you were dead or alive. For all I knew, you could have had another family somewhere else. You could have been in love with someone else. You could have forgotten all about me," she said, feeling the sting of tears threaten her anger. "I had no reason to believe you'd ever come back. Why should I have waited for you?"

"Then why did you?"

Silence. Jessica's heart pounded in her chest as his gaze held hers. His brown eyes softened, misted, looked at her the way he used to look at her, as if she was someone so very special to him. As if she was the only woman in the world for him. As if he couldn't wait to take her in his arms and hold her. Dear God, how often she had thought about that look, how often she had prayed to see it again, just one more time.

But how could she trust it now? How could she trust her own emotions when memories of the past were so strong at that moment she could almost reach out and pluck one from the air between them?

She let her anger blaze to life again. "I didn't wait," she denied. "I was busy working, raising my son, providing a stable home for us both. I was busy growing up, learning how to make my own decisions and realizing that I had no one to rely on but myself. Look around you, Pierce. I did all this *by myself*. I didn't wait for you. I've gone on with my life. Max and I are happy. We're a family. We don't need—" She broke off, realizing what she had almost said.

His brow arched upward, twisting slightly from the scar. "You don't need me? That's what you were about to say, isn't it? You have changed, Jessica. I remember a time when you would never have tried to hurt me like that."

Pierce's face looked like a cold, hard mask. At that moment, he seemed more than ever like a stranger to her. A stranger who had shared her life once, who had helped create a son with her. A stranger who had walked back into her life just when she was beginning to feel good about herself again.

"Five years is a long time, Pierce," she countered. "People change. I've changed. I'm not the same woman you left behind."

"Yes," he agreed quietly, "but I never would have imagined you could have changed that much."

Jessica lay wide awake, staring at the ceiling, thinking how strangely quiet the house seemed without her son. She could hear the soft whir of the ceiling fan overhead, the chime of the Tompion grandfather clock down in the foyer, the rustle of leaves in the trees outside her window. If she listened closely enough, she could almost imagine she could hear the sound of Pierce's breathing.

She turned her head and gazed at the side of the bed that had been his. She'd slept on the same side all these years, never giving it a second thought, even when Pierce's would have been more convenient for getting up in the middle of the night with Max.

Had she unconsciously been waiting for Pierce to come back? Had she known all along, somewhere deep inside her heart, that he wasn't dead? That he was alive...and still loving her?

Don't, she told herself harshly. Don't believe everything he says. How could he have loved her and left her like that? How could he have loved her and not gotten in touch with her all these years? How could he have loved her and forgotten all about her?

Maybe there was a perfectly logical reason to explain where he'd been all these years. Maybe he hadn't left by choice, just as he claimed. Maybe he'd been in an accident and hadn't remembered her at all until now.

Surprising how that thought gave her very little comfort. Her own husband couldn't remember her? Couldn't remember what they'd had together? Maybe because it hadn't meant as much to him as it had to her, Jessica thought with a new flash of anger. Maybe because—

Oh, God, stop it! she commanded herself. What good did it do to go over and over all the possibilities in her head? Whatever had happened to Pierce didn't change anything. Not really. Five years had gone by. Five years of her growing and maturing and taking charge of her own life. She hadn't meant to hurt him earlier when she'd said she and Max didn't need him anymore, but it was the truth, wasn't it?

She'd learned everything there was to know about Pierce's business, and it had flourished in the past few years. She'd redecorated the house to suit her own tastes, and the result was elegant and beautiful, if a little cold. She'd raised Max all by herself, with no help from anyone, and he was an adorable, well-adjusted, happy little boy.

Jessica's life was ordered now. Completely secure. For the first time, she felt in control of her own destiny. She didn't have to depend on anyone else for her security and happiness. She'd made a safe, stable life for herself and Max, and she wouldn't let anyone, not even Pierce, threaten her peace of mind.

What right did he have to come back here now?

A little thread of guilt wove through her anger as Jessica punched her pillow, then turned her back on the empty side of the bed that had once been Pierce's.

If only he didn't look so hurt, so badly in need of someone to take care of him. She sniffed, telling herself she must be catching a cold.

If only he didn't have those horrible scars to remind them both that the past five years hadn't been kind to either of them. If only she didn't have to wonder how he'd gotten them, about the pain he must have endured.

She tried to harden her heart at the rush of emotion that swept through her. She'd suffered, too, hadn't she? She had her scars, too. She'd taken charge of her life and become her own person, but not without a price. She'd grown harder, colder, even bitter at times. She seldom laughed anymore, except with Max. It wasn't a pretty image she drew of herself, she knew. Perhaps this change in character wasn't one of her finer triumphs, but it was life. It was reality.

It was just the way things were now.

And Pierce, well ... Pierce would learn soon enough that you can never go home again.

It was good to be home.

Now that he was back, Pierce didn't intend to ever leave again.

He didn't care what the hell the agency said. He'd paid his dues. Five years of his life gone, and Pierce had no idea what purpose they had served. What good he might have done.

Standing in the shadows of the backyard, he let his gaze roam over the familiar, yet changed, surroundings. The cherry trees he and Jessica had planted together had grown so tall, so thick and hardy. The flower beds were neatly tended, the grass freshly cut.

With a sharp pang of guilt, Pierce wondered if Jessica hired someone to come in regularly to do the chores that he'd once done. He'd always hated yard work, but now he found himself resenting yet another usurpation of his position here at home.

His home.

He sighed deeply. He only had to look at his reflection in the mirror to know that wherever he'd been in the past five years, it wasn't a place he would have called home. The scars, the gauntness, the haunted look in his eyes suggested he'd been through hell.

He grimaced, remembering the first time he'd seen himself in the mirror. He certainly wouldn't be winning any beauty contests, that was for damned sure. No wonder Max had been so afraid of him this morning.

Max.

Pierce still couldn't believe he had a son.

He smiled into the darkness, recalling the little boy's face, the dark hair, the brown eyes, the solemn expression. He might have been looking at his own mirror image thirty years ago, Pierce thought.

His smile disappeared, replaced by a brooding frown. He hoped the resemblance ended with the physical appearance. He'd hate to think his own son might be as unhappy and lonely as he'd been at that age.

But surely Max and Jessica had fun together. Surely Jessica spent time with their son, saw to the special needs of a little boy, made him feel wanted and loved—unlike Pierce's own parents who hadn't had a clue how to raise a child, he thought bitterly.

A boy should be allowed to have friends over, Pierce thought, remembering the hours he'd spent alone as a child. A boy needed to be able to get dirty and roughhouse once in a while without being reprimanded for it. Surely Jessica understood all that. But as Pierce stood there gazing into the darkened backyard, an image of the immaculate interior of their home flashed through his mind.

The house was beautiful, but so different from the way it used to be. He missed the casual mix-and-match furnishings they'd begun their married life with. Jessica had gotten rid of all the old stuff. He wondered if she'd even kept the antique pine bed they'd found together at an estate sale.

Pierce let his gaze drift up to their bedroom window, imagining Jessica lying in that bed, fast asleep, her hair fanning across the pillow like a dark, misty veil. How he wished at that moment that he could see her, touch her...be with her.

Would it ever happen for them again?

Would he ever be able to hold her as he'd once held her, kiss her as he'd once kissed her? Would he ever be able to make love to her again?

He closed his eyes, feeling the old familiar need rush through him. She looked so different now. So sophisticated and mature and... womanly. She'd let her hair grow long, he thought. So long and lustrous... He wondered what it would feel like beneath his hands or brushing against his bare chest.

Dear God, he could remember vividly the way she tasted, the way she kissed, the way she felt beneath him. He could remember everything about the way it used to be between them, and the images tormented him now, just as her words had earlier.

It'll never be the same again.

A mild breeze drifted through the cherry trees, stirring the leaves and bringing to his nostrils the nostalgic scent of honeysuckle and clover. It reminded him of all the summer evenings they'd spent out here, planning the rest of their lives together.

He should have told her the truth about himself long ago. Maybe none of this would ever have happened. Maybe he wouldn't have left her on that fateful day five years ago.

The assignment he'd been on was supposed to have been his last, Pierce reflected. He'd given his notice to the agency. The rest of his life belonged only to himself and to Jesse and the child she was carrying. One last assignment, and then Pierce would be free.

So what the hell had gone wrong? What had happened to him? Why couldn't he remember?

As much as he hated to bring that part of his past back into his life, Pierce knew that he could never truly be free until he learned what had happened the day he'd left the house five years ago.

And there was only one way to do that.

With one last glance at Jesse's window, he turned and noiselessly slipped through the darkness, taking care to keep to the shadows. Thankfully he still knew how to blend with the night. At least he hadn't forgotten that.

Within minutes, Pierce had located the familiar phone booth on a secluded street a few blocks from the house. He'd often used it years ago, and had wondered earlier when he'd let himself out the back door if it might have been removed while he'd been gone. So many things had changed.

But there it stood, an old-fashioned glass booth where many a message had been given and received. He'd gotten a phone call in that very booth on his way to the grocery store the day he'd disappeared, Pierce recalled.

The memory shocked him. For a moment, time stood still, then reversed. The day had been cloudless and brilliant with a mild breeze stirring the leaves in the cherry trees that lined the street where the phone booth was located. Pierce crossed the cobblestone street, opened the phone-booth door and stepped inside. Within two minutes, the phone rang and he picked up the receiver.

"Hello?"

Silence on the other end. After a few seconds, Pierce began to grow uneasy. Automatically he recited the code, but the caller still didn't respond.

The sound of a car engine was Pierce's next alarm. His instincts kicked into action. He jerked open the door and dived for the street, but not fast enough. A blinding flash of light and a stunning blow to his shoulder sent him sprawling to the ground. In his last seconds of consciousness, he lay on his back and stared at the blue sky. A bird—an eagle he thought—soared against the brilliant light of the sun.

Then ... nothing.

Pierce closed his eyes, trying to summon more. Memories and impressions ripped through him as sharp as a knife, followed by the echo of emotions long forgotten. Betrayal. Fear. Guilt.

And pain. Blinding pain. Pain so intense he'd had to retreat into the darkness. Into a blackness so complete that nothing else had existed for him. He couldn't let it.

That same pain slashed through him now. He put his hands to his head, pressing his temples as if he could squeeze away the hurt. But there was only one way to stop the pain, and he knew it. Only one way to save his sanity.

He had to fade to black.

Within moments, the pain inside his head subsided. The memories vanished. And Pierce was left standing in the darkness, feeling more helpless than ever. He crossed the street and entered the phone booth. Inserting the coin, he dialed the number and waited.

"Tremont House." The voice sounded as if it belonged to an old woman. Pierce had a sudden image of gray hair pulled back into a severe bun, a ramrod-straight backbone and dark, wary eyes. Had he met her before?

"I'd like to speak to the manager."

"Whom should I say is calling?" she asked curtly.

Pierce hesitated, choosing his words carefully. "Tell him an old friend is in town. Tell him I've been ... away for several years. Tell him I'm in desperate need of a room."

"Wouldn't do you any good to talk to him," the old woman answered coolly. "We're booked solid."

The line clicked, then went dead, but Pierce had his answer. He gazed bleakly down the remote, empty street.

Help would not be forthcoming as he'd hoped.

Hell, he couldn't even be sure the number he'd called was even a contact anymore. Things inside the agency could change within five minutes' time, much less five years. The agency itself might no longer exist, and if that were the case, Pierce might never be able to find out the truth.

It was a nightmare, he thought. He felt as if he'd been trapped in the Twilight zone for too long or, like Rip van Winkle, had fallen asleep for half a decade while the rest of the world had passed blithely by him.

No time for self-pity, though. He had Max and Jessica to think of, and the possibility that they might somehow be in danger. Maybe he had brought the danger with him, Pierce thought. Maybe the best thing he could do for his family would be simply to disappear again.

But even as the idea formed, he dismissed it. No one would take care of his family the way he could. No one could protect them the way he would.

Somewhere down the street, Pierce heard the distant hum of a car engine. His heart accelerated as the car turned the corner and its headlights caught the phone booth in their full glare. Automatically he tensed.

The car slowed as it passed by the phone booth. Pierce glanced around. The car was a dark green Ford Taurus, but the windows were tinted so that he couldn't see the occupant—or occupants—inside. It was exactly the kind of innocuous-looking vehicle that the agency furnished its operatives.

Were they already checking him out?

Steady, he cautioned himself. By all indications, he'd been out of the mainstream for a long time now. Even though he had no memory of the past five years, Pierce couldn't imagine that he would still be a threat to anyone. The double agent he'd been after before Pierce had disappeared would have surely long since been trapped. The codes, the contacts, even the targets would have all changed by now.

Pierce Kincaid was a dinosaur. A washed-up agent without a memory. No one would want him anymore. Dead or alive.

Not even Jesse.

But even that grim thought couldn't dim the deeply ingrained need for caution. Pierce gripped the handle of the glass door, readying himself to yank it open and make a dive for cover. The car seemed to slow even more, then with a burst of acceleration, it sped down the street.

Pierce waited for a moment, watching the taillights disappear into the night. He felt a keen mixture of relief and disappointment. For a while there, with the adrenaline pumping and all his senses working precisely as they'd been trained, he could almost believe that *he* hadn't changed that much. That there was still something left of the man he'd once been. The man Jesse had once loved.

But that man had been a lie. That man hadn't really existed. If Jesse had known the truth about him then, she might never have loved him at all.

Burdened with guilt, regret and an almost overwhelming need to return to his family, Pierce opened the glass door, stepped out into the cool night air and quickly headed for home.

The ringing of the telephone awakened Jessica at a few minutes past two. She pushed herself up, certain that a call at that time of night could only mean one thing. Something had happened to Max.

In full-blown panic, she grabbed the phone in the dark. "Hello?"

When no one answered, Jessica first felt relief, then a strange uneasiness. Someone was on the line but wouldn't answer her. For some reason, the silence seemed eminently threatening. She could hear the soft breathing, almost sense the caller listening intently to her voice. A shiver crawled up her spine as her heart accelerated.

She swung her legs off the side of the bed and sat on the edge as if poised to flee. "Hello? Are you there? Who is this?"

Still silence, and then very softly the line clicked dead.

Jessica hung up the phone, her hands trembling in spite of herself. She'd gotten hang-up calls before. Everyone did. No reason to be upset or frightened. No reason to suspect anything was amiss. No reason to think that call had anything to do with Pierce's return.

But what if it did?

What if someone from his past—his immediate past—had found him? What if—

Jessica got up and paced the room, wringing her hands. Dear God. What was she going to do? The unanswered questions, the suspicions, the *not knowing* were going to drive her crazy. Every little thing out of the ordinary would take on new significance for her now. She knew she wouldn't be able to stand this kind of limbo indefinitely, but what could she do? Ask Pierce to leave?

She felt guilty at even contemplating such an action, but really and truly, how could they go on like this? How could they live in the same house now that they were nothing more than polite strangers?

Perhaps not even polite, because Pierce was now someone she could no longer trust.

After crawling back into bed, Jessica huddled beneath the covers, unable to fall back asleep. Images, both of the past and the future, crowded her mind. She tried to tell herself that things had a way of working themselves out, but Jessica had never been much of an optimist. Pierce's glass was the one that had always been half-full.

There was only one thing she could do. Only one way to handle such an impossible situation. She had to think of her son, after all. His emotional, as well as his physical security had to be her first priority. She had to do what was best for him.

And the sooner she let Pierce know her decision, the better it would be for all of them.

Chapter 5

"I'll give you a month." Jessica said the words aloud in her bedroom, testing the way they sounded as she tried to decide exactly what to say to Pierce when she saw him this morning. "I'll give you a month. Not one day longer."

"A month should be long enough to get your affairs in order." Jessica flinched at the prissy formality of her words. There was just no easy way to say it, she decided, but the fact remained that she wanted him out of here. They couldn't possibly go on living in the same house indefinitely. Not after all these years.

A month seemed reasonable to her. More than reasonable, actually. Perhaps a little foolhardy, considering that for all she knew, he could be a common criminal now.

She sat up in bed. Hugging her knees, she chewed on her lip. A thief on the run. That would explain a lot. The scars. His appearance. What if he'd been in prison or...

But wouldn't she have known that? Wouldn't she have been contacted? Maybe he used aliases. Maybe he was like one of those men she'd seen on Oprah who had different identities and different families in several cities. Maybe she should call Jay and have him do some kind of a check, run Pierce's fingerprints through a government computer or something.

It was strange how that idea made her feel just the tiniest bit like a traitor when she had absolutely no reason to. Yet she'd be a fool not to do everything in her power to protect herself and her son. She'd be a fool to trust Pierce again after all these years.

"Mo-o-m? Mom, where are you? I'm home!"

The sound of her son's voice startled Jessica into action. She swung her legs off the bed and reached for her robe just as her door flew open and Max launched himself toward her.

"Why are you still in bed?" he demanded. "You have to find me clean clothes for school. I had a bath at Allie's house, but I didn't have no clean clothes to put on," he said accusingly. "Hurry, Mom. I'll be late."

Still functioning at only half speed, Jessica let her son pull her to her feet and drag her down the hallway to his bedroom. Rummaging through his drawers and closet, they managed to come up with a pair of denim shorts—the only kind he would wear—and his favorite Superman T-shirt. Mollified somewhat, he dutifully brushed his teeth and combed his hair without complaint.

Jessica watched as he bent over his black high-tops, laboriously tying the laces. She resisted the temptation to help him, knowing that the best gift she could give to her son was the ability to be self-reliant.

Oh, but how she wanted to take him in her arms at that moment, to shield him from the hardships of the world. How she wished that she could turn back the clock and make this morning as peaceful and unthreatening as she had tried to make all his other mornings.

Seeming to read her thoughts, Max looked up at her. His dark eyes, eyes so like Pierce's, narrowed slightly as if he was concentrating on something he didn't quite understand. "Why is that guy still here, Mom? I saw him downstairs. He's in the kitchen making coffee."

The image jolted Jessica. Obviously Pierce was making himself at home, but then to him, this was still his home. Jessica ran her fingers through her mussed hair. "He spent the night in the guest room, Max. He had nowhere else to go." She winced, realizing how lame her answer sounded. She'd have to do better than that.

But Max, as usual, was one step ahead of her. His frown deepened. "I been thinking," he said. "That guy—he's the one in the pictures you showed me when I was a little kid, isn't he? He's my dad, right?"

Jessica's heart pounded more rapidly. She and Max used to look at Pierce's pictures together. She'd tried to instill in her son a sense of his father, tried to make him understand that Pierce would have loved him just as much as Jessica did, if he had lived.

But what did she tell him now? she wondered desperately. How did she explain Pierce's resurrection? How did she keep Max from hating his father because there was no plausible explanation for his absence from their lives?

She took a deep breath and said simply, "Yes, Max, he is."

"Then why isn't he dead?"

"I don't know. Something happened to him. He…might have been in an accident. He doesn't remember anything about the years he was away."

"You mean he's got anesia?"

Jessica stared at her son, amazed. "*Am*nesia and where did you learn that word?"

Max shrugged. "From Superman." His tone implied "Where else?" Aloud he added, "Once, Lois Lane couldn't even remember who Clark Kent was 'cuz she got conked on the head by these bad guys." Max scratched the side of his nose. "That guy downstairs—my dad—does he remember you?"

"Well . . . yes."

"Does he remember me?"

"He never knew you, Max. You hadn't been born when he le—disappeared."

Max seemed to mull over the information, but something in his eyes made Jessica uneasy. A glint of excitement that made her stomach flutter with dread. Already, she thought. Already Max was starting to think of Pierce as his father. Already Jessica could feel just a tiny bit of her son slipping away from her.

"Is he gonna stay here with us?"

"I'm . . . not sure what his plans are."

"Does he know how to play baseball?"

Jessica's heart sank. "I don't know."

Max's dark eyes lit up. "That would be great, wouldn't it? Because then you wouldn't have to get your clothes all dirty. Girls don't like that, do they?"

"Some don't, I guess. I've always enjoyed our time together, though."

"Yeah, but you can't catch the ball very good, Mom. I bet he knows how to play baseball," Max concluded. "I bet he knows how to fight, too, just like Superman. I bet that's how he got all those scars. Marcus Tate's father's an accountant. He sits in an office all day behind a great big desk. He don't have no scars." Marcus Tate's father, the T-ball coach and once one of Max's heroes, had certainly been cut down a peg or two. Jessica didn't like the way the conversation was going.

She brushed her fingers across Max's silky hair. "Honey...." She trailed off, grasping for words. "I don't think you should get your hopes up too much about, well, about baseball and all that. I told you, I don't know what Pierce's plans are."

"But if he's my dad," Max said, frowning, "don't he have to stay here with us? Isn't it a law or something like that? Maybe I should ask Uncle Jay. I bet he'd know." Max's Uncle Jay was another point of pride with him. He was sure his Uncle Jay was a super-duper agent of some sort. Jessica had tried to explain that just because Jay worked in the Pentagon didn't mean he was a spy, but Max wouldn't hear of it. "Mom," he'd complain, "haven't you ever heard of a cover?"

Jessica sighed, bringing her thoughts back into focus. "Can we talk about this later? The bus will be here any minute, and I don't want you to miss it again."

"Okay." Max shrugged into his leather backpack, then looked up at her, his gaze solemn. "Can I ask you a question, Mom?"

"Sure, sweetie."

Sudden tears glinted in Max's dark brown eyes. Most of the time he tried to act so cool and grown up, but he was still just a little boy with a whole list of questions Jessica didn't know how to answer. "Don't you want my dad to stay here with us?"

"Oh, Max." Jessica knelt and folded him in her arms, and for just a while, he was once again her baby, the one person in the world whose love she had been able to count on. Jessica tightened her arms around him, holding him close, trying to blink back the hot tears before they could spill down her face. At that moment, she didn't know what she wanted. "It's not that easy," she whispered. "He's been gone for five years. Things...change."

"Carly Wilson went away to her grandmother's house for two whole weeks," Max said, tolerating Jessica's embrace for only a second or two longer before he pulled away. "When she came back, she'd lost her two front teeth." He grinned, tapping his own front teeth with his finger. "She looked real funny. Is that the kind of change you mean?"

Jessica managed a smile, ruffling his hair. "Not exactly," she said. "But we'll talk some more later. Now get a move on before you miss that bus."

Jessica quickly dressed, too, slipping on blue jeans and an old faded shirt. Hand in hand, she and Max walked to the bus stop and greeted the other children and mothers who were already waiting for the bus.

Sharon, dressed in a light blue sundress, her blond hair glistening in the sunlight, gave Jessica a knowing look.

"Didn't get much sleep last night, eh?"

Jessica grimaced. "How can you tell?"

"The dark circles are a dead giveaway." She tugged at one of Jessica's rolled-up shirtsleeves. "And I haven't seen you wear this lovely ensemble out on the street before."

"I dressed in a hurry this morning," Jessica murmured. "I...overslept."

Sharon's brows soared. "You? I've never known you to be anything but disgustingly punctual in your whole life."

"I never claimed to be perfect," Jessica snapped, then immediately regretted her bad temper. Sharon McReynolds was the best friend she'd ever had. She and her husband, Frank, had helped Jessica with Max on more occasions than she cared to remember, and she owed them a lot. She gave Sharon an apologetic smile. "I not only overslept, but I got up on the wrong side of the bed this morning. I'm sorry."

Sharon studied her thoughtfully. "Don't worry about it."

Jessica gazed at the children playing at the curb. "I hope he behaved himself last night," she said.

"Who, Max?"

Jessica shot her a look. "Of course Max. Who else?"

"Max was a perfect angel, as always." Sharon hesitated, then said, "You aren't going to say a word, are you?"

"About what?"

Sharon shook her blond head. "I have never known anyone as infuriatingly closemouthed as you are. Don't you know I'm positively *dying* to know why you overslept this morning and why you got up on the wrong side of the bed? And who, for God's sake, is that gorgeous man standing on your porch?"

Jessica whirled. Sure enough, there he stood on her front porch, in broad daylight, for all the world to see. Dressed in faded jeans and a white T-shirt, Pierce leaned against the railing with a proprietary casualness that instantly brought a frown to Jessica's brow.

When he saw her looking, he lifted his arm and waved as if nothing in the world was amiss. Jessica had to keep reminding herself that for him nothing was wrong. Everything was just the way it had been five years ago when he'd left the house to go get ice cream. When they'd still be in love.

She whipped her head around, looked at her friend, then glanced away.

"Well?" Sharon demanded. "Is that the strange man Max told me about? The one who obviously spent the night at your house last night?"

Jessica gave her a nervous smile. "It's not what you think."

"It never is. But you'd better explain real quick," Sharon warned, "because he's coming this way and I might just be inclined to ask *him* instead."

Coming this way? What in the world was he thinking? How was she going to explain his sudden appearance to all her neighbors? Jessica had told them long ago that her husband was dead, and now here he was, obviously not a ghost, but a real flesh-and-blood man.

Obviously a man.

Too obviously.

The group of chattering mothers fell silent as Pierce approached the group. There was something different about him this morning, Jessica thought. In the bright sunlight, he looked taller. Broader. Tougher. More confident.

More like the old Pierce.

She felt her heart stop for a moment.

The sunlight caught the scar on his cheek, highlighted it, but somehow the effect was less daunting than when she'd first seen it. He didn't look like a man who needed taking care of at all this morning.

What he looked like, Jessica thought with a catch in her throat, was a man very much in control.

Their eyes met and clung, and Jessica's heart started beating again, almost painfully. No, she silently denied. I don't feel anything for him. Nothing at all. I *can't*.

But the butterflies in her stomach wouldn't listen to her. They were going crazy. They were making her feel weak and helpless and out of control, and Jessica wouldn't stand for that. Not anymore. She lifted her chin and eyed him with chilly annoyance.

That's when she realized that the whole group of mothers and children were still silent and staring at the scene unfolding before them with avid curiosity.

Out of the corner of her eye, Jessica saw Max move away from his friends and start toward them. Oh, no, she thought. Not here. Not like this. What would this kind of scene do to him? Pierce should have known better. What if

Max got upset? What if he started to cry in front of his friends? He'd hate that later.

But it was too late to head off disaster now, because Max was already standing beside her. He slipped his little hand in hers and squinted up at Pierce, his expression as inscrutable as his father's as they stared at each other for a long, tense moment.

Max bent and scratched a scab on his knee. He kicked the dirt with the toe of his new running shoe. He looked Pierce straight in the eye. "Hi, Dad," he said, and smiled.

The group had been silent before, but now everyone looked stunned. Max had spoken right up so that everyone at the bus stop had no trouble at all in hearing what he'd said.

Pierce felt his heart give a funny little twist. He stuck his hand casually into the pocket of his jeans. Then he grinned. "Hi, Max."

Dad. Max had called him Dad. Pierce couldn't believe it. It was too much to ask for, this soon. It was too good to be true....

And then he turned and glimpsed Jessica's thunderstruck expression. She looked as stunned as he felt, but not in the same way. There was no elation in Jessica's eyes. No joy in her face. Just a rigid determination to see this scene through with as much dignity as she could muster. He couldn't help but admire her resolve because Max's easy acceptance of him must have been like a slap in the face to her.

He tried to catch her eye, wanted to smile at her in reassurance, but Jessica wouldn't look at him. Instead she turned and watched their son as he boarded the school bus.

As Max climbed the steps, the little boy behind him said loudly, "Wow! That's your *dad?*"

"Yeah," Max said. "Did you see all his scars?"

"Yeah! How'd he get 'em?"

"Fightin' bad guys, a course."

"Cool," the little boy said with reverence.

Pierce grimaced. He was afraid Max's assessment had hit a little too closely to the truth, but he hardly had time to worry about that now. As the bus lumbered down the street toward the next stop, the crowd of mothers reluctantly began to disperse. Several of them smiled and waved at him as they turned in various directions toward their homes. A tall, attractive blonde, who stood just behind Jessica, glowered at him with open distrust.

"Jessica," the woman said, "are you all right?"

"I'm fine, Sharon," Jessica said quietly. "I'll call you later, okay?"

"Please do." The blonde gave Pierce one last disapproving look before she turned and strode up the sidewalk of the house next door to theirs.

Without a word, Jessica started down the cobblestone walkway. Pierce caught her arm as she tried to brush past him. "Jesse—"

The look she gave him stopped him cold. Her gray eyes frosted over as she glared at him. "Are you satisfied?" she demanded. "Do you see what you've done?"

"I didn't do anything," Pierce said. "I came out here to say goodbye to our son. What's so wrong with that?"

"What's *wrong* with it? Oh, please. You can't be that dense." Impatiently Jessica brushed the windblown curls from her forehead. Her manicured nails flashed pink in the sunlight. "Don't you see what you're doing to him?"

Pierce kept an easy pace beside her as they headed for home. "Why don't you tell me what I'm doing to him? I've barely met him."

"My point exactly. You just met him." Jessica turned on the top step of the porch to face him. Her hands went to her slim hips as she stood there glaring at him. Anger had warmed the chill in her gray eyes, and now they sparked with silver fire. Two rosy spots of color tinted her high cheekbones, and her lips—those gorgeous lips—trembled with indignation.

Standing on the top step put her at an even level with him. Their eyes were flush, their mouths only inches apart. Even in anger—perhaps even more so in anger—she was still the most beautiful woman Pierce had ever known. He had to resist the urge to reach out and cup the back of her neck and pull her to him, not gently, until he could claim her lips with his. He wanted to kiss her, hold her, touch her in such a way that she would have to remember she belonged to him.

Only to him.

Something of his thoughts must have shown on his face, because Jessica's eyes turned wary, almost frightened. She reached out a hand and grasped one of the white porch pillars for support.

"Your son is five years old and you just met him, Pierce." She took a deep breath, her eyes filling with tears, but Pierce didn't reach for her or try to comfort her. He didn't dare. "Max has always wanted a father like all his friends have. Someone to play baseball with, someone to take him swimming, someone to teach him the things all the other little boys know how to do. And now suddenly here you are, after all these years, ready to step in and make all his dreams come true. You're setting him up for a big fall, and I'm the one who'll have to pick up the pieces."

"What are you talking about?" Pierce demanded angrily. "I would never do anything to hurt our son. Why can't I do all those things with him? Why can't I be the father he always wanted?"

"Because I don't even know if you're going to be here," Jessica burst out. She seemed stunned by her own words, her own anger. Her fingers trembled as she lifted her hand to her mouth.

Pierce had a sick feeling in the pit of his stomach. He took a step toward her, and when she would have backed away, his hand shot out to grasp her arm. Reluctantly her gaze lifted and met his. "Are you asking me to leave, Jessica? Is that what all this is leading up to?"

Her gaze flickered. "I don't...not exactly," she faltered, but she could no longer meet his eyes. She made a helpless gesture with her hand. "This is an impossible situation, Pierce. We have to talk, decide what's best for...all of us."

"I thought we talked last night," Pierce said, frowning. He didn't like the way she kept dancing around his question. *Did* she want him to leave?

"Things got a little too tense last night," she said.

He smiled sardonically. "No kidding. It's not every day I return from the dead, you know."

"It's not every day my long-lost husband walks through my back door," she countered, her gaze leveling on him once again. But her eyes softened just a hint. Pierce felt enormously encouraged. "We do have to talk, Pierce, but not out here. I think we've given the neighbors enough to gossip about for one day."

"Worried your reputation will be tarnished, Mrs. Kincaid?" he teased softly.

Jessica gave him a defiant look as she tossed her dark hair over her shoulder. "How do you know it wasn't already?" she asked.

Then she turned and left him standing on the porch, swearing beneath his breath.

* * *

Jessica decided she didn't want to have such a serious discussion with her husband while she looked like the waif he'd once rescued. That insecure young woman was long gone, thank goodness. Jessica wanted to make sure Pierce knew they were on equal footing now. She gazed critically at her reflection in the mirror.

The narrow black skirt and white rayon blouse she chose were simple yet elegant, and the French twist that tamed her hair made her look sophisticated and businesslike. Jessica decided she looked like a woman ready to face the world. Or, as Pierce had said, a husband who had just returned from the dead.

When she talked to him this time, Jessica didn't want to let her anger get the better of her. She wanted to present her plan to him clearly and concisely in as straightforward a manner as she could muster. She wanted to make him see that she had thought it all out, and it really was the only viable plan for their rather peculiar situation. She wanted to make this as painless as possible—for all of them.

Pierce would cooperate. How could he not? What reasonable alternative could he possibly come up with?

Yet that reassurance didn't calm her nerves in the least as she walked down the stairs. It annoyed her to find that her palms were sweating and her throat was suddenly, achingly dry.

The aroma of freshly brewed coffee greeted her as she shoved open the swinging door and stepped inside the kitchen. She let the door swish shut behind her. It barely made any noise, but Pierce, who had been standing at the sink, whirled around as if she'd just fired a gun.

It wasn't that he was startled, she noticed. There was no look of surprise in the dark gleam of his eyes. No jumping pulse in his throat. He eyed her with what she could only call steely readiness. A determination to face…whatever he had to face.

Her own heart leaped to her throat. Jessica's hand went to her neck, as if to quiet her own rioting pulse. As she stood there, Pierce's gaze softened and moved over her.

"Is that the way you always dress on your day off?" he asked approvingly. "At least, I assume the shop is closed today. I always closed it on Mondays."

Jessica cleared her throat, stepped across the room to the counter and poured herself a cup of coffee, somehow managing not to spill the steaming liquid as she clutched the cup with hands that still trembled. "I don't do everything at the shop the way you used to, Pierce." She shot him a challenging glance. "In fact, I have my own policies now. My own rules and regulations."

"I see."

Jessica shrugged. "You used to complain yourself that the way your parents ran the shop was archaic and inefficient. You just never took the time to implement change. In fact, in many ways you were a very lax businessman," she said with cool disapproval.

"Is that so?" He didn't seem perturbed in the least by her criticism. "And you are the very epitome of efficiency, I imagine."

Jessica fought the flash of hurt his flippancy brought on. "Yes, as a matter of fact, I am. Is that so hard to believe?"

"A little," he admitted. "I never thought of you as a businesswoman, Jesse."

"I used to work for you," she observed, annoyed. "That's how we met."

His gaze softened. "I remember. But you seemed happy to quit when we bought this house. You wanted to be a wife and mother. You had no interest in the business."

"Things change," Jessica said.

"So you've said."

"In fact," she continued, "I think you'll be quite surprised by the margin of profit The Lost Attic now enjoys."

"Are you going to show me your books?" Somehow he managed to make the innocent question sound like a sexual proposition.

Jessica frowned as she carried the cup to the table and sat down, crossing one leg over the other and then carefully smoothing her napkin across her lap.

"So," Pierce said as he leaned back against the sink. His eyes lingered on her legs for a moment, then lifted to meet her gaze. "*Are* you going to work today?"

"Actually, no," Jessica admitted. "I still close on Mondays."

"Aha. Something that *hasn't* changed around here." He made it sound like some kind of marvelous discovery.

Jessica decided she'd better nip that train of thought in the bud right now. "Why don't you sit down?" She gestured toward the chair across from her. "I have a few things I'd like to say."

He ignored the chair she'd indicated and pulled out the one next to her. His knees brushed hers under the table, and Jessica quickly shifted hers aside.

She lifted her chin, ignoring the tiny thrill that raced up her spine. "I think what we should do first is set some ground rules for our...cohabitation."

Pierce's brow rose almost imperceptibly. "Cohabition?" he said in a voice that was faintly mocking. "Is that what we have here?"

"For lack of a better term," Jessica said. She took a deep breath, throwing him a defensive glance before averting her gaze to her coffee cup. "In fact, I have an ultimatum for you. Sort of a two-part one, you might say."

"Let's hear the first part." His voice was oddly devoid of emotion. Jessica gave him another glance. Then a second one. He looked so... clean this morning, she thought fleetingly. She could smell the barest hint of soap on his skin, and his dark hair gleamed in the morning sunlight, begging to be touched. She could still remember the texture of his hair, she realized. Could almost feel the softness as she ran her fingers through it while they—

Stop it, Jessica! she admonished herself as she tore her eyes from his rugged profile. He's a stranger now. Worse than a stranger—a counterfeit.

A counterfeit husband, that was a good description for Pierce Kincaid.

"Well?" Pierce prompted, jerking her thoughts to the present.

"I'd like you to see Dr. Prescott," she said. "Today, if possible." Dr. Prescott had been their family doctor ever since he'd administered Pierce and Jessica's blood tests before they got married. A few years later, he'd delivered Max. Seeing him seemed like the logical first step to Jessica.

"You think Dr. Prescott can prescribe some miracle drug that will cure me, Jesse?"

"I don't know what he can do," she said. "But I certainly think you should have a thorough examination. All those scars...." Her voice trailed off as her gaze lit on the jagged line that marred the left side of his face. "I... think you can understand why I would want you to see a doctor," she said uneasily.

Pierce smiled. "I understand more than you think," he said softly. "If it'll make you feel any better, I'll go see Dr. Prescott. Just don't expect too much. Don't get your hopes up."

Jessica looked him straight in the eye. "I never do that."

Pierce's gaze flickered with something Jessica thought looked a little too much like pity. That was the last thing she wanted from him. She cleared her throat. "The second part of my ultimatum is this. I'll give you one month."

His scarred brow twisted. "To do what?"

"To stay here. To come up with the right answers. To explain to me why you left five years ago and why you haven't been in touch since. I think a month is more than reasonable. Don't you?"

Pierce shrugged. "I'm hardly in a position to bargain." He sat back, staring at her. "All right, supposing at the end of this month, I still don't have any answers for you. Supposing my memory still hasn't returned. What then, Jessica?"

"Then . . . I don't see that there can ever be any hope for us. Maybe you didn't leave me on purpose, Pierce. Maybe there were extenuating circumstances. But if you never get your memory back, then we'll never know for sure, will we?" She locked her hands together in her lap, trying to stop the trembling. Might as well face the truth, hadn't they? Get it all out in the open? No use pretending that things could ever be as they used to be.

Pierce's chair scraped against the tile floor as he shoved it away from the table and stood. Jessica jumped at his sudden movement, at the look he gave her. His dark eyes glittered like black diamonds as he placed his hands on the table and leaned toward her. His face was only inches from hers. His lips only a breath away . . .

Jessica's heart thundered in her chest. What was he doing? What right did he have to look at her like that? As if he wanted to . . .

Surely he didn't think she would let him kiss her? Not after the discussion they'd just had.

But he was so close she could hear the slight quickening of his breath, could see the warmth of desire in his eyes. His lips were moving closer and, dear God, it had been so long. So very long since he'd kissed her. Jessica's eyes fluttered closed....

"One month," he said, his voice low and seductive. "I'll give *you* one month, Jesse."

Jessica's eyes flew open. She gazed up at him, and the hint of amusement she saw on his face made her anger flare to life once again. "What are you talking about?" she demanded, her face heating in embarrassment at his rejection.

He smiled. Slowly. Mysteriously. He smiled just like he used to. "I'll give you one month to fall in love with me again," he said softly.

Then he turned and strode from the room, leaving Jessica sitting alone with an open mouth and a pounding heart.

Jessica fumed all the way to the bank. What nerve! How dare he challenge her that way? Fall in love with him again? Not bloody likely. What kind of fool did he take her for?

She should just turn the car around, drive back home, march inside the house, and demand that he leave the premises immediately. Letting him stay a month was just prolonging the agony. Both she and Max would be better off making a clean break now.

At the thought of her son, Jessica sighed. How would Pierce's return affect her relationship with Max? She'd never had to share him with anyone. Their devotion to each other had been complete and uncomplicated. Max's love was the only love Jessica had ever been able to depend on. To trust. The thought of sharing it, of losing even a little bit of his affection, was more than she could bear.

Why? she asked herself bitterly, biting her lip to hold back her emotions. Why did Pierce have to come back?

You sound disappointed, Jesse.

Unbidden, his accusation came back to her, and Jessica realized with a sinking sensation in her stomach that it wasn't disappointment she felt at that moment. It wasn't anger or resentment or even confusion.

What she felt was fear. Cold, mind-numbing terror.

I'll give you one month to fall in love with me again.

Jessica parked the car in front of the bank, then sat staring out the window. There was no way, she promised herself. No way on earth she would ever let herself fall in love with Pierce Kincaid again. She was over him. She'd been over him for a long time.

But things change, a little voice in the back of her mind taunted her.

Pierce wouldn't let himself consider the possibility that it might really be over. For just a moment this morning, for just a split second of time, he'd seen the hint of desire in her eyes. The flicker of memory that told him she hadn't forgotten how it used to be between them.

It wasn't love, he admitted grimly. It wasn't even affection, but it was something. Something he could hold on to while he grappled with all the other losses.

She'd given him a month. Not much time when you considered the five years in which he'd lost ground. He could almost smile at the image of her sitting beside him, dressed so prim and proper, issuing her two-part ultimatum with what seemed like all the confidence in the world.

How she'd changed, he thought in wonder. How she'd matured.

There was hardly anything left of the woman he'd fallen in love with and married, of the woman who had once looked up to him with a hero worship that had made him feel ten feet tall. Jessica had grown into her own woman, as he always knew she would. What he hadn't counted on in those days was that she might one day outgrow her need for him.

Of course, he had to admire what she'd done. Running a business and raising their son single-handedly couldn't have been easy. He admired and respected her more than ever, but when he thought about the way she used to be, he couldn't help feeling something of the loss she must have felt when he disappeared five years ago.

One month, he reminded himself grimly. He had one month to counteract all the negative feelings the past five years had generated inside her. He had one month to win back his wife. One month to regain his memory.

One month to fight for his life.

Chapter 6

"Doctor, can a person pretend to have amnesia when in fact he really doesn't?"

Dr. Prescott raised an eyebrow as he settled back in his leather chair. "Are you saying you think that's the case with your husband, Jessica?"

Jessica squirmed under his unwavering stare and tried to settle more comfortably into her own chair. She'd been in Dr. Prescott's office for several minutes now while Pierce waited in the examination room. She wondered if he was as nervous as she was.

She made an aimless gesture with her hands. "I don't know what I'm saying, Dr. Prescott. It just seems so strange to me that he could leave one day, be gone for five years, then show up out of the blue thinking he'd only been gone for thirty minutes. I mean, is that really possible?"

"I'll admit it seems a bit...extreme, but selective amnesia— if that's what he's suffering from—is a complicated illness, Jessica. There's still a lot about it we don't understand. I know of several documented cases, not unlike Pierce's, where the amnesia victim loses an entire block of time from his memory, nothing else, just a particular period of time. The rest of his memory remains intact.''

"What would cause that?"

Dr. Prescott leaned forward and folded his hands on the top of his desk. "Any number of things, actually. An accident. A serious illness. Sometimes a blow to the head is all it takes to bring on some form of amnesia. Selective amnesia, however, is a bit trickier. Sometimes the cause can be more mental than physical, the result of a severe shock or trauma. Something so painful the victim has to block it from his or her memory in order to deal with it. Sometimes in order to survive.''

Jessica thought about the scar on Pierce's face and on his arm. Would his wounds have been traumatic enough to make him block the memories? Or had it been something else? A different kind of shock? Jessica took a deep breath, avoiding Dr. Prescott's kindly stare. "During this five years, could...could he have been leading another life? Could he have forgotten about...you know, his real life during that time?"

"It's entirely possible," Dr. Prescott said. "You see, sometimes when a person recovers from total amnesia, he won't remember anything about the interval of time when his memory was gone, not even the people he met or the places he went to. His mind simply reverts to the person he was before he lost his memory. Do you follow me, Jessica?

"What I'm saying is that something could have happened to Pierce five years ago to bring on a complete memory loss. He might not have even known his own name. Then five years later, something might have triggered the recall. Gradually his memories returned, but the period of time in which he suffered from amnesia, the interval, could be gone forever.''

"You mean...we may never know what happened to him?"

Dr. Prescott must have read Jessica's distressed reaction, because he added softly, "That's not necessarily conclusive, Jessica. I'm merely reciting some textbook cases. As I said before, there's still much about amnesia we don't understand. Each case is different. Sometimes memories will manifest themselves in dreams. That can be extremely helpful." He stood and picked up the folder on his desk. "We can talk some more later if you like. I know it sounds complicated and confusing, but right now I think I better get to our patient.''

The sound of the office door closing behind Dr. Prescott barely registered with Jessica. She sat staring straight ahead, her mind reeling with all she had learned.

Something could have happened to Pierce five years ago to bring on a complete memory loss. He might not have even known his own name.

Jessica closed her eyes, letting the impact of the doctor's words sweep over her. It was entirely possible that everything Pierce had told her was true.

One thing I do know. I didn't leave you because I wanted to.

Jessica put her hands to her face, overcome with emotion. Did she dare believe it? Did she dare believe that Pierce hadn't left her because he wanted to? That he hadn't just abandoned her because he didn't love her anymore?

And if it was true, if she did accept it, where did that leave them? Five years had gone by. Five long years of learning to live without him, of being happy with the person she had become. She wasn't the woman Pierce had left behind, no matter what his reason for leaving had been.

Jessica knew she would never be content again to stay at home and be the perfect wife for him. She would never be able to tolerate his overprotectiveness, his treating her as if she were some rare and fragile flower.

She was older, stronger, more mature now. She was capable of taking care of herself and her son, and if truth be told, she had no idea where Pierce, with or without his memory, was going to fit into her life.

"My God, son, what the hell happened to you?"

"If I knew that I probably wouldn't be here," Pierce said dryly as he sat, shirtless, on the examination table. He knew Dr. Prescott was staring at his back. He could see the shock on the nurse's face beside him as she glanced around, then hastily averted her eyes.

It had been quite a shock to Pierce last night, too. After his shower, he'd studied himself in the mirror—not out of any particular sense of vanity, far from it—but to try to reacquaint himself with a body that seemed very much a stranger's to him.

The mass of thin, crisscrossing scars on his back had only served to confuse him even more. When he'd tried to remember how he'd gotten them, he had experienced a headache so severe, so blinding, Pierce had feared he might black out.

Dr. Prescott whistled softly. "You know what this puts me in mind of? Some of the POWs I saw as an army doctor during and after Korea." He hesitated for a moment, then said, "Step outside for a minute, will you, Sue?"

The nurse nodded and quietly left. Dr. Prescott came around and took a seat in front of Pierce. "Has Jessica seen your back?"

Pierce flinched, reaching for his shirt. "No, and I'd just as soon she not know about it."

Dr. Prescott raised a brow. "She'll have to sooner or later, won't she? That is, if you two plan to resume a normal married life."

"That doesn't seem too likely at the moment," Pierce muttered, buttoning his shirt.

"Pretty emotional time for you two, I would imagine," Dr. Prescott observed kindly. "Five years is a long time to be separated from one another. A lot can happen. Things change. People change. If I was inclined to offer something other than medical advice, I'd say it's not the time for anything but complete honesty."

Pierce frowned at the terrazzo floor. "If I was inclined to accept unsolicited advice, I'd say you could be right. But complete honesty is not always all it's cracked up to be, Doctor."

"I wouldn't share that bit of wisdom with Jessica if I were you. She . . . well—" he searched for the right words, gesturing with his hand "—let's just say she has her doubts about your condition."

"She doesn't believe I have amnesia."

"She's skeptical."

"And you?" Pierce asked bluntly.

"Now that I've examined you? No. Judging from your back alone, I'd say you've been through enough trauma in the past five years to want to block it from your memory in any way possible." He paused, eyeing Pierce with an understanding but not pitying look. "Make no mistake, that's purely a gut instinct from someone who's been there, and not the professional opinion of a medical doctor. I'll reserve that judgment until we have all your test results in."

"Fair enough," Pierce said, shoving himself off the examination table. "But one more thing, Dr. Prescott. I don't want you to mention the scars to Jessica. The one on my face is bad enough. I'd like to tell her about the others my-self, when the time is right."

When he thought she could handle it without looking at him in pity and disgust, Pierce mentally added.

When the door to the office opened again, Jessica jumped to her feet, a testament to her agitation. Her gaze went first to Dr. Prescott, then to Pierce who followed just behind the doctor.

"Have a seat, you two," Dr. Prescott began. He seated himself behind his desk and opened Pierce's chart, studied it for a moment, then closed it and laid his folded hands on top of it. Jessica wasn't sure why but the gesture seemed fraught with symbolism. An open-and-shut case. Nothing more to be done.

Reluctantly she sat down again, and Pierce took the seat next to her. She cleared her throat and stared ahead at Dr. Prescott, but it was Pierce who dominated her thoughts. She could *feel* him beside her, and her overwrought nerves seemed to scream with awareness.

"As I just told Pierce," Dr. Prescott explained, "I want to withhold my final opinion until we have all the test re-sults in, but I do have one recommendation I'd like to make at this time."

"What is it, Dr. Prescott?" Jessica asked nervously. Pierce remained silent as if he, too, was withholding final judgment.

"I'd like to give you the name of another doctor, a psy-chiatrist, I think you should see."

Jessica wasn't looking at Pierce, but she felt his almost violent reaction to Dr. Prescott's suggestion. Dr. Prescott scribbled the name and number on a piece of paper and handed it across the desk. When Pierce made no move to accept it, Jessica reached out and took the paper from the doctor's hand, glancing at the Georgetown address.

"His name is Dr. Layton. He just moved here recently from Chicago. He's cut back on his patient load, but I think he'll be willing to see you with my recommendation. His work with amnesia victims is well-known and respected in the medical community. I really hope you'll go see him, Pierce. At the very least, he can help you cope with the stress."

"We'll call him," Jessica promised as they all stood, concluding the meeting.

Pierce said nothing. He opened the door for her and they walked out of the office together, but still he remained ominously silent. When Jessica tried to question him about the examination on the drive home, he answered her questions as curtly and evasively as possible. Once home, he went straight to the guest room. He was still there when Jessica left to go pick up Max at the baby-sitter's.

Jessica pondered his reaction on the drive to Mrs. Taylor's house. It seemed to her that Dr. Prescott's suggestion that Pierce see a psychiatrist had brought on some sort of anxiety attack, but why? Why would he be so reluctant to see a psychiatrist, someone who could help him, unless...

Unless... he was afraid of what he might reveal.

Jessica blocked that idea from her mind. She wouldn't think about it now. Not when her son was hurling himself at her like a speeding bullet. She caught him up and spun him around. It felt so good to hold him in her arms today.

"Do you have a kiss for me?" she asked.

"Uh-huh." He dutifully pecked her cheek. "Did you bring my cape?" he demanded.

"It's in the car, Mr. Kent."

"Good." He wiggled out of her arms and looked up at her, squinting one eye. "Can we go see my dad now?"

Jessica said nothing as she and Max climbed into the car. All the way home, Max kept up a running commentary on the day's events. Alan Michael had brought a dead turtle to school that morning which had greatly impressed Max. By lunchtime, though, it had started to smell so the teacher made them give it a decent burial in the playground.

"It was real cool," Max said. "Cari Thompson cried but everyone knows she's just a big baby, anyway."

Jessica murmured the proper response, and Max launched into a new topic. "I made a new friend today," he informed her. "I think his family's gonna move into the house next to Mrs. Taylor's. At least I hope so. He was real cool."

Jessica made a mental note to check with Max's baby-sitter about her potential new neighbors. "Is he about your age, Max?"

Max thought for a moment. "He's older, I think. But we played a really cool game called secret mission."

"Secret mission? What kind of game is that?"

Max instantly clammed up. He locked his lips together and stared out the window as if he'd said more than he should have. "It's just a dumb kid game," he muttered. "No big deal."

"You mean like the superhero games you and Marcus sometimes play?"

Max brightened. "Yeah. Like that."

"Well, don't get too carried away with it, okay? Remember, it's just pretend."

"Okay, Mom. Are we almost home? I promised Allie I'd help her build a house for Snowflake today. Course, cats don't like houses, you know. Dogs do, though."

Jessica ignored the bait. Her mind was still on their previous conversation. She hoped Max's imagination wouldn't get the better of him with this new game. She supposed she should be relieved that his obsession with superheroes might be waning, but secret missions? What would he come up with next?

She slanted him a look as she braked for a traffic light. Was it her imagination, or did he seem a little secretive tonight? A little evasive? Oh, he was talking ninety to nothing as usual, but there was something about the way he almost skillfully led the conversation onto topics he knew Jessica wouldn't object to that bothered her. Made her just a tad suspicious.

He reminded her a little too much of the way Pierce used to be when he came home from one of his buying trips, she thought with a start. Pierce would dazzle her with attention from the moment he walked in the door until Jessica would soon forget all about the questions she'd intended to ask him when he got home.

Maybe she was just being overly suspicious in hindsight, she concluded, but her gaze strayed back to her son.

He's only a little boy, she reminded herself. It was only natural he'd have secrets from her. Nothing sinister in that. Probably had a frog stashed somewhere up in his room. Or dirty underwear stuffed under his bed.

He caught her looking at him and smiled Pierce's smile. "I love you, Mom," he said sweetly.

"I love you, too, son."

Oh, dear. Something was definitely up. Jessica had a feeling that the next time she cleaned his room, she was in for some nasty surprises.

"Why don't we just order a pizza?"

Jessica stared at the meager selection in the refrigerator, trying to ignore Pierce and his comment as he hovered over her shoulder.

"You love pepperoni."

Jessica slammed the refrigerator door, annoyed with herself for not having gone to the grocery story after leaving the doctor's office and annoyed with Pierce for being...well, for being Pierce. She couldn't seem to get his reaction to the suggestion of his seeing a psychiatrist out of her mind. It seemed to her that he should be willing to do whatever it took to restore his memory. She didn't understand his reluctance.

"For your information," she said, turning to confront him, "I haven't eaten pizza in years. It's loaded with fat and cholesterol. Max is a growing boy. He needs proper nutrition."

"Just trying to help," Pierce said, throwing up his hands. "Why don't we go down to Kelly's," he proposed, referring to a cafeteria where they used to eat once or twice a week.

"Kelly's went out of business three years ago," Jessica said. "I'll just have to go to the grocery store."

"But, Mo-o-m," Max complained as he materialized in the doorway. His red cape fluttered behind him. "I'm starving!"

"Surely pizza just this once wouldn't hurt," Pierce murmured.

"Pizza?" Max's spirits immediately perked up. He tossed his cape over his shoulder. "Do we get to have pizza for supper, Mom?"

Jessica could almost see the little boy's mouth watering. Even though she'd always worked, Jessica had tried to give Max balanced meals, at least at dinnertime. It was a point of pride with her. But her head was hurting tonight, her stomach was clenched with tension, she was tired, and she had to go to work tomorrow. A trip to the grocery store was the last thing she wanted to make.

"Oh, all right. I'll call in the order," she conceded, giving Pierce an exasperated look that said "You may have gotten your way this time, but don't try it again" as she brushed past him to reach the phone.

Max clapped his hands in glee. "Yippee! Pizza! Get a real big one, Mom. I can eat five hundred pieces all by myself."

The sound of Pierce's laughter drew Jessica's gaze. The quality of his laughter had always affected her so strongly. She realized now how long it had been since she had heard it. How much she had missed it.

Pierce ruffled Max's hair affectionately. "That's quite an appetite you have there, Superman."

Max beamed proudly. "Mom said I got that from you. She said I got your smile, too." He grinned broadly. "Didn't you, Mom?"

Jessica could feel Pierce's eyes on her as she avoided his gaze. "I...I don't remember."

"Sure you do. We were watching the wedding movie, remember? The part where you were feeding each other cake. Mom said you could've eaten that whole cake all by yourself on account of your teeth are sweet or something like that. We used to watch that movie all the time, didn't we, Mom? 'Cept we had to stop, 'cuz it always made her cry."

Max rattled on, oblivious to the tension in the room. He twirled his cape over his arm. "'Specially that part where you put the ring on her finger and said you would always be together till death has a party or something like that. Didn't you always cry, Mom?"

Jessica could feel Pierce's stare, and almost against her will, she lifted her gaze. His eyes were deep and dark and liquid with emotion. *I'm sorry,* they seemed to tell her. *I'm so sorry for your pain.*

And at that moment, all Jessica wanted to do was drown in those eyes, melt inside his arms, and rejoice in the miracle that had brought her husband back to her. He was *alive.* Dear God, Pierce was alive. All those years of agony. All those days of uncertainty. All those nights of loneliness.

Pierce was alive.

Shouldn't that be all that mattered?

But it wasn't, Jessica thought with a pain deep inside her heart. There were too many unanswered questions. Too many memories. Too much time between them. Too much doubt and suspicion.

Nothing would ever be the same again.

Jessica dropped her gaze and turned away. "I'll place the order," she murmured, reaching for the phone.

"Come on, Max," Pierce said quietly. "Let's make ourselves useful. Do you know how to set the table?"

"Sure I do," Max readily agreed. "I learned when I was about . . . four."

"You can probably teach me a few things," Pierce said wryly, casually putting a hand on the little boy's shoulder. Jessica's heart almost stopped when she saw the way Max gazed up at his father.

"Okay," he said, grinning. "I bet we could teach each other a lot of things. I got lots of comic books. You can borrow them if you want. Maybe you could even read them to me sometime on account of I can't read yet. I like to look at the pictures, though."

Pierce smiled back, then glanced at Jessica. For a moment back there, he'd almost imagined he'd seen a glimmer of warmth in those gray depths. A trace of some of the joy he'd felt this morning, but it was all gone now—if it had ever been there in the first place. Her eyes were like twin glaciers. Frozen. Hard. Impenetrable.

And they seemed to be saying, *One month, Pierce. You have one month.*

He felt Max's little hand in his, and he looked down at his son's earnest face gazing up at him. Dear God, he thought, how would he ever be able to leave them now?

While they waited for the pizza, Jessica went upstairs to change into jeans and a sleeveless cotton blouse. After dinner, she planned to do some work on the games room before bedtime. Her goal was to have it completely remodeled by Max's birthday in July, but work at the shop had taken up most of her time lately, plus she had a buying trip planned in two weeks, which would throw off her schedule even more.

At the thought of the trip, she frowned as she climbed the stairway to the third floor and stood in the doorway. She'd have to postpone it now. There was no way she could leave Max at a time like this.

Actually, Jessica had always hated leaving Max at any time. Since he'd started kindergarten, she couldn't take him with her as she used to, so she had come to rely more and more on Brandon Chambers, an antiques buyer who traveled extensively all over the world. Brandon was good and he was reliable, but he'd never had quite the nose for the unique, as Pierce did. Jessica scowled. As Pierce had once had, she amended. She had no idea where her husband's talents lay these days.

Nor did she care.

But why did he still have to be so handsome? she thought morosely. So...masculine? The scars on his face and arm didn't diminish his good looks at all. In fact, in some strange way, they only added to his appeal. Made him seem invincible somehow. Strong and solid and...permanent.

For God's sake, hadn't she learned anything in the past five years? What was the old adage? You shouldn't judge a book by its cover? How a man looked wasn't important. It was what he was like *inside* that mattered. It was how trustworthy he turned out to be that counted. And she'd learned the hard way that Pierce was not to be relied upon.

Take Brandon, for instance. He was nice-looking, but not handsome like Pierce, and not nearly so tall. Silver accented his brown hair and his hazel eyes were light, open and honest. Not mysterious and soul-stabbing dark like Pierce's.

But what mattered to Jessica was that Brandon Chambers had been extremely kind to her. He'd helped her out when she'd been at her wit's end. He'd stepped in and taken over the buying trips from her when she had almost had to close the shop because she couldn't be both entrepreneur and mother at the same time.

Of course, she paid him a healthy commission for his finds, and she wasn't the only dealer in the D.C. area he bought for. But it seemed to Jessica that he always gave her a more than fair deal, and even more importantly, she trusted him completely.

So why didn't she feel anything else for him? she wondered forlornly. She knew Brandon would like for their relationship to evolve into something more than the friendly business arrangement they shared now, but Jessica had been reticent to encourage him and she didn't know why. He was perfect for her—successful, attractive, trustworthy and kind. What more could she want in a man?

Sparks, she thought immediately. A racing heart. Sweaty palms. The whole nine yards of falling in love again. That's what she wanted and what she didn't have with Brandon.

That's what she'd had with Pierce, and look where it had gotten her, she thought bitterly, kicking at a piece of broken tile. She almost wished she could get down on her hands and knees now and start chiseling away at the tile floor. The physical exertion she had to put into the project might ease some of her mounting frustration at the impossible situation she found herself in.

Instead she crossed the room and made sure the French doors to the balcony were secure. Yesterday she'd noticed that some of the railing had rotted through, and she'd cautioned Max to stay away from this room until she could get a carpenter in to replace the railing. Just to be on the safe side, she'd also shoved a sawhorse in front of the doors.

With the toe of her tennis shoe, Jessica sent another piece of white tile flying toward the opposite wall. Memories of the plans she and Pierce had made for this house came rushing back to her. Turning the converted attic into a game room had been Pierce's idea. When the children had company over, the little beggars could all go upstairs and Mom and Dad could still have their privacy, he'd said.

Children. They'd planned to have several to compensate for both their lonely childhoods. Jessica had long ago given up that dream, but at least she had Max.

No one could ever take him away from her.

When Jessica returned downstairs, the table had already been set and the pizza waited in the center. Pierce had lit candles and turned down the lights, and the room looked beautiful, soft and romantic with the panes in the stained-glass window sparkling like rubies and emeralds and aquamarines and the crystal candelabra flashing like diamonds. The dining room no longer seemed cold and perfect, but vibrantly alive and rich with color. Jessica realized with a start that it was the first time she'd seen the room by candlelight since she'd redecorated a few years ago.

She'd given up all the little luxuries that she and Pierce had once indulged in. It seemed too frivolous for just her and Max, and besides, she was always short on time. Most nights it took everything she had just to get a decent meal on the table after working all day, but somehow Pierce had managed to turn pizza and Coke into an elegant feast for three.

"Why is it so dark in here?" Max asked curiously. "Are we gonna tell ghost stories?"

"Eating by candlelight is a tradition," Pierce explained. "It's considered refined and ... romantic."

"You mean like kissy face? Yuk!" Max screwed up his face in distaste.

"I thought your mother might enjoy it. She used to like to eat by candlelight."

"Why?" Max demanded, climbing into his seat. "That's girl stuff."

"Your mother is a girl. A woman," Pierce said slowly, his eyes on Jessica.

Jessica cleared her throat. "It's ... very nice," she said. "Shall we sit down?"

Pierce pulled out her chair and Jessica sat down. She reached for her napkin and unobtrusively wiped her damp palms on the linen.

"Can I have the first piece, Mom? That one," Max said, reaching across the table to stick his finger into the center of a fat, gooey slice.

Jessica put the choice slab of pizza on his plate. "Max, your napkin," she reminded him quietly. She may have forgone the amenities during the past few years, but she'd at least taught Max basic table manners. It just didn't always show.

"I can use my cape," Max informed her.

Jessica shook her head. "I don't think so."

Max shrugged and stuffed his napkin into the neck of his T-shirt, and Jessica winced. "In your lap, Max."

"This is the way Nicky Perrelli's grandfather does it," Max explained. "That way, he never gets s'ghetti on his shirt." With both hands, he picked up the pizza slice, took a huge bite, then held it out as far as his arms could reach, trailing cheese across the antique white lace tablecloth. Her best one. Jessica grimaced but didn't comment. Obviously Pierce had never eaten dinner with a five-year-old.

Smiling and looking pleased with himself, Pierce placed a huge slice of pizza on Jessica's plate, then took one for himself. Jessica took a tentative bite, then sighed. *Heavenly.* She'd forgotten how divine pizza could be. It was almost a religious experience. She ate the rest of her piece with almost as much gusto as Max did, and had to restrain herself from reaching for another one.

Especially when Pierce kept urging her to eat more. "Come on," he said. "You haven't eaten enough to keep a bird alive."

"Better not," she said, sipping her drink. It wasn't even a diet Coke, she noticed. It was good. What a shame Pierce had to remind her in just one meal of everything she'd been missing lately.

"You can't be watching your weight," he commented innocently. "You look wonderful, Jesse. I like your hair that way."

In spite of herself, Jessica warmed to the compliment. What woman wouldn't? It had been so long since she'd felt attractive. Since she'd felt like a woman.

But she reminded herself just as quickly that Pierce had always known how to charm the socks off her. She wouldn't let him get away with it this time. It would take more than a few pretty phrases to sway her from her decision.

Pierce had a month, and not one day longer.

Their gazes met in the candlelight and suddenly, without warning, Jessica's mind swept her back in time, to another candlelit table, but this one in Paris. Pierce had seemed just as mysterious to her then. Just as handsome and charming, and when he'd proposed to her, Jessica had accepted wholeheartedly. She had been willing to take a chance then because she had loved him so much....

But what about now? What did she feel for him now?

With an effort, Jessica tore her gaze from Pierce, and the memories drifted away. She tried to turn her attention back to the meal, but a chill was in the air, an emptiness, as if she'd lost something precious. Jessica didn't understand it. Didn't understand why, at that moment, she should miss Pierce more than she had in years.

She gazed around the table, her husband at one end, her child at the other. She sat between them. It was such a homey scene, she thought. So innocent and normal-looking. Anyone eavesdropping on them would never have suspected the undercurrents flowing around the table.

How many times had she prayed for such a night? Jessica wondered. How many times had she wished that Pierce would come home so they could be a real family?

But Pierce hadn't come home. At least, not when she'd wished for it. Now didn't count, she thought bitterly. Now was too late.

Losing interest in his second piece of pizza, Max stared at the candles in fascination. He waved his hand, making the flames dance wildly. "Do we get to blow them out when we're done?" he asked hopefully.

"Not like you mean," Jessica told him. "These are not like birthday candles."

His expression was crestfallen. "We don't get to make a wish?"

"Yeah," Pierce echoed, his eyes darkening in the flickering light. "We don't get to make a wish? I know exactly what I would wish for."

Jessica's heart thudded against her chest at the look he gave her. "You," his eyes seemed to be saying. "I'd wish for you again, Jesse."

And what would she wish for? Jessica asked herself sternly. For yesterday? Might as well wish for the moon, because yesterday was gone forever.

"I know what I'd wish for, too," Max chimed in. "I'd wish for a dog. A real big one. Like a sheep dog, or something like that. Every kid in my class has a pet 'cept me," he mourned. "I don't even have anything to bring to the pet show next week, and Alan Michael says it's because I'm still a baby. I'm not a baby, Mom. I could take care of a dog."

"We've been all through this," Jessica said with a sigh. "I know you're not a baby, Max, but you're too young to take care of a pet all by yourself, and I just don't have the time. I'm sorry."

"Maybe I could help."

"You?" Jessica's and Max's voices piped up at the same time, hers edged with suspicion, Max's with hope.

Pierce shrugged. "I like dogs. I wouldn't mind giving Max a hand. You wouldn't have to worry about it at all, Jesse."

And what happens when you leave? Jessica wanted to scream at him. Then I'll be stuck with your responsibility, just like I was the last time. Only she had never felt that she was stuck with Max. Quite the contrary. He'd been her lifeline. Her salvation.

But he still couldn't have a pet.

She said with quiet determination, "I've already made my decision."

"But Mo-o-m!"

"I don't want to hear any more about it, Max. If you're through eating, you may be excused."

Sullenly he pushed back his chair, but as he did so, his arm dragged across the table, upsetting his glass. Dark, sweet liquid poured out all over the antique lace tablecloth.

"How many times have I told you not to set your glass so near the edge of the table?" Jessica admonished as she jumped up and began dabbing at the puddle with her napkin.

Max's lips quivered as he stood beside his chair. "I'm sorry."

"It's all right," Pierce said, coming to stand beside them. His hand reached out, but Jessica noticed he restrained from touching his son. "Everyone makes mistakes."

Gritting her teeth, Jessica ignored him. "Go on upstairs, Max, and start your bath. I'll be up there in a few minutes."

His little shoulders slumping, Max left the room. Even his cape looked wilted.

"It was just an accident," Pierce said again. "Why are you making a federal case out of it, Jesse?"

Jessica whirled on him. "That particular accident has happened almost every night for the past two weeks. He wasn't paying attention to what he was doing. He was being careless."

"He's only five years old," Pierce said, clearly annoyed.

Jessica threw the napkin onto the table. "You don't have to tell me how old my son is. I was there when he was born, remember? And for your information, five years old is not too young to begin learning about responsibility."

"Then why not let him have a dog?" Pierce countered. "What better way to teach him about responsibility?"

"And what happens when he gets tired of the animal?" Jessica flared. "The responsibility would end up being mine, and I have more than I can handle at the moment."

"All the more reason why you should let me help you."

"And what happens when you leave?" she asked coldly. "What happens if you get tired of your responsibilities? I'd have to pick up the pieces for both Max and me, and I won't do that again, Pierce. I can't." Eyes stinging with tears, Jessica turned her attention to the table and began scrubbing fiercely at the stain.

"Let me do that," Pierce said softly, putting his hand on top of hers. "It's my fault. I shouldn't have used this tablecloth. I remembered it was always your favorite. We got it in Brussels, remember?"

"Stop it."

"Stop what?"

"Stop trying to make me remember. I know why you used this tablecloth. Why you lit candles. Why you made such a production out of a simple meal." She gazed at him with cold contempt.

Pierce shrugged. "I just wanted to make our first meal as a family special."

Jessica sniffed, turning away from him. "I know exactly what you were trying to do. You were trying to make things the way they used to be. You were trying to become a part of our lives again, trying to win over Max by taking his side against me. Well, it won't work, Pierce. I won't let you use my son that way. I said you could stay here a month, and I won't go back on my word. But don't think that means I'll let you insinuate yourself into our lives any more than you already have. I won't let you take my son away from me. Max is mine."

Pierce stared at her in shock. "Is that what you think I want to do? Max is *our* son, Jessica. I don't want to take him away from you. I just want to share him with you. I want to be part of his life. And yours, too, if you'll let me."

"Then tell me where you were for the past five years," she demanded.

"You know I can't do that."

"Can't or won't?"

It was Pierce's turn to throw down the napkin. His dark eyes blazed with anger. "You think I'm lying about this?"

"That thought has crossed my mind," she admitted. "Why else would you be so unwilling to see a psychiatrist?"

His eyes glinted dangerously. "This is crazy, Jessica. You're being unreasonable."

"*I'm* being unreasonable! If I had amnesia, I'd try every way possible to get my memory back."

He shook his head. "This isn't you talking, Jesse. This sounds like Jay."

"No, it *is* me," she insisted. "You just don't know me anymore. Of course I have suspicions. I can't help it. I can't just ignore the years you've been gone. I can't pretend you've been here all along because that's the way it is for you." She paused for a breath. "I can't turn back the clock, Pierce. I can't be the woman you left behind. I don't want to be."

"I'm not asking you to be," Pierce said. He turned away, frowning. "Look, I know this is hard for you. It is for me, too. All I'm asking is for you to give me a chance to prove to you how much I love you and Max. How much I want to be a part of this family." He turned to look at her, his gaze earnest. "Isn't that all that matters?" he asked quietly.

Jessica refused to answer. She walked over to the window and crossed her arms as she stared blindly into the darkness. I don't know, she thought. I don't know what matters anymore.

"I'm not trying to threaten your independence, Jesse." His voice lowered. "I wouldn't want to diminish anything you've accomplished."

What she'd accomplished. Images of the past five years flashed through her mind. The long nights spent walking the floor with Max when he couldn't sleep. The grueling hours at the shop the next day when she was dead on her feet. The endless juggling of hours when there were never enough in one day.

What she'd accomplished, Jessica thought, was to feel like a robot half of the time. Hardly ever like a woman. Why, after all these years, did that fact bother her so much?

She sensed Pierce's presence behind her. Could almost imagine his arms steadfastly around her. Her heart began to beat a little faster. His hand touched her arm, a tentative caress, and Jessica closed her eyes.

Please, she thought, don't make me care again. But her pulse was racing at even so slight a touch.

"Jesse." His breath warmed her cheek. "Don't you see? I'm not a threat to you. You're the one who holds all the cards now. You're the one who's in control."

But you're wrong, Jessica cried inwardly.

She had never felt less in control.

Both of Pierce's hands were on her arms now, and he pulled her back until she was leaning against him, her head nestled against his shoulder. For just a moment, Jessica let herself relish the support, allowed herself the luxury of his strength, but then she remembered that he was the man who had left her without an explanation, and she stiffened, tried to move away.

But Pierce held her. He whispered against her ear. "Let me hold you. Just for a minute."

The ragged desperation in his voice made Jessica's eyes sting with tears. Almost unwillingly she felt herself relax against him, and Pierce's arms tightened around her. In his embrace, it was almost too easy to remember how much she had once loved him, needed him.

Desired him.

Dear God, she prayed. Don't make me want him again.

"Have you been lonely, Jesse? Did you miss me?"

His hands were so warm and comforting against her bare arms, but his words brought the past back to her, made her remember the hurt and the doubts and the endless tears.

She pulled herself away from him and stared bleakly out the window. "The first few weeks after you were gone, I wanted to die. I didn't think I could go on without you. I wanted to give up." Jessica sensed his reaction to her words. His despair. She turned to face him. "But I couldn't give up," she said. "I had our child to think of. Max was born exactly two months after you disappeared."

"Were you alone?" His dark eyes flickered with pain.

He'd asked the question as if dreading to know the answer, but Jessica didn't try to shield him. Why should she? She lifted her chin and looked him in the eye. "Yes. Jay was out of the country. There was no one."

Pierce was silent for a moment, then he said, "You'll never know how much I wish I could have been there with you. God, Jesse, I've lost so much more than just memories. I've lost a part of our life together that I can never get back. I'm so sorry. I'm sorry I let you down."

"Sorry is an easy word, Pierce," Jessica said, forcing back the tears. She wouldn't let him get to her. No matter what he said or did, she wouldn't allow herself to forget what he had done to her.

"But what else can I say?" he asked with an edge of desperation in his voice.

"Nothing. There's nothing you can say," she said, but there was a numb, hollow feeling inside her. "What's done is done. I can't help feeling the way I feel."

"Do you hate me that much, Jesse? Are you that bitter? Can it be," he asked softly, his eyes dark and intense, "that you would forgive me for dying but not for living?"

Chapter 7

"And they lived happily ever after."

Jessica closed the book she'd been reading to Max and bent to kiss his satiny cheek. "I'm sorry I yelled at you earlier, sweetie. I've had a lot on my mind lately, and I took it out on you. That was unfair of me."

Max yawned widely, his eyes starting to droop. He snuggled under the covers. "It's okay, Mom. I forgive you. Everyone makes mistakes." His tone mimicked his father's perfectly, and Jessica's heart turned over.

She couldn't get Pierce's accusation out of her head. It echoed through her mind and pounded against her temples as relentlessly as a drumbeat.

Can it be that you would forgive me for dying but not for living?

Jessica closed her eyes, feeling the pain of his words deep down inside her. She hugged Max tightly, tucked him in, then walked down the hall to her own room. But she knew she wouldn't be able to sleep. Pierce's words, the pain in his voice wouldn't let her.

"It's not true," she whispered into the darkness.

But even as she denied it, deep in her heart she knew that Pierce was right. She couldn't forgive him for being alive because that meant that he'd deserted her, just as everyone else in her life had. She couldn't forgive him for being alive because that meant he'd stopped loving her, just as all the others had. She couldn't forgive him for being alive because that meant he could leave her again.

And Jessica was very much afraid she wouldn't be able to stand it a second time.

Voices. He heard voices.

Were they coming back? Would he have to endure their torture all over again?

In some ways, Pierce welcomed their return because that meant they hadn't gotten what they wanted yet. That meant he hadn't succumbed to the pain. The intense psychological training he'd undergone early in his career had worked. He could fade to black and the secrets he carried in his head would remain protected. Pierce knew that he would die before revealing them. That was what he was trained to do. That was what the agency expected him to do.

The door to his cell slid open and two men entered. They grabbed Pierce by the arms and jerked him up off the damp stone floor. He could barely walk, but they didn't seem to notice. They dragged him across the filthy floor, shoved him out into the murky corridor, and when he fell to his knees, one of them kicked him in the side, where at least two of his ribs had already been broken.

They spoke in low, covert tones. In spite of the fact that Pierce was fluent in Spanish, he lost much of their rapid-fire dialogue. One word kept cropping up. *Traidor*. Traitor. Were they talking about him?

They hauled him down the corridor and into a small office where they shoved him down onto a straight-back wooden chair, blindfolded him, and secured his hands and feet to the slats and rungs of the chair. The room grew silent as the men left. Pierce was in complete darkness. He knew better than to struggle against the ropes. The men were experts, just as he was. The more he moved, the tighter the bindings would become, and when at last they released him, the pain would be excruciating.

But the pain was the least of it. He could tolerate the pain. What he couldn't stand was the not knowing. The uncertainty of his position. Jessica must be going crazy by now. What had they told her? Did she know the truth about him now?

Pierce groaned, wishing he could have told her himself. She must feel so betrayed, he thought. So angry. He had to get away from here and somehow make it right with her again.

But where the hell was he? What had happened to him? What had gone wrong? One moment he'd been standing in the sunshine, the next thing he knew he'd awakened in a dark, stinking cell with a lump the size of a baseball on the back of his head.

That had been three days ago, the best he could tell.

Since then he'd been beaten twice, and each time the previous wounds had reopened. Pierce suspected that infection had set in. He was very much afraid he would die in this place, that he would never see Jesse again. Never see his child.

The door opened and closed. Automatically Pierce turned his head toward the sound. Two men stood talking in low voices at the door, but it wasn't the same two who had

brought him here. Though he couldn't distinguish any of
their words, he could tell by their tone that they spoke with
authority. They were men in control, used to giving orders
and having them obeyed. They both spoke in Spanish, but
one of them had an accent. An American accent. Pierce
strained to hear. Did he recognize that voice?

He sat listening to the slow, measured footsteps as one of
the men crossed the wooden floor toward him. The steps
paused in front of him, and Pierce tensed.

"Are you ready to talk?" a voice asked. But it wasn't the
American. This man's English was flavored with the barest
hint of a Spanish accent. Cuban to be precise. Pierce's pre-
dicament was beginning to make a grim sort of sense.

"I don't know what you want," he said.

"Then you are a very stupid man," the voice said. "How
long do you think you can hold out to our...questioning?
Sooner or later you will have to tell us what we wish to
know."

"When hell freezes over," Pierce said.

"As you wish."

The American laughed. Again Pierce wondered if he recognized the voice. If he knew the man.

The Cuban's footsteps beat a staccato against the wooden
floor as he crossed the room and opened the door. He
barked an order, and then Pierce heard more footsteps. Two
other men entered the room, the two goons who had man-
handled him earlier, he guessed.

"Do what you want with him," the man in charge told
them. "But don't kill him. Yet." Then the door slammed as
he and the American left the room.

Pierce knew what was coming. He'd been through it before. As he mentally braced himself for the pain, a picture
of dark hair, gray eyes and a shy smile flashed through his
mind, and Pierce knew that he could endure just about

anything if it meant he would some day be able to see Jesse again.

He savored her image for just a moment, then he gave himself the command that would make his mind shut down.

"Fade to black," he whispered.

"Fade to black. Fade to black," Pierce mumbled over and over.

Jessica sat down on the edge of his bed and grabbed his shoulders. His skin felt red-hot to her touch. His head thrashed against the pillow, and he was trembling all over. Jessica tried to shake him awake, but he flinched away from her touch as if she had hurt him.

"Pierce, wake up," she said. "You're having a nightmare."

At the sound of her voice, he seemed to calm down for a moment. His eyes flickered but didn't open. "They're coming again, Jesse. I can hear the footsteps."

"It's all right," she soothed. "It's only a dream."

He clutched his head with both hands. The grooves around his mouth and eyes deepened. "I have to forget you now, Jesse. I'm sorry, but I have to forget everything. I have to fade to black."

"Pierce, wake up," Jessica said, more firmly this time. She reached out and shook his arm. Pierce's eyes flew open as he grabbed her. Jessica gasped, frightened. She tried to scramble away from him, but Pierce's hand pinned her to the spot.

His hair was all mussed and his eyes gleamed in the dim light from the hallway. He looked savage and dangerous as he glared at her like a wild animal caught in a trap.

Jessica's heart pounded with fright. His hand seared her arm, branded her. Made her all too aware of the flimsy nightgown she wore, the state of his own undress. His chest and arms were bare, thinner than she remembered, but still strong. Still muscular. Still able to hold her, even if she should struggle.

But Jessica wasn't struggling. She was staring at her husband, at the stranger who looked for all the world like a man who could just as easily kill her as kiss her. She wondered wildly if he had the notion to do both.

"What are you doing in here?" His voice was dark with suspicion. His eyes flashed deadly in the pale light. Jessica shivered, unable to tear her gaze away from him.

"I heard you call out. You were having a nightmare," she said. "Wh-what were you dreaming about?"

"I don't remember." He cocked his head, listening. "What's that noise?"

"It's just the rain," Jessica said, nodding toward the window. "A storm blew in awhile ago." She felt his hold on her arm ease, but he didn't release her. She looked down at his hand, then back up at him. "You said my name in your sleep. You said, 'I have to forget you now, Jesse.' What did you mean, Pierce? Why did you have to forget me?"

His hand dropped from her arm. He lifted both his hands to his temples, much as he'd done in his sleep. "I don't know."

Jessica leaned forward. "What does fade to black mean?"

He dropped his hands and looked at her. "What?"

"You said 'I have to fade to black.' What does that mean, Pierce?"

He was looking past her toward the window, staring blindly into the wet darkness. Something flickered in his eyes, a flash of recognition. Then he shook his head. "I don't remember."

"But you have to," she said desperately, reaching out impulsively to touch his arm. "Dr. Prescott said that sometimes memories manifest themselves in dreams. If you were dreaming about what happened to you, then you must remember something. Think about it, Pierce. Try to bring back the dream. Try to remember why you had to forget me.''

"I can't, dammit," he exploded, shoving her hand away. "Don't you understand? I don't remember anything. Beyond two days ago, my mind is a complete blank for the past five years."

"But you remember things that happened *before* five years ago."

"Obviously." His gaze roamed over her with the same possessive gleam she was beginning to recognize.

Jessica ignored the insinuation. She didn't want to get sidetracked from their conversation. It was too important. Too crucial to her peace of mind. "Then you must be purposefully blacking out those five years. For some reason, you don't want to remember."

"You don't know that."

"I'd say it's a reasonable assumption," she said. "Look at all the scars you have, Pierce. On your face and on your arm. You must have been in terrible pain at one time. Maybe that's why you can't remember. Maybe you're trying to block out all that pain. A psychiatrist might be able to help you," she said. "Pierce, you have to go see Dr. Layton. The sooner the better."

"Do you think I'm crazy?" His tone was bitter, almost mocking, but Jessica sensed something deeper in his voice, an uncertainty that matched the flash of fear in his eyes. Then he shuttered his expression, once again closing her out.

"I think we both need help in dealing with this situation," Jessica said helplessly. "We can't go on like this indefinitely."

"I didn't think we were. You gave me a month, as I recall." Pierce sat up in bed and the cover slipped even lower. Jessica tried to keep her eyes on his face, but light from the hallway pooling on his shoulders and chest drew her gaze downward, where the dark hair narrowed and disappeared beneath the quilt. She could remember with vivid detail—

Her gaze flew back up to his. Her face flamed. What was she doing, ogling him like an infatuated teenager? Like a…a love-starved widow? What in the world was *wrong* with her?

Nothing, Jessica thought. Nothing was wrong with her, and that was the problem.

"Would you like to reopen negotiations?" Pierce asked, sensing her reaction. His voice was low and deeply sensual. His eyes darkened, burned with an intensity that made her tremble. His lips curved into the barest hint of a smile. "A month isn't much time, Jesse."

It might be too long, she thought. "Pierce…." Her voice trailed off as his hand lifted and caressed her cheek. Jessica closed her eyes at the tenderness. At the quiver of emotion inside her. "Pierce?"

"I'm right here, Jesse." His fingers wove through her hair and lifted the curls as if carefully testing their weight. He let the silky strands slip through his fingers, and Jessica heard the sharp intake of his breath just before he pulled her to him.

The moment his lips touched hers, the tenderness vanished, replaced by a deep, aching need that slashed through Jessica's defenses with stunning velocity. With his hands on her arms, Pierce urged her up, until they were both kneeling on the bed. His pajama bottoms were cotton, almost as thin and revealing as the satin nightgown she wore. They both might as well have been naked.

The heat scorched through the fabric of their nightclothes and fused their bodies together until Jessica could no longer distinguish her own heartbeat from Pierce's. She clung to him, letting him part her lips with his tongue, allowing him to delve into the velvet recesses of her mouth, permitting him to touch her wherever and whenever he wished. Her body came alive beneath his hands.

Five years, she thought. Five years she had waited for this kiss. She would have waited an eternity, she realized. No one could ever have made her feel this way. No one but Pierce...

He lifted his mouth from hers, and Jessica sobbed a breath. She was trembling all over, her body on fire with need. Pierce's hands tunneled through her hair, holding her face still as his eyes caressed her every feature.

"Again," he whispered heatedly, dipping his head to hers. This time Jessica was ready for his kiss. This time it was she who parted his lips, tangled her tongue with his until Pierce groaned. He cupped her bottom with his hands, pulled her even more tightly against him as the second kiss turned into the third and then the fourth....

His hands were all over her, making her burn with a passion she had buried for so many years. Making her want him as she had never wanted anyone. Making her lose control and loving it. His hand found her breast, massaged the swollen peak until Jessica arched against him.

"My God," he groaned. "It was never this way before."

Jessica barely heard him. Her lips ached for his kisses and she reached for him, but Pierce's hands closed around her wrists, stopping her.

"Wait a minute," he said.

His tone had changed. Something was wrong. Confused, Jessica gazed up at him. His eyes, hot with desire only moments before, now gleamed with cold suspicion. Her own passion cooled as a chill of dread crawled up her spine.

"It was never this way before," Pierce repeated slowly, still holding her wrist. "*You* were never this way."

"I don't know what you mean." Jessica glanced away, embarrassed. She was all too conscious now of the way they were dressed. All too aware of the echoes of passion still throbbing inside that room. Dear God, what was the matter with her? Had she completely lost her senses?

"You were never that easily aroused." He made it sound like an accusation. As if there was something wrong with her.

Hot anger poured over her at his insinuation. Jessica jerked her hands from his hold and jumped from the bed. "Just what are you accusing me of, Pierce? What right do you have to talk to me that way?"

"I'm your husband," he said with icy calm. "I have every right to know what you were doing while I was gone. Who taught you to kiss like that, Jessica? Who showed you how to lose control? God knows, it wasn't *me.*"

"How dare you?" she screamed. "How dare you accuse me of being unfaithful to you? And what if I was? You were the one who left *me.* You have no claim on me anymore."

"Don't I?" The look in his eyes frightened her. Made her tremble all over again.

"No," she said uncertainly. She backed away from him, shoving her hands in her hair. "I can't believe I let you kiss me that way," she whispered, tears scalding her eyes.

"Which part can't you believe?" Slowly Pierce got up and stalked her across the room. "That you let me kiss you or that you enjoyed it?"

"I didn't enjoy it." She was lying and they both knew it. Jessica felt the wall behind her back and realized she had nowhere else to run. Pierce knew it, too. He planted his hands on the wall on either side of her face and entrapped her until she was forced to look up at him, forced to meet his suspicious eyes.

"You're mine," he said, not tenderly. "Make no mistake about that."

"You're the one who's mistaken," Jessica told him. Her voice shook with anger and frustration and a thousand other emotions she didn't dare name. She brushed the tears from her face with the back of her hand. "I've changed, Pierce. I don't need you to tell me what to do anymore. I don't need you for anything."

"Not even for this?" His finger traced the outline of her lips, and Jessica sucked in her breath. Even so light a touch could send thrill after thrill spinning through her. She shoved his hand away.

"No," she denied, as much to herself as to Pierce. "Especially not for that."

"Because there's someone else?"

"I told you last night there's no one else."

"But there has been. You don't kiss the way you used to kiss, Jessica."

"I don't do a lot of things the way I used to do them."

His eyes hardened. "Such as?"

"I don't owe you any explanations."

She tried to brush past him, but Pierce caught her arm and stopped her. "This isn't over yet, Jesse. Not by a long shot."

"Yes, it is," she said, trying to jerk her arm from his grasp. "You just don't want to believe it. Now let go of me."

"Not until—"

"You leave her alone!"

Pierce and Jessica whirled in unison. Max stood in the doorway, his little hands doubled into fists at his side as he eyed Pierce with all the bravado a five-year-old boy could muster. He wore his Superman cape over his pajamas, and the cowlick at the crown of his head stuck straight up, giving him a comical yet vulnerable appearance. But his eyes—

his father's eyes—were dark and steely with disapproval. His bottom lip quivered but remained defiant.

"It's okay, Max," Jessica soothed. Both she and Pierce started across the room toward their son, but the little boy backed away. His angry gaze focused on Pierce. His fists tightened at his side.

"I thought you were my dad," he said, his voice trembling with tears. "I thought you were a good guy, like Batman or...or Superman. But you're not. You're a bad man. You tried to hurt my mom."

"I didn't, Max," Pierce denied, spreading his hands in supplication. "I would never hurt your mom. I promise."

"Yes, you did," Max accused, standing his ground. He trailed his pajama sleeve across his nose. "I saw you. You made her cry. You're not a hero at all. You're a bad guy," he shouted. "I hate you! I wish you'd never come back here! I wish you were dead again, that's what I wish!"

Max turned and raced down the hallway as fast as his little legs would carry him. An awkward silence fell over the room. Stunned, Jessica looked over at Pierce and started to say something—she wasn't sure what—but the stricken look on his face stopped her.

Behind her, she heard her son's footsteps on the staircase, heard his bedroom door slam shut.

But still she hovered in the doorway, torn between her husband's pain and her son's fear. Max needed her. She had to go to him, but the look on Pierce's face, the agony in his eyes—dear God, how would she feel if Max had turned against her like that? What would she do if her son didn't love her, didn't want her, didn't need her?

"He's just a little boy," she whispered. "He didn't mean it."

"He meant it," Pierce said, his eyes distant and bleak. "He meant every word of it. But you know what hurts the most, Jesse? I've seen that same look on your face. I've seen that same wish right there in your eyes.''

Without another word he turned, grabbed the jeans that had been draped across a chair, went into the bathroom and closed the door.

Jessica took a deep breath, opened her son's bedroom door and stepped inside. The room, with its crowded shelves and toy-strewn floor, had a forlorn look to it. Superman, Batman and a host of other human and superhuman heroes stared down at her accusingly from the walls. She'd failed him, they seemed to be saying. She'd failed her son.

On the floor at her feet, Max's cape lay in a red puddle. Jessica stooped and picked it up, smoothing the satiny cloth beneath her fingers. He must really be upset to have abandoned his cape, she thought.

She turned toward the bed with trepidation. What in the world could she possibly say to him? Naturally it was all her fault. She'd always thought Max's fascination with superheroes a harmless game, but now she saw it for what it really was.

Max had been looking for a father in these men. He'd been looking for someone to look up to, someone to admire. A role model. He'd been looking for Pierce, and he'd learned the hard way tonight that his father was only a man. A man who made mistakes.

You're not being fair, Jessica told herself. You can't blame all this on Pierce.

But if he'd never come back—

If he hadn't made her want him—

She put her hands to her face. If only she could turn back the clock, wake up yesterday morning and find the world normal and safe again. If only she could protect her son not just from this hurt but also from all the pain he was bound

to experience throughout his life. She didn't have the power
to do that, though. No one did.

Jessica walked over to his bed, holding his cape. He'd
pulled the cover up over his head and was trying to ignore
her. He lay perfectly still, not making a sound. They'd been
through this routine before.

"Max? Can I talk to you for a minute? Honey, I know
you're upset...." She sat down on the edge of the bed and
reached for her son. She found only a pillow. Frowning,
Jessica jerked back the covers. The bed was empty.

She jumped up and looked anxiously around the room.
"Max? Where are you? Come on, sweetie. I want to talk to
you."

No answer.

Jessica crossed the hall to the bathroom. The night-light
revealed the sink, the toilet, the bathtub—but no Max.

"All right, Max, I know you're upset, but you get out
here this instant." She tried to keep the panic out of her
voice, but her concern was growing by the minute. Jessica
hurried up and down the hallway, opening doors and turning on lights.

She stood at the top of the stairs, her hands planted on her
hips. How could he have just disappeared like that? She
couldn't have been more than two or three minutes behind
him. He couldn't have come back down the stairs without
her seeing him. He had to be hiding someplace up here.

But she'd looked everywhere except the unfinished game
room on the third floor, which was off-limits to Max. He
wouldn't have gone up there. He wouldn't have deliberately disobeyed her. But what if he had? What if he'd
somehow managed to open the balcony doors...

Jessica whirled and ran down the hallway and bounded up
the stairs that led to the third floor. She threw open the door,
flipped on the light and searched frantically for Max. But

the French doors were still closed, the sawhorse still in place, and Jessica let out a breath of relief. She turned and started to switch off the light when she heard a muffled noise. A very slight sound but it lifted the hair on the back of her neck.

"Oh, God." Jessica was across the floor in one second. She shoved the sawhorse out of the way and reached to unlock the French door, but the latch had already been turned. Max had used the sawhorse—her barricade—to stand on in order to reach the lock. He'd opened the doors and gone outside.

Jessica ran out onto the balcony, almost slipping on the rain-slick boards. Thunder crashed in her ears, and lightning blazed a fiery trail in the eastern sky. Then all was black again. But in the instant when the night was lit up, Jessica had seen what she had feared the most. Her heart stopped in midbeat. A whole section of the railing had fallen away at the end, revealing nothing but a gap of darkness and a thirty-foot drop to the stone terrace below.

"Max!" She screamed his name into the wind.

His pitiful little voice weakly answered her. "Mom? I fell down, Mom."

"Oh, God." Jessica was on her hands and knees, peering over the balcony. A part of the railing was still fastened to its support, but the other end hung freely, and this flimsy hold was all that kept Max from falling to the stones below.

Another flash of lightning revealed his form to her, and Jessica caught her breath in terror. His legs dangled in midair, and when he turned his face up to her, she saw his hands slip on the board.

"Hold on, baby," she said. "Please, Max, hold as tightly as you can until I tell you to let go. I'm going to grab hold of you now, okay? Don't be frightened."

"I'm falling, Mommy!"

"No, you're not, Max. You're very strong, remember? I know you can hold on." Jessica continued to coach him as she lay on her stomach on the wet balcony. She stretched her arms down toward Max. Inches remained between them. She slid more of her body through the opening, but the slippery floor was treacherous. She had to be careful.

"Think what Superman would do if he were here. He'd hang on, wouldn't he, Max, until someone could reach him? He wouldn't let go for anything."

She still couldn't reach him. The board creaked beneath his weight. The railing slipped even farther away from its remaining support. Jessica was hanging so far over the edge now that she feared even if she could grab her son, she wouldn't be able to hold his weight. They both might fall. She tried again, making a desperate attempt as her body slid dangerously close to the edge.

Dear God, she prayed. Help me.

"Move out of the way." Strong hands grabbed her, pulled her back from the edge. She rolled away as Pierce took her place on the balcony floor, stretching his long arms through the opening to find his son.

"I've got you, Max," Jessica heard him say calmly. "Let go, son."

"No! You'll drop me!" Max cried. Jessica heard the ominous squeak of the support as it pulled farther away from the balcony.

"I won't drop you," Pierce said. "I promise."

"No!" Max cried again, wrenching his arm free.

Jessica scrambled to her feet and leaned over the balcony, until she could see Max. The part of the railing he clung to was slipping farther and farther away. Pierce's hand was reaching out to him, but every time Pierce tried to grab him, Max would move away, causing the board he clutched to swing precariously.

"Max," she called, trying to keep the terror from her voice, "listen to me. Let Pierce take your hand, sweetie. It's okay. Let him take your hand, Max."

Max shook his head, but when Pierce's hand closed around his arm again, he didn't try to move away. He still clung to the broken railing with all his might.

"Let go of the railing, Max," Jessica urged. "Pierce has you. He won't let you fall, I promise."

"Trust me, son. I won't let you fall," Pierce coaxed quietly.

Max hesitated, then with a pitiful "Mommy!" he let go of his handhold, and Pierce lifted him up to safety.

A split second later, Max was in Jessica's arms. Small, cold hands came up and clung to her neck. "It's okay," she whispered. "You're safe." He was shaking so badly Jessica could hear his teeth chattering. She wrapped her arms around him, holding him close.

Over Max's shoulder, she looked up at Pierce. Rain lashed his face and ran in rivers down his skin. Jessica could barely distinguish his features in the darkness, but she knew, somehow, that he was as shaken as she was.

"Thank you," she said. "If you hadn't been here—"

"Don't think about that," he said. He knelt and put his hand on Max's head. "I *was* here. That's all that matters."

"But I couldn't reach him—"

"And I couldn't make him let go. He needed us both tonight, Jesse," Pierce said quietly.

If Pierce hadn't been there—

Jessica closed her eyes, feeling her body tremble all over. She was still in the throes of shock and couldn't seem to shake it. Max could have been killed tonight, she thought. Her baby could have died because she couldn't reach him. Couldn't save him.

If Pierce hadn't been there—

Her legs refusing to support her, Jessica sank onto the floor beside Max's bed and watched her son sleep. Only moments earlier, she'd helped him change into dry pajamas, then fixed him a cup of hot chocolate. Max had gulped down the drink, eaten the last of the marshmallows from the bottom of the cup, then promptly fell asleep.

But Jessica couldn't bear to leave him. Not yet. She had to be able to look at him whenever she wanted, to touch him if she needed to in order to reassure herself over and over again that he was really safe. That everything was all right.

But if Pierce hadn't been there—

She would have found a way to reach him, Jessica tried to convince herself. She would have found a way to save her son. She had always been able to take care of him by herself. They'd never needed anyone else.

He needed us both tonight.

Dear God, tonight she hadn't been enough. She *had* needed someone else. She'd needed Pierce, and he'd been there. He'd been there for her when she'd needed him the most.

Shouldn't that be all that mattered?

Jessica felt a tear slip from the corner of her eye and trail down her cheek. She wrapped her arms around her knees and hugged them tightly as she rocked herself back and forth beside her son's bed. Not since that awful day when her sister had left her at the orphanage could Jessica remember feeling so lost and confused.

And so terribly frightened because she knew, without a doubt, that tonight her world had been changed forever.

Chapter 8

"*Punished?* You mean I gotta be punished?" Max glared at Jessica in disbelief as he shoved the last bite of his blueberry waffle into his mouth. "But, Mom, I coulda been killed last night. I coulda been smashed into a million pieces on the terrace. My head coulda been knocked off." He grabbed his throat dramatically. "There woulda been blood everywhere—"

"Enough," Jessica said, putting up her hand to halt the gruesome tirade. The image of her son dangling from the balcony last night was still too fresh in her mind to appreciate Max's graphic embellishments this morning. But at least he didn't appear any the worse for wear, she noticed in relief. In fact, he looked pretty happy with himself this morning. Almost glowing.

Until she'd mentioned the little matter of punishment, of course. Now he scowled at her with dark, disapproving eyes. "What do you think a reasonable punishment would be for your disobedience, Max?"

"My what?"

"For your having gone out on the balcony last night after I told you, more than once, to stay away from the third floor until I could get that railing fixed."

"Oh, that." Max swirled the syrup on his plate with his finger, then lifted it to his mouth.

"Yes, that," Jessica said. "I was thinking no TV for a week. What do you think?"

Max eyed her in horror. "Starting when?"

"Immediately."

"But Mo-o-m. Superman comes on tonight."

Jessica sipped her coffee. "Sorry. You should have thought about that last night."

"But a week's a long time," Max wailed. "I'll be thirty-eight by the time I get to watch Superman again."

"Could be," Jessica agreed, "if you don't stop arguing with me. One week without TV and that's final. End of discussion."

Max's bottom lip jutted out in defiance, but then his eyes lit up as he gazed past Jessica's shoulder.

"Good morning."

The sound of Pierce's voice startled her. He always entered a room so quietly, she thought, almost as if he were sneaking up on her.

Jessica's heart raced as she turned toward the door. He stood with one hand propped against the frame as he smiled across the room at Max. Then at her. And her heart beat even faster.

He was dressed in jeans and a navy cotton sweater with the sleeves pushed up, and Jessica's first thought was that he looked good this morning. Real good. Except for the fact that the clothes hung a little too loosely on his lean frame, he looked almost like his old self.

She smiled timidly at him. "Good morning," she answered. "Did you manage to get any sleep last night after the excitement?"

He grinned, and she realized too late that he'd deliberately misinterpreted her words.

"Not much," he murmured.

A memory of that kiss they'd shared instantly popped into her head, and Jessica's face flamed as she stuttered, "I—mean after the—the rescue and all. I want to thank you again for everything you did."

His eyes darkened for a moment as he stared at her. "Don't thank me, Jesse. Max is my son, too, you know."

"Yes, I know." Her gaze dropped, and she toyed with the topaz ring on her finger. It was a fact she had grappled with for days now.

"Did you save my life last night?" Max chimed in.

"I don't know," Pierce said, straightening from the doorway. He crossed the kitchen and sat down at the table with them. "What do you think?"

"I think you did," Max said, bursting with excitement. "Wait'll I tell all the guys. You were just like Superman. Can you fly?"

Pierce laughed. "Only in my dreams."

"Know what? Me and Marcus Tate already figured out how you got all those scars. I bet it was from fightin' bad guys, right? 'Specially that real big one on your face."

"Max!" Jessica was appalled by her son's lack of tact.

Max's eyes widened guilelessly. "What'd I say wrong? I like scars. I want a bunch of 'em all over. Maybe even a tattoo someday." He rubbed his nose with his sticky finger. "Do you have any more scars? Can I see them?"

Jessica cringed but Pierce appeared undaunted. He said, "Not at the breakfast table, I'm afraid. I don't think your mom would approve."

He grinned at Max, man to man, then turned and met her gaze. For a moment, for one split second, their eyes held and something special passed between them. A mutual affection for their son that created an undeniable bond. No matter what happened in the future between them, Max would always be there to remind them how very much they had once loved each other.

Jessica felt a knot form in her throat, and she had to look away. Had to sever the hold Pierce had on her this morning, because no matter how grateful she was to him for last night, she was still very much afraid of him. Afraid of the man he might have become.

"I can't watch no TV for a whole week," Max moaned, eyeing Pierce hopefully. "Can you believe that?"

"I can't watch *any* TV," Jessica corrected.

"Yeah, but you don't even like it," Max said. "A week's a long time, isn't it?" He turned his big, dark eyes on Pierce. Jessica was familiar with the tactic. She felt her own resolve weaken, but instantly hardened it. She couldn't let Max charm her out of this one. His disobedience could have gotten him killed last night. She shuddered, remembering the close call.

Unfortunately Pierce hadn't had as much experience dealing with their son's devastating appeal. "Well. . . ." he hedged, eyeing Jessica doubtfully.

Don't say it, she thought. Don't you dare say it.

"It *does* seem a bit harsh."

He said it. Jessica pursed her lips. All the good feelings she'd had for Pierce last night and this morning evaporated in the twinkling of an eye. She folded her napkin precisely, creased it, and set it on the table. "I told you earlier the subject is closed, Max," she said, trying to keep a firm rein on her anger. After all, Max was only a little boy. She could hardly blame him for trying to capitalize on his newly forming relationship with his father. Kids always played one parent against the other when they could get away with it.

It was Pierce she blamed. He should have known better. "If I hear another word about it, I'll make it two weeks." She looked up and defiantly met Pierce's gaze. Instead of looking contrite, he merely stared back at her.

Incensed, Jessica pushed her chair back and stood. "Time to catch the bus, Max. Go find your backpack."

Dutifully Max left the room. As soon as the door swung closed behind him, Jessica whirled. "How dare you undermine my authority like that? What do you think you're doing?"

Her attack seemed to catch Pierce off guard. He gazed at her thoughtfully for a moment, then shrugged. "You're right. I shouldn't have said anything in front of Max. But you know, Jessica, you really should have discussed his punishment with me first."

Jessica's mouth flew open. "Discussed it with you? Why would I do that?"

"Because I'm his father. Because I should have a say-so in these kinds of decisions. I happen to think the punishment is too harsh, considering the circumstances."

Jessica planted her hands on her hips. "No TV for a week is too harsh for deliberately disobeying me? He could have been killed last night. At the very least, seriously injured. I can't let him think that kind of behavior is acceptable."

"Yes, but you set awfully high standards, Jessica."

Jessica couldn't believe what she was hearing. "Are you saying you *condone* what he did?"

"No. But I'm saying there were extenuating circumstances. He'd seen us fighting. He was upset and confused, and he did something he knew would get our attention."

Jessica turned away and started clearing the table. He might have a point, but she didn't want to see it. "Extenu-

ating circumstances is always a convenient excuse for doing
something we know we shouldn't.''

"Are we talking about Max now or me?''

Jessica set down the stack of dishes and turned. "All
right,'' she said, "let's talk about you. You've been back in
this house for less than three days and already you expect to
be included in the decisions I make regarding my son.
You've undermined my authority with him more than once.
You've made it seem as if it's you and him against me.
You're trying to bribe him into loving you, but what happens when you leave, Pierce? What happens when you're no
longer here for him to count on?''

"You mean what happens when my month is up?'' he
challenged. Anger sparked in the dark depths of his eyes.

"Yes,'' Jessica said, "that's exactly what I mean.''

Pierce's gaze narrowed. "Let's get a few things straight,
Jessica. You're the one who set the deadline, not me. You're
the one who seems obsessed with my leaving. If and when I
do leave, it'll be because *you* want me to. Our relationship
may end, if that's your choice, but I won't give up Max.
He's my son, and now that I've found him, not you or anyone else will ever take him away from me. Is that clear?''

Crystal clear, Jessica thought, stunned. She watched
Pierce turn and exit the room as she sat back down at the
table, her legs shaking. Would it come to that? she wondered desperately. Is that how it would finally end between
her and Pierce? In a bitter battle over their son?

Memories drifted through her mind—the day she'd told
Pierce she was pregnant, the elation he'd felt, the elaborate
fuss he'd made over her. They'd looked forward to the arrival of their first child with such joy and anticipation. A
child had seemed the perfect way to cement their union. A
precious gift that only they could give to one another.

Now everything seemed like such a mess. What if Pierce decided he wanted more of Max than Jessica was willing to share? What if he decided he wanted to raise their son himself? What if he tried to take Max away from her?

Panic mushroomed inside her at the thought, along with a determination so fierce it almost took her breath away. Jessica clutched the edge of the table so tightly her knuckles whitened.

There was no way she would ever allow that to happen. Max was hers, and the sooner Pierce realized it, the better off they'd all be.

But over the next few days, Jessica began to feel her old life slipping further and further away from her grasp. Gone were the quiet, routine, uncomplicated days of the past. Now all her waking thoughts centered on Pierce, her mixed feelings toward him, and her concern about his growing closeness with their son.

Much to Jessica's chagrin, every day Max seemed to become more and more attached to Pierce. In the evenings before dinner, they took to playing baseball together in the backyard. Sometimes Sharon's daughter, Allie, would join them, and the yard would be filled with shouts of laughter and childish squeals of triumph.

Reluctantly Jessica had to admit that Pierce was wonderful with the children. Sometimes she would watch them from the kitchen window, and a bittersweet tightness would form in her chest. How often she had dreamed of such a scene.

But all she could think of these days was how more and more Max was turning to Pierce for attention instead of her. How more and more her son wanted to spend all of his free time with his father instead of her.

The first time Max had asked her if Pierce could read him his bedtime story had nearly broken Jessica's heart. Story time had always been her and Max's special time together. They would cuddle in bed at the end of the day and enjoy an adventure together.

Not so anymore. Now Max wanted Pierce to tell him "real-life" stories, as he called them. He wanted to know everything there was to know about his father. His interest in Superman waned, then disappeared altogether. His little cape remained discarded on his closet floor, forgotten and abandoned for a "real-life" hero, as Jessica knew he had begun to think of Pierce.

And what made matters even more difficult was the fact that everyone in the neighborhood had seemingly accepted Pierce back into Jessica's and Max's lives just as easily as her son had. Pierce had become a regular fixture at the bus stop in the mornings. Once, when he was late coming out, Jessica saw several of the women watching her house expectantly, waiting for his imminent arrival. And just yesterday morning, Jessica had noticed, rather in disgust, how many of the mothers had started putting on their makeup and doing their hair before they brought out their children.

Obviously the added primping was for Pierce's benefit, and Jessica couldn't help feeling just the tiniest twinge of jealousy. She began getting up a little earlier to spend extra time on her own appearance, though she wouldn't allow herself to analyze the reason why.

Only Jessica's friend, Sharon, remained reticent toward Pierce. Only she seemed to understand Jessica's qualms about Pierce's return.

"Doesn't it drive you crazy?" she asked Jessica one day. "How can you stand him living in the same house with you and not knowing where he's been for the past five years? Or who he's been with," she added slyly. "Watch yourself,

Jessica. There's something about him . . . something in his eyes. . . ." She paused, then said, "I have a feeling there's a lot more to that man than any of us can imagine. Even you, Jessica."

Jessica hardly needed Sharon's warning. She was consumed with her own doubts and suspicions. She thought about Pierce all the time. She couldn't even forget him in her sleep. The kiss they had shared a few nights ago filled her dreams except, in these dreams, they didn't stop with the kiss. They made love over and over and over again until Jessica would wake up in the middle of the night, so aroused and frustrated and confused she would sob into her pillow.

How much longer could she go on like this? she would ask herself helplessly. How much longer could she live in the same house with Pierce, sit across from him at meals, see him with their son, imagine him downstairs in his bed—and not succumb to the mounting need inside her? How much longer could she bear not to have him touch her again, to have him hold her again?

Twenty more days, Jessica thought, as she x-ed through yesterday's date on the calendar in her office. That's how long she would have to fight this yearning inside her. This . . . desire, she thought, putting a name to it. She closed her eyes for a moment as a wave of panic washed over her.

"Sleeping on the job, Jessica?"

At the sound of the masculine voice, Jessica's eyes flew open. She cleared her throat, straightened some papers on her desk, and smiled self-consciously at Brandon Chambers as he stood in front of her desk.

"Penny for your thoughts," he said, smiling down at her.

Jessica felt her face warm. She closed the ledger on her desk and stood. "You might feel shortchanged," she tried to say lightly. "When did you get back from Europe?"

"Yesterday afternoon. I have some real treasures for you this time. The bulk of the shipment won't arrive for a few more days, but in the meantime, feast your eyes on this." He pulled an intricately designed gold and aquamarine necklace from his pocket and displayed it on the desk in front of Jessica. "Lovely, isn't it?"

"It's beautiful," Jessica breathed. "Am I going to be able to afford this?"

"It was a steal," Brandon assured her. "I knew it was perfect for you the moment I laid eyes on it. And there's even a story behind it. I'd love to tell you about it over dinner tonight."

Jessica fingered the necklace, avoiding Brandon's gaze. "Sounds very intriguing," she murmured evasively.

"Shall I make reservations at Justine's? How does eight sound?"

"I'm afraid I can't make it tonight," she said. "Perhaps another time. . . ." Honestly, Jessica chided herself, she and Brandon had had dinner countless times together. Why, all of a sudden, did she feel the need to put him off? To make sure he knew their relationship was strictly business?

Because of Pierce, that's why.

Everything had changed since he'd returned. Even her feelings toward her friends.

Brandon reached over and caressed the necklace. "This would make a handsome addition to your collection, Jessica. You could even feature it in the ads you were telling me about."

"That's a wonderful idea," she agreed, anxious to return their conversation to a less awkward subject. Mentally she changed the layout for her full-page spread in *Antiques Quarterly* to incorporate the necklace. She wished Brandon would just go ahead and tell her the story behind the necklace instead of dangling it in front of her like bait.

The history, even more than the age of a piece, was always an irresistible lure to potential customers and an invaluable selling tool once you got them into the shop. Pierce had taught her that.

Pierce had taught her a lot of things, she thought with a funny little catch in her throat. But that was a long time ago. A lifetime ago.

"You could even model it yourself," Brandon suggested. "You've certainly got the looks for it. Try it on. Here, let me help you." He took the necklace from her fingers and, standing behind her, draped it around her neck as Jessica lifted her hair.

"How does it look?" she asked, turning to face him.

"Lovely," Brandon said softly, reaching to touch one of the stones. "Exquisite."

Jessica's first reaction was to pull back from his touch, but before she could, a movement at the doorway drew her attention. Pierce stood scowling at them both, his dark eyes flashing with anger. His gaze dropped from her face to the necklace, then back up to her eyes. Jessica felt herself blushing guiltily, even though she hadn't done anything wrong. She lifted her chin and stared back at him. He didn't say anything, just walked slowly into her office.

Brandon said, "Can we help you?"

Pierce's gaze shifted, very briefly, to the other man. "I seriously doubt it."

"Then perhaps you'd care to wait outside," Brandon said stiffly. "This is a private office."

"Uh, Brandon," Jessica began, putting her hand on his sleeve, "it's okay. I know him. I mean he's...this is Pierce. Kincaid."

"Kincaid?" Something flickered across Brandon's features. Something that looked like recognition. Or fear, Jessica thought, though she couldn't imagine why he would be afraid of Pierce. Brandon said in a disbelieving voice, "You mean, he's your *husband?*"

Jessica refused to look at Pierce. She took a deep breath. "Yes."

Brandon's gaze darted to Pierce. "But I thought—"

"That I was dead? That seems to be the general consensus around here." Pierce smiled lazily, but there was no humor in his eyes. Quite the contrary. Jessica felt a tremor of fear in her stomach. She didn't like the way he seemed to be sizing Brandon up.

Pierce walked around the desk and stood directly behind her, putting a hand on her shoulder in a deliberately casual but unmistakably familiar gesture. Jessica resisted the temptation to shake it off.

"Well, I...hardly know what to say," Brandon said, straightening the knot in his tie. He looked thoroughly disconcerted.

Pierce said, "How about 'welcome back'?"

"Yes, yes, of course." Brandon extended his hand. "Brandon Chambers. I'm an associate of Jes—of your wife's."

"Really?" The two men shook hands, then Pierce placed his hand back on Jessica's shoulder.

"So...where've you been?" Brandon asked awkwardly.

"It's a long story," Pierce murmured. He bent and kissed Jessica's neck. "Is that a new necklace, sweetheart?"

Jessica jumped. Her hand flew to her throat. She felt as though she had been stung by a wasp. Burned by a fire. Kissed by a lover. Her heart was beating all over the place as she carefully removed herself from her husband's grasp and retreated a few steps away.

"It really is a beautiful piece," she told Brandon. "If the price is right, you have yourself a buyer. In the meantime,

I'd better return it to you." She lifted her hands to unclasp the necklace.

"Let me help you," Brandon said quickly.

At the exact same time Pierce said, "Turn around, Jesse." It didn't surprise her to find Pierce's hands at her throat as he undid the chain, lifted it away, and held it out to Brandon. The aquamarines sparkled in the overhead lighting as Pierce let the necklace slither into Brandon's open palm.

The two men eyed each other for a moment with open hostility, then Brandon smiled. He placed the necklace very carefully on Jessica's desk. "The price is immaterial, Jessica. The moment I saw that necklace, I knew it had to be yours." He flashed Pierce a brief, dismissing look as he paused significantly at the door. "I'll phone you later?"

"Please do," Jessica murmured, sinking down into her chair. She toyed with the necklace for a moment until Pierce reached out and took it from her hands. He perched on the edge of her desk and examined the necklace in the light.

"Circa 1920, I'd guess. Ten karat gold. At least two of the aquarmarines are chipped, and the clasp has obviously been replaced. Not a quality piece, but it does have a certain... pretentious appeal, I suppose."

Annoyed, Jessica reached out and snatched the necklace from his fingers. "I happen to like it," she snapped. "And for your information, big, intricate pieces are very popular right now."

"I noticed you'd added a jewelry case out front. I never could muster much interest in it myself. Except for the ring I bought you, of course." His gaze flashed to her left hand and her bare third finger.

Jessica folded her hands together, feeling naked. "Yes, well, truth to tell, you never mustered much interest in the shop at all, Pierce. Except for the travel, of course. You always loved that."

"Only when you went with me," he said softly. "We had some good times, didn't we? Remember Venice and that little hotel we stayed in right off the—"

Abruptly Jessica stood, shutting off the memories. "I don't have time for this. I have work to do. Three crates of Austrian crystal came in this morning and it all has to be unpacked, cataloged and shelved. So if you'll excuse me—"

"Who is he?"

Jessica glanced up. "Who?"

Pierce lifted one brow at her obtuseness. "This Chambers guy. What's he to you?"

"He's an independent buyer," Jessica said, not liking Pierce's tone.

"Having a middleman must eat into the profits," he said, still fiddling with the necklace.

"Yes, but it cuts down on a lot of traveling for me. Brandon's been very helpful, and he's given me some really good deals."

"Oh, I'll bet he has."

Jessica planted her hands on top of her desk. "And just what does that mean?"

"Is he the one?"

"Is he the one what?"

"The one who taught you to kiss the way you kissed me a few nights ago."

Heat flooded over her at Pierce's words and at the memory. Jessica crossed her arms as if to stave him off. "I have no idea what you're talking about. My relationship with Brandon is strictly business," she said primly. Then realizing how defensive she looked, she immediately dropped her arms to her sides.

Her nervousness didn't go unnoticed by Pierce. His gaze narrowed on her. "Relationship, huh? Interesting choice of words, Jessica. Was his dinner invitation a part of this *business* relationship? Do you go out with him often?''

''That's none of your concern,'' Jessica snapped. ''I'm getting awfully tired of these innuendoes, Pierce.''

''I'm getting tired of making them,'' he said. ''So why don't you convince me that I have nothing to worry about?'' Somehow his tone had changed in no more than a heartbeat. His voice had lowered, deepened, become even more sensuous.

Jessica's heart started to pound a warning. Don't let him do this to you, she cautioned herself. Don't let him sidetrack you as easily as he used to.

But from his perch on the desk his hand was already closing around her wrist. He exerted just the tiniest bit of pressure until he had pulled her toward him and she was standing between his thighs. He lifted her hand to his lips and kissed her palm.

Jessica closed her eyes and clenched her fist. ''Don't,'' she breathed.

''Why? Because of him?''

Her eyes flew open. ''Why must you always think the worst of me?''

''Maybe I could ask you the same question.'' His thumb lazily caressed her wrist. ''We've been apart too long, Jesse. We don't know how to act with one another anymore. We're afraid to trust each other. Afraid to trust our instincts.''

''I don't know what you mean.''

''Sure you do.'' He tugged her even closer, until he could slip his arms around her waist. Jessica's hand was free now, but instead of using it to push him away, she rested it lightly on Pierce's shoulder. ''You want to kiss me right now, almost as much as I want to kiss you, but you're afraid to, aren't you?''

"You...want to kiss me?" Her own timidness confused Jessica.

"More than anything."

"But Pierce—"

"I know," he said, his deep gaze searching her face. "You've changed. You're not the same woman I left behind. You're independent now. You have a career. You don't need me anymore. And I still want to kiss you, Jesse. More than ever."

"But I don't think—"

"Don't think, sweetheart," he whispered. Their gazes clung for a moment, then he cupped her neck and brought her head forward until their lips slowly merged.

Jessica felt quivery all over. Where the kiss had been desperate and almost violent a few evenings ago, today the joining was soft and tender and fraught with emotion. Her lips trembled beneath his.

In that exquisite moment, Jessica remembered how it felt to be loved and wanted and utterly protected. She remembered how it felt to be Pierce's wife.

When they broke the kiss, she rested her head against his shoulder, unable to look at him, afraid of what he might read in her eyes.

His hand slipped beneath her hair to caress her neck. "You see, Jesse?" he whispered. "It's still there. What we had, what we felt for each other is still there. We just have to give ourselves time to find it again."

Jessica turned her head so that she could look up at him. She resisted the urge to trace the scar on the side of his face with her fingertip. She fought the temptation to wrap her arms around him and kiss him again, but long and deep and hard this time. Her emotions were in a jumble right now, and Jessica knew she had to be very, very careful.

With an effort, she lifted her head from his shoulder and pulled herself free of his arms. "Please don't read too much into what just happened," she said.

"It's hard not to," he said, "when it's something I'd like to believe so badly."

"But it doesn't mean anything," she protested. "Not really. We were married, Pierce. We have a son together. We're bound to still have feelings for one another. I don't deny that. But that doesn't mean I'm willing just to forget everything that's happened. I still need answers. I have to know what happened before I can even begin to think about a future... together."

"You have to learn to trust me again. I understand that," Pierce said. He eyed her steadily. "I know all this is scary for you, Jesse. It is for me, too."

Jessica looked at him in surprise. "You're scared?" She'd never known Pierce to be afraid of anything. He thrived on risk. Or used to.

He smiled. "Of course, I'm afraid. What do you think this is like for me, losing five years of my life? It scares me to death to think of those missing years, but it frightens me more to think of losing even another day with you and Max."

At the mention of their son, Jessica's gaze hardened, became defensive, but before she could speak, Pierce put up his hand to halt her words. "I know where part of your fear is coming from, Jesse, but believe me, I'm not trying to take Max away from you. I would never do that. He loves you. He needs you. I couldn't take your place even if I wanted to. You've done a fantastic job, both at home and here at the shop, and I'm proud of you."

In spite of herself, Jessica felt a small glow of pleasure at his words. High praise from a man like Pierce. She tried to warn herself that she was setting herself up for another fall, but Jessica's heart had already made up its mind.

Pierce got up and came to stand behind her at the window. He slipped his arms around her, holding her close. She tried to quiet the trembling inside her, but it felt so good to be in his arms again.

To be held by the only man she had ever loved.

He said softly, "I don't expect you to be the woman you were five years ago, sweetheart. I did at first, naturally, because the time hadn't passed for me. But I understand now how you feel, and you can relax about all that. I'm not trying to take anything away from you. I know I've tried to rush you into something you weren't ready for. I know I've tried to make things the way they used to be when that's impossible. You were right that first night. Things will never be the same again. I understand that now."

A feeling of loss settled over Jessica at his words. She had to close her eyes to blink back sudden tears.

"But just because things have changed, just because *we've* changed doesn't mean the feelings we had for one another are all gone."

Jessica cleared her throat and attempted to strengthen her resolve. "What are you trying to say, Pierce?"

"I'm saying we should give each other another chance. I'm saying we should try to get to know each other again without any promises and without any pressure. We have over two weeks left in your thirty-day ultimatum. If at the end of that time you still want me to leave, I will. I'll fade quietly out of your life."

"And Max's?"

She felt him stiffen at her challenge, but he didn't release her. If anything, he tightened his embrace. "Max will always be my son. Just as he is yours. But no matter what happens between us, I would never try to take him away from you. You can trust me, Jesse, whether you realize it or not."

At that moment, Jessica wasn't even sure if she dared to trust herself.

"Tremont House."

"I'd like to speak to the manager." Pierce shifted the receiver to his other ear as he glanced around. It was just after five, and the traffic on Jefferson Avenue was starting to bunch up. As the line of cars crawled by, Pierce suddenly felt exposed at the open-air pay phone.

The voice, the same one he'd spoken to the other night, asked, "Who's calling, please?"

"A friend who needs a room."

"We're booked solid," came the standard reply.

"Look, damn you, I want to talk to the manager, and I want to talk to him now." Pierce's voice was low and calm but deadly insistent. This time, he wouldn't be put off. He wanted some answers, and he'd do what he had to do to get them. "If he's not on the line in, let's say the next five seconds, I'll take my story to the press."

There was a brief pause, maybe all of two seconds, then another voice said tersely, "This is Walker."

Pierce smiled grimly. The man had been listening all along, as he'd suspected.

"Are you the manager?" Pierce asked, sticking to the routine.

"Are you the same *friend* who called a few evenings ago?"

When Pierce responded in the affirmative, the man who called himself Walker said, "I got the message. I've been wondering when you'd make contact again. Welcome back, Kincaid."

The friendly exchange shocked Pierce. He said uncertainly, "Do I know you?"

"We've met. Actually we worked together five years ago on the Alpha project."

Flashes of memory were starting to dart around in Pierce's head. "Alpha—"

"Code name for a certain operation in the Caribbean. Is it coming back to you now?"

"Not exactly. I need a few details filled in. I want to talk to someone," Pierce said. "Face-to-face. I need some answers, and you damn well better give them to me."

Walker paused, then said, "That can be arranged at a later date."

"Why not now?"

"Security reasons," he said evasively. "Certain precautions have to be taken where you're concerned. You understand."

Pierce didn't understand a damn thing. He said angrily, "Just what the hell am I supposed to do in the meantime? I've lost five years of my life, Walker, and I don't even know how or why. But I'm willing to bet the agency's behind it. At the very least, you people owe me an explanation."

"'You people,'" Walker repeated. "You sound as if you think we're the enemy, Kincaid."

There was something in the man's voice that sent a chill of warning through Pierce. He was treading on dangerous ground, and he knew instinctively he had to proceed with caution.

As if to reiterate that point, Walker said, "For the time being, I suggest you sit tight, and don't talk to anyone. I mean anyone. It's a matter of national security. At the highest level."

Pierce expelled a vicious curse. "If my family's in danger, I want to know it, you son of a bitch."

"They're not," Walker said immediately. "You don't need to worry about that."

Pierce wasn't convinced. "I'll give you forty-eight hours," he said. "If I don't hear from you by them, I'll start looking for the answers myself. And believe me, no stone will be left unturned until I find them."

"You still work for the agency," Walker warned. "I'm advising you to stay put and keep your mouth shut until further notice. When the time is right, you'll be contacted. You have your orders."

"And you have yours. Forty-eight hours," Pierce said and hung up the phone. He drew a long breath and looked around, feeling the invisible eyes of the agency tracking his every move. What Pierce couldn't figure out was why those eyes felt so unfriendly. And so dangerous. He was supposed to be one of the good guys.

Wasn't he?

Chapter 9

Forty-eight hours had come and gone, and Pierce was still as much in the dark as he'd ever been. The agency had ignored his ultimatum. At least, the man calling himself Walker had.

Pierce realized he had taken a big chance, laying all his cards on the table, not just with Walker but with Jessica as well. She could easily have turned even further away from him, but at that point he hadn't known what else to do. He couldn't stand seeing the fear in her eyes every time he and Max were together. It seemed to him the only thing he could do was to try to allay her worries. Let her know that he wasn't a threat to her. In any way.

But was that true?

Pierce hadn't overtly heard from the agency, but at times he had the distinct feeling that he was being watched, followed. Yet no one made contact.

Sometimes, especially in the dead of night when he lay in bed wide-awake, trying to remember, trying to sort out the fragmented pieces of memories floating around in his head, he had to wonder if he should just leave again. If he should disappear from Jessica's and Max's lives until he could sort out what had really happened to him. Until he could find out the truth.

But Walker had warned him to stay put, and even though Pierce had no reason to trust anyone from the agency these days, he had to agree with that course of action. The thought of leaving Jessica and Max alone and unprotected sent cold chills through him. In spite of what Walker said, Pierce had a very strong feeling of danger, and somehow he knew that if he left his family now, they would be vulnerable to that danger. Only he could protect them. Only he could keep them safe from the threat that he had brought with him. A threat he didn't even recognize.

Meanwhile, Pierce was following through on his own threat. He'd very quietly set the wheels of his own investigation in motion. He'd even broken down and called his brother-in-law at the Pentagon.

"What do you know about Brandon Chambers?" had been his first question.

After a couple of seconds of stony silence, Jay had said, "Is this personal or professional?"

"What do you think?"

It took a few minutes of wangling before Jay finally conceded. "All right, I'll tell you what I know. He showed up at the shop a few months after you'd disappeared. I was suspicious myself at first, but his credentials all checked out. He buys for dozens of antique shops all over the area. As far as I can tell, he's on the up-and-up. And Jessica certainly seems to trust him," he added slyly.

Pierce had hung up the phone, not feeling a damn bit better. Regardless of what Jessica and Jay thought, Pierce *didn't* trust Brandon Chambers. There was something about the man's eyes, the way he had looked at Pierce as if—

"D-a-ad! Keep your eye on the ball!" Max admonished as the baseball went whizzing by Pierce's head.

Pierce nodded and grinned, returning his attention to the game. "Sorry, Max. I'll try to do better."

"Here, Mr. Kincaid." The little girl from next door came running up to him, holding out the ball. "I catched it for you."

"Thanks, Allie. That's quite an eye you have there."

She beamed and squinted up at him. "My mother says you're strange," she said, bending to scratch a scab on her knee, "but you look okay to me."

"Thanks. I think."

"Are you coming to our party tonight?"

"Well, I'm not sure," he said, tossing the ball back to Max. "I'll have to check with Max's mother."

He nodded toward the picnic table where Sharon and Jessica sat talking quietly in the shade. The morning breeze lifted Jessica's curls and settled them around her face, setting off her creamy complexion and her wide gray eyes. She wore white shorts and a sleeveless yellow top, and Pierce felt a tenderness well inside him as he stared at her. She looked so young and relaxed this morning.

She looked exactly the way he remembered her.

And maybe it was his imagination or wishful thinking, but her attitude seemed to have lightened since their conversation at the shop. The hostility was gone from her eyes as if she was genuinely making an effort to keep an open mind. To get to know him again.

And once or twice he could have sworn he'd seen a flicker of interest in those gray depths. Maybe even a spark of desire, Pierce thought hopefully, feeling his pulse quicken just looking at her.

"Jessica's pretty, isn't she?" Allie said, following his gaze.

"Very."

"She's nice, too."

Pierce grinned. "She sure is."

Allie giggled. "I bet I know what."

"What?"

"I bet you'd like to kiss her."

Pierce felt his face redden. Since when did five-year-olds get so wise?

Allie clapped her hands to her mouth, suppressing more giggles.

Max called crossly, "Move out of the way, Allie. No girls allowed in this game."

"Hey, young man," Jessica admonished from the sidelines. "Since when did you get to be such a chauvinist?"

"Since he wants to have his father all to himself," Sharon suggested. Her blue eyes regarded Jessica thoughtfully. "I must say, you're certainly taking all this in stride, Jessica."

"You think so?" Jessica smiled, tucking a stray lock of hair behind her ear. She stared at her sandaled feet for a moment. "I'll let you in on a little secret. The first few days Pierce was back, I was terrified he might try to take Max away from me. But I realize now I was just overreacting. I was projecting my past into my feelings."

"You sound so wise," Sharon commented, sipping her iced tea. "So analytical. Now tell me how you really feel."

"What do you mean?"

"Are you in love with him?"

Jessica looked up, surprised by her friend's bluntness. "I—I'm not sure. I still have feelings for him," she said reluctantly, "but I'm not sure how much of that is just memory."

Her gaze went to Pierce as he pitched the ball to Max. Over the past couple of weeks, he'd filled out a little. His jeans were beginning to fit him more snugly and the lines in his face had softened a bit. That dark, haunted, hungry look in his eyes had vanished. When he laughed, he looked ten years younger, and he laughed a lot when he was with his son. They both did.

It hurt Jessica to realize how little laughter there had been in her and Max's life. She'd concentrated so hard on being a success at work and being the perfect mother all round that she was very much afraid she had never learned how to be a mom, the kind who relaxed and enjoyed life.

But Pierce was teaching her that.

He was teaching her and her son how to have fun.

"It doesn't bother you that you may never know what happened to him all those years ago?" Sharon asked softly.

"It bothers me," Jessica admitted. "But what can I do about it?"

Sharon shook her head. "You amaze me, Jessica. You're always so levelheaded. It doesn't worry you that you'll be alone with him for the next few days?"

Jessica whipped her head around. "What?"

Sharon's blond brows rose slightly. "Don't tell me you forgot. Max is supposed to go camping with us this week, remember? We're leaving tomorrow."

Jessica had completely forgotten the plans she'd made with Sharon over a month ago. It seemed impossible that Memorial Day weekend was already here. It seemed impossible that Pierce had already been home over two weeks and that they had only a little more than a week left of the ultimatum she'd given him.

What then? Jessica wondered. Where did they go from there?

He'd said he wanted to get to know her again, without promises and without pressure, and true to his word he'd been nothing more than casually friendly since their conversation at the shop. He hadn't so much as come near her.

Much to her disappointment, Jessica acknowledged to herself.

Her gaze strayed back to Pierce, and suddenly she couldn't help remembering the way it felt to be in his arms.

It was never this way before.

A wave of warmth washed over her as she remembered the night she'd gone to his room, the way he'd kissed her and the way she'd kissed him back.

It was never this way before.

Who had changed? Her? Pierce? Or both of them? And if a kiss had done that to her, what would it be like to make love with him now? Would that be different, too? Would it be even more passionate than before? More intense? More powerful?

Jessica felt a tingle of anticipation in the pit of her stomach. Pierce glanced her way and their gazes met. Something electric passed between them. Something purely sexual. It seemed as though he could read her every thought. Jessica's face reddened as his gaze moved over her, lingering for a long moment on her bare legs.

"...and I know the kids would be disappointed if Max didn't get to go. What do you say, Jessica?"

Jessica tried to turn her attention back to Sharon. "What?"

Sharon gave her an odd look. "Can Max come camping with us or not?"

Alone with Pierce for a whole week. Jessica's heart began to pound like a drum. She felt her palms moisten. "I—I'll have to check with Pierce," she stammered.

Sharon's brows soared, but she refrained from comment. "Okay," she agreed. "Can you come over early tonight and help me set up? The others guests will be arriving at six, so if you could come around five-thirty, that'd be great."

"Sure," Jessica said absently, fanning herself with her hand. Was it her imagination or had the temperature suddenly gone up a few degrees, even in the shade?

Sharon stared at her for a long moment, then grinned. "Gee, I'm worried about you, Jessica. A decreasing attention span, glazed look in your eyes, red cheeks, shortened breath. Sounds like a heat stroke to me." She stood to go but then turned and said softly, "Or is it just love?"

Or is it just love?

Jessica felt a little tremor of fear in her stomach as she contemplated Sharon's question. Could she be falling in love with Pierce again? So soon? In spite of all the unanswered questions?

You amaze me, Jessica. You're always so levelheaded.

Jessica didn't feel levelheaded now. Not at all. She felt all trembly inside and out of control. She felt like a woman on the verge of falling in love who didn't give a damn about responsibility. Didn't give a damn about the future, only the present.

Except that Jessica couldn't afford the luxury of acting on impulse, of letting her emotions rule her life. She had a son to think about. She had their future to worry about. She didn't want Max to get hurt because of a decision she had made in a moment of passion.

It was all so confusing, she decided. With the palm of her hand, she tested the cake cooling on the rack. She found a can of frosting in the pantry, opened it and sampled a bit on the tip of her finger, shrugging. Not as good as homemade, but not bad, especially considering she was in a hurry. It was after four, and she still had to bathe and get ready for Sharon's party.

Feeling the time slip away, she sighed as she slathered the frosting on the cake. She hoped that Max was already in the bathtub, scrubbing off the grime from his and Pierce's baseball game, but you could never tell with him. Her son was easily diverted when it came to bath time.

Pierce came in just as she was putting the finishing touches on the cake.

"Looks good," he said, his eyes raking her up and down.

"Where's Max?" Jessica asked, trying to ignore the suddenly close confines of the kitchen.

"Outside with one of his friends. They found a dead lizard, last I heard."

Jessica groaned. Dead animals were always an irresistible lure to her son. "He's supposed to be in the bathtub. I'll never get us both ready in time now. Sharon wants me to come over early, and I still have to make a salad—"

"Relax," Pierce said, putting his hands on her arms. "I'll go and find Max and make sure he gets his bath. You do what you need to do in here, and then go get yourself ready."

"But I—"

"Jessica," Pierce said in an admonishing tone. "You don't have to do it all by yourself anymore. I'm here now. I want to help you if you'll let me."

"But—"

He swiped her mouth with his fingertip. "There. See?" He held up his finger, showing her a streak of chocolate across it. "I'm already helping you out. Wait a minute. I missed a spot." Before she had time to realize what he was doing, Pierce bent and retrieved the rest of the chocolate from her lip with his tongue. "Mmm, delicious. Tastes even better than it looks."

Jessica froze. "What are you doing?"

"What does it feel like I'm doing?" Pierce murmured.

"But you said no pressure. You said. . . ."

His arms slipped around her waist, and Jessica's protest died on her lips. The look in his eyes sparked too many memories of too many nights spent in his arms.

She drew a long breath, telling herself her heart shouldn't be racing and her pulse shouldn't be jumping so erratically just because he had touched her. Just because she was remembering something they had once shared.

And because she knew he was remembering, too.

And because it felt so good to be in his arms again.

"Remember the last time I did that? It was at our wedding," he said softly. "I was in such a hurry to get the reception out of the way that when I fed you your cake, I got frosting all over your mouth."

"You barely gave me time to throw the bouquet," Jessica reminisced.

"I was in a hurry to start our honeymoon," he admitted with a grin. "I'll never forget our wedding night, Jesse. You looked so sweet in that white frilly thing you wore to bed. I had the devil of a time getting it off, though. Probably because I was so damned nervous."

Jessica gazed up at him, enjoying the closeness. The comfort of shared memories. "You nervous? I don't believe it. You always seemed so experienced to me. So sure of yourself."

"An act," he confessed, his arms settling more possessively around her. "I was nervous, all right. I'd never been with a virgin before."

Jessica blushed as she always did when that particular subject was mentioned. She pushed at his arms but not forcefully enough to push him away. "Do you have to remind me of that? A twenty-year-old virgin must have seemed pretty weird to someone like you."

He smiled down at her, his eyes deep and intense. Incredibly dark. "You seemed very special to someone like me. You seemed like the woman I'd been waiting for all my life. Do you know what it's always meant to me that I was the first for you, Jesse? It was like the rarest, most precious gift you could ever give me."

Jessica began to relax even more, basking a little in the glow of their shared past. It had been so long since they'd reminisced together. And Pierce had always had a way of making her feel good about herself, in spite of her childhood.

She lifted her hands to his shoulders, feeling the hard definition of his muscles beneath his shirt. "Do you know what I thought the first time I ever saw you?" She teased him with a smile. "I thought you were the most dashing, the most sophisticated, the most handsome man I'd ever seen."

"You were such a naive little thing."

"You always seemed so mysterious to me. As if you had done things you couldn't share with me. As if there were secrets from your past you couldn't reveal even to me. That made you even more irresistible," Jessica said, laughing softly.

Something flickered in Pierce's eyes. A flash of regret?

He said, "I don't want to have secrets from you, Jesse. I want to share everything with you now. There are so many things I want to tell you, but I can't. I... can't."

"I know," she said softly. "Because you don't remember."

His smile seemed rueful. "I don't deserve you, you know. I never did."

Jessica started to protest, but his eyes stopped her. They were so dark and unfathomable. So intense. So deeply probing she could feel his gaze all the way to her soul. She knew she should move, break the spell, remember that this was the man who had hurt her so badly. But a sweet contentment was slipping over her. A languor that made her want to remain exactly where she was. In Pierce's arms. Forever.

She closed her eyes and whispered his name.

"I'm here, Jesse," he murmured as he threaded his fingers through her hair. "I'll always be here. If you'll let me."

For an eternity it seemed, he just held her, giving her the comfort she needed. Jessica wasn't sure when their bodies began to shift, edging beyond comfort to something else— something that bordered on sexual awareness. But suddenly she was conscious of a dozen different sensations. The feel of his jeans against her bare legs. The flicker of desire warming his dark gaze. The delicious torment of his fingers in her hair. And his mouth. His mouth only inches from hers.

She closed the distance, parting her lips in anticipation.

She heard Pierce's breath catch, then he groaned as his hands fisted in her hair and he drew her mouth the rest of the way to his. She opened for him immediately, and Pierce sent his tongue deep inside her mouth, shocking Jessica and then thrilling her.

The kiss was deep and hard and electric, and it made Jessica remember exactly what she had been missing for five years. Abstinence had never been a problem for her, but now she was suddenly, achingly aroused to the point of desperation. To the point of not caring. To the point of no return.

She rubbed against the front of his jeans, feeling the heat of his erection through their clothing. Jessica's legs began to tremble. It would be so easy, she thought. So easy just to give in to her need, allow Pierce to lead her upstairs and undress her, make her want him until she begged him for release.

Her thoughts shocked her. Was she that desperate? That aroused?

It was never this way before.

Pierce broke the kiss and stared at her with a look so hot and so hungry that Jessica felt a thrill of alarm race through her. What had she done? she wondered. What had she started?

"Sweetheart," he murmured, letting out a long, ragged breath. He reached for her again, but this time Jessica managed to put up a token resistance.

"Pierce, it's broad daylight and we're standing in the middle of the kitchen."

"I don't give a damn where we are."

His lips nipped hers, sending a sensuous shiver down her spine. "But there's no time...I mean, I still have to get dressed and all...." Jessica knew she was babbling, but she couldn't seem to string two coherent thoughts together. Not when Pierce was looking at her the way he was looking at her.

He lifted a hand and raked it through his hair, sighing deeply. "You sure as hell can kiss, Jesse. See what you've done to me? In broad daylight. In the middle of the kitchen."

Jessica's gaze slid downward to the front of his jeans. There was no mistaking his meaning. "I'm...sorry."

"Don't be. I just wish we had time to pursue this elsewhere. Or...do we?"

Jessica tried to shake off the lingering remnants of her arousal. "We don't. And besides, I don't think it's a good idea to rush into anything. I think we should wait until we're both sure we're ready."

"In case you haven't noticed, I'm as ready as I'll ever be," he said in a pained voice. "In fact, if I was any more ready—"

The back door slammed, and they both jumped apart like guilty teenagers. Max appeared in the doorway, eyeing them with avid curiosity. Jessica put up a hand to smooth her hair. Max's dark eyes didn't miss a move.

She said nervously, "Where've you been, sweetie? It's time for your bath."

Max gazed first at Jessica, then at Pierce, then back to Jessica. She had the feeling that they hadn't fooled him at all. He knew that something was going on. He held up a dead lizard and dangled it by the tail. "Can I keep this?"

Automatically Jessica stepped back, right into Pierce's arms. His hands went around her waist, steadying her against his body and making Jessica all too conscious of what had just gone on between them. "Please get that thing out of my kitchen," she said, her voice not quite as steady as she would have liked.

"But, Mom—"

"No buts. Get it out of here this second," Jessica ordered.

Max turned around and left without further protest.

Behind her, Jessica heard Pierce laugh. She spun around to face him. "What's so funny?" she demanded.

"Nothing," he said. "But for a minute there, I was afraid you might be talking to me."

Chapter 10

"Can I go camping with Allie and her mom and dad? We'll only be gone till Saturday."

Pierce sat on the edge of the bottom bunk bed in Allie's room as he tucked the covers around Max. Allie hung halfway out of the top bunk, listening avidly to Pierce and Max's conversation. The sounds of the party outside drifted in through the open window, making the children too restless to sleep.

"We got enough food and bug spray and toilet paper for everybody. You don't have to worry about anything, Mr. Kincaid," Allie said solemnly, her blond hair swinging back and forth like a silk curtain in a stiff breeze. "Can he go with us? Please, can he?"

"Can I, Dad? Please, can I?"

Pierce's heart skipped a beat or two. It never failed to thrill him every time Max called him Dad. He had to resist the temptation to give in to his son's every whim, but that urge had gotten him in trouble with Jessica more than once.

Not that her anger wasn't justified. It was. But it was just so damned hard not to want to make up for all those years he'd missed with his son.

Pierce said cautiously, "What did your mother say about this camping trip?"

"She said she'd have to talk to you about it. Did she?"

Talk to him about it? Pierce stared at his son in surprise. Jessica was asking for his opinion? His advice? He didn't want to read too much into it, but he couldn't help feeling encouraged by this latest development. Maybe his talk with her had helped, after all.

He ruffled Max's hair and reached up to tickle Allie's ear. "I tell you what, you two. I'll talk to Jessica about it tonight, and we'll let Allie's mom and dad know before we leave the party. How's that?"

"Okay, but will you come and tell us?" Max demanded. "I won't be able to sleep until I know."

Pierce grinned. "You got it."

Max grinned back. "Thanks, Dad. I love you."

Pierce felt his throat tighten with emotion. Keep it light, he advised himself. Don't embarrass him in front of his friend. He said, a little too gruffly, "I love you, too, son."

Allie's blond head popped up over the railing again. "I love you, too, Mr. Kincaid."

Then she collapsed on her bed in a fit of giggles, but the tension inside Pierce eased up. He and Max met each other's gaze in conspiratorial silence, shaking their heads in a man-to-man agreement about the incomprehensible behavior of women in general.

The pool glistened aquamarine in the glow of the torches Sharon had planted around the edges of the yard, and citronella candles flickered on the tops of picnic tables lining the covered terrace. Everyone had abandoned the water in favor of the tables once dinner had been served, and now soft music was playing on the stereo and a few couples were dancing. Jessica sat away from the crowd at the dark end of the pool, enjoying the cool evening breeze and the pleasant drone of the distant chatter.

She nursed a glass of wine in one hand as she dangled her feet in the water. It had been a pleasant evening, and she felt content and mellow and just a little bit lazy. Pierce had put Max and Allie to bed upstairs in Allie's room a little while ago, and now all Jessica had to do was relax and enjoy the rest of the night. Automatically she searched for Pierce in the crowd.

She spotted him at the other end of the yard, where the light of the torches hardly reached. Like her, he was all alone, standing apart from the crowd. She remembered a time when Pierce would have been the life of the party. Not that he'd ever been loud or boisterous or sought attention, but back then, people had just naturally gravitated toward him. Now he seemed to shy away from crowds as fervently as Jessica did. It wasn't like him to be such a loner.

But he'd been acting strangely toward her all evening, Jessica reflected. Ever since that scene in the kitchen, he'd made it a point to keep his distance from her. In fact, he hadn't even sat by her at dinner, choosing to sit with Max and his friends, instead. He didn't seem angry, just reserved. Pensive.

Jessica couldn't help wondering what he was thinking about.

See what you've done to me? In broad daylight. In the middle of the kitchen.

She flushed slightly as his words came back to her. His arousal may have been more apparent, but it had been no more thorough than hers had been. No more intense. She shifted, feeling her body tingle in all the places that had been too long ignored.

The wine was making her have thoughts she oughtn't to be having, Jessica decided, and it was making her feel a little too warm. Perhaps she should jump into the pool and cool off. Maybe Pierce would come and join her—except he hadn't been swimming all evening. He was wearing trunks, an old navy blue pair he'd had years ago, and a white T-shirt, but even when Max had asked him to come into the water earlier, Pierce had declined. He'd sat at the edge of the pool instead, enthusiastically applauding his son's swimming ability. He hadn't even taken off his shirt when the kids' splashing had gotten him soaking wet.

Curious, Jessica thought. Pierce had never been the modest type before. Of course, he had lost some weight, but he still looked better by far than any man at the party. Jessica could feel the warmth easing over her again as she watched him from a distance, willing his gaze to hers.

Pierce sat in the shadows, trying to keep his gaze off Jessica, but it was damned near impossible, the way she looked tonight. The way she'd kissed him earlier.

It had never been that way before, that instant arousal, that almost overpowering need. Jessica had always been a little reticent about lovemaking, a little reluctant to take pleasure from the physical side of their relationship. Pierce had always tried to be gentle with her and as understanding as he could be under the circumstances, but he'd always had the disquieting feeling that there was a part of her he had never been able to touch.

But she'd changed, he reflected. The way she kissed, the way she moved against him led him to believe that she was now as eager for their lovemaking as he was. The question that bothered him, though, was *why?* Why had she changed?

Or more to the point—*who* had caused her to change? Who had taught her the things she would never allow him to teach her?

She'd said there was no one else, but in five years? Had she abstained from sex for five whole years? Maybe that explained this new boldness in her. God knows what five years of celibacy had done to him, he thought with a grimace.

How can you be so sure there wasn't someone else in all that time?

Jessica's question returned to haunt him, and Pierce didn't have an answer, just a feeling. Just a certainty deep inside him that there had never been anyone else for him since Jessica. And there never would be.

He watched her with a brooding frown as she lifted the glass to her mouth, and he suddenly wanted to taste the wine from her lips. To let his tongue continue the exploration he had begun in the kitchen earlier that day. To see just how much they had both changed.

She trailed her feet in the water, then lifted her hair from her neck. The innocent action accentuated the line of her breasts in the white one-piece swimsuit she wore. The cut of the suit was no less tantalizing because it was modest. Her body had filled out in all the right places since he'd been gone. Not that she hadn't looked great before. But now . . .

Pierce took a long swallow of his cold beer, suppressing a groan. She looked so damned sexy it was all he could do to keep his hands off her.

I'm saying we should try to get to know each other again without any promises and without any pressures.

Pierce muttered a curse under his breath. What the hell had he been thinking? No promises? No pressure? No sex?

That wasn't what he wanted at all. The longer they kept their intimacy at bay, the easier it would be for Jessica to walk away from him at the end of the thirty days. And Pierce had no intention of letting that happen.

He studied her now, so cool and aloof, so prim and proper, but he remembered the way she'd been this afternoon. Warm and trembling and ready.

For him.

He got up, tossed the beer can into the trash and slowly walked toward the pool.

Jessica watched him. The pool lights had been turned off, and the torches cast dancing shadows across the surface of the water. Standing at the opposite side where the light barely touched him, Pierce stripped off his shirt and dived into the cool water. He surfaced at her feet, his hand coming up to snare her wet ankle.

"Why don't you come in?" he invited. "The water's great."

"I went in earlier," she reminded him. "But I was beginning to think you didn't like to swim anymore."

"I just don't like crowds."

"Seems as though I'm not the only one who's changed," she said pointedly.

Pierce shrugged. "I've never denied that. Sometimes when I look in the mirror, I hardly recognize myself."

"I'm not talking about the physical changes, Pierce," she said quietly.

"I know. But I guess what I'm trying to say is, I realize I look different, Jesse. I know I'm not exactly easy on the eyes. If you don't want to be with me, if you can't stand—"

"Don't say that," Jessica whispered. "Please don't think that."

Impulsively she slipped into the pool. It was cool and dark and gave them an instant illusion of privacy. The music and laughter faded into the background as Jessica stood in shoulder-high water facing Pierce.

"The scars don't matter to me."

"They matter to me," he said, "because I don't know how I got them." He hesitated, then said, "I probably should warn you. There are others."

Jessica looked at him, feeling the impact of his words all the way to her heart. She asked hesitantly, "Worse ones?"

"Yes."

"I'm sorry," she said, her voice tremulous. "I'm so sorry for what you must have gone through. I can't imagine what could have happened to you, but I...." Her words trailed off and she took a shuddering breath. "Is that why you didn't want to go swimming earlier? Because you didn't want to take off your shirt?"

"Yeah. It's not a pretty sight. I'm sorry, Jesse."

Jessica couldn't help herself. She lifted her hand and trailed her finger down the scar on the side of his face. "You're still the most attractive man I've ever met, Pierce."

Even though he wasn't touching her, she could sense his reaction to her words. His pleasure. "And you are undoubtedly the most beautiful woman I have ever seen. You take my breath away."

It was so easy to let the water carry her toward him. The darkness hid them, wrapped them in a blanket of intimacy that made Jessica feel daring and desperate, a very dangerous combination.

Pierce's hands rested lightly on her shoulders, then slid beneath the water till he found her waist. He pulled her toward him and Jessica floated against him without resistance. The water felt cool against her skin, but inside she was burning up. She wanted Pierce to kiss her in the worst way and she wanted it now, this instant....

Pierce's lips found her neck, teased her ear, then trailed across her cheek, barely skimming her mouth. She tasted like wine and chocolate and something a little more decadent. More sinful, except that it wasn't sinful because she was his wife, and that notion excited Pierce even more. She was his. And she always would be. . . .

As if to prove it to her, Pierce kissed her more forcefully, angling his head so that he could part her lips even farther. He wanted in. Now. And Jessica offered no resistance.

Her mouth was so sweet and hot and wet that it reminded him of other areas he would like to explore. Other places he wanted in. His hands slipped through the water to skim the edges of her swimsuit. Even in the water, she felt warm to his touch.

He broke the kiss, his fingers still gently exploring under the water. Jessica's head dropped forward to rest against his chest. He could feel her trembling, shuddering as his fingers probed more deeply, more thoroughly. She clung to him desperately, her breathing deep and ragged. He shot a glance across the yard toward the terrace. If anyone looked over here, they would just see shadows. At the most, a kiss. He'd break things up in a minute, but not quite yet. Not when she felt so delicious against his fingers. So hot. He drove deeper and felt her shudder against him. Just a minute more—

A peal of laughter rang out across the yard, an irritating intrusion into their little island of privacy. Pierce let out an unsteady breath, forcing his hands away from Jessica as he realized how far he'd let things go. The wine and, he hoped, the kiss had lowered Jessica's inhibitions, but he never should have taken advantage of her vulnerability. She would hate herself for her loss of control, and she'd very possibly hate him, as well.

He lifted his hand out of the water and smoothed her hair. She remained against him, but Pierce could tell that she had withdrawn from him. She was gathering her poise, he suspected, before she could face him, let alone the crowd of people on the terrace. He heard her draw a breath that sounded almost like a sob.

He forced a casual note into his voice. "Looks like the party's winding down. Maybe we should collect Max and be on our way, too. If you'd like to go on ahead, I'll make our goodbyes."

Jessica lifted her head from his shoulder, but her eyes didn't quite meet his. "No, it's okay. I'll tell Sharon we're leaving."

Pierce watched her pull herself up out of the pool and grab a towel from a nearby lawn chair. She walked across the yard toward the terrace, not once looking back at him.

Jessica followed Pierce up the stairs as he carried Max to bed. They hadn't said two words on the way home from Sharon's, and the silence between them was rapidly turning into awkwardness. She suspected they were both reflecting on what had almost happened between them a little while earlier.

How could she have done it? Jessica asked herself over and over.

How could she have lost control like that?

How could she have behaved so...wantonly in public?

And now what would Pierce think of her? What would he expect from her? And what did she want from him?

Tonight had changed everything. After what had almost happened in the pool, Jessica knew they could never go back to being polite strangers. They would no longer be satisfied with casual dinner conversation or a few chaste kisses. The question now wasn't so much if they would have sex, but when. And not if it would change her life, but how much?

And was she ready to face such a change?

Jessica leaned against the door frame and watched Pierce with their son. He was so gentle with Max, so tender and so loving that it made her heart ache just to watch them together. Max trusted Pierce wholeheartedly. He had no reservations at all about letting him back into their lives. Jessica wished she could be so sure. She wished her own feelings for Pierce were so uncomplicated.

Max stirred in his sleep as Pierce tucked the covers in around him. "Dad?"

"I'm here, son."

"Did you ask Mom about the camping trip?"

"Why don't we both ask her now?"

Max sat up in bed, rubbing his eyes as he looked around the dimly lit room. "Is it okay, Mom?"

Jessica crossed the room and stood beside the bed. Pierce was sitting on the edge, and he and Max were both gazing up at her. They looked so much alike that Jessica felt a tenderness for them both well up inside her. She said, "You know you'll be gone until Saturday, sweetie. That's five whole days. Almost a week. Are you sure you want to be away from home that long?"

"Are you afraid you'll get lonely for me?" Max asked solemnly.

Jessica smiled. "A little."

"But I know a trick," Max said. "If you think about me every night before you go to sleep, then you won't be so lonely for me."

"I know that trick, too," Jessica said, bending to kiss his cheek. "And I will think about you every night before I go to sleep."

"I'll think about you, too, Mom," he promised. "Just like I used to think about my dad every night until he came back home."

Jessica met Pierce's gaze. She could see his eyes shining in the moonlight and knew that he was as moved by their son's revelation as she was. Jessica wanted to take his hand and tell him how she used to think about him, too, every night before she went to sleep. She wanted to tell him how she used to pray for his safe return, wish with all her might that she could see him just one more time.

She felt a tear trickle down her cheek as waves of emotion swept over her.

"I guess it's all settled then," Pierce said. His voice was strangely subdued. "I'll help you pack in the morning, Max. How's that?"

"Good," Max said contentedly. He settled down under the covers, but almost instantly bolted upright again, his eyes wide with alarm. "When I get back from camping, you'll still be here, won't you?"

"I'll always be here, son. I'm not going anywhere."

"Never again?"

"Never again. I promise." His words were reassurance for Max, but his eyes were on Jessica. Something settled inside Jessica, a feeling of peace that at least one obstacle had suddenly been cleared from their path. She believed Pierce. She trusted him. And she wanted him to stay.

She wanted to tell him so much of what she was feeling and more, but Max was clinging to his hand as if he, too, was suddenly aware of how much he meant to him.

"Will you stay with me until I fall asleep?" he asked.

A few days ago, such a request would have torn Jessica up inside because her son was turning to someone else for comfort where he had once turned to her. But now as she watched Pierce stretch out beside their son and pull him into the protection of his strong arms, Jessica knew only a feeling of deep contentment.

Yet another barrier had fallen between them.

* * *

Jessica expected the knock on her bedroom door, but when it came, her stomach knotted in apprehension just the same. She laid the hairbrush on the dressing table and stood, then tightened the belt of her robe as she crossed the room to open the door.

"I just came to say good-night," Pierce said, when she drew open the door. "Max is finally sleeping."

"Good."

Their eyes met in the lamplight, and in that instant, awareness leaped across the space that separated them. Pierce leaned one arm against the door and took a moment to gaze around the room, his eyes lingering just a fraction too long on the king-size bed they had once shared.

She should have gotten rid of it a long time ago, Jessica realized. It held too many memories for them, and she wasn't sure it was a good idea to have such an intimate reminder of what they'd once shared. Maybe it would have been better to start new memories where old ones didn't exist. Where comparisons weren't inevitable.

His gaze returned to her and he smiled a little half smile that sent her heart racing. "You know, Jesse, of all the things we've talked about since I've been back, there's one subject we've pretty much avoided."

"What?" Her voice sounded breathy, a little too excited.

"We haven't talked about sex. I think maybe it's time we did."

Jessica let out a shaky breath. "Don't you think it's a little late for conversation? I mean considering...what almost happened earlier...." She glanced away, embarrassed.

Pierce walked into the room and closed the door. The sound of the latch clicking shut made Jessica even more nervous. The room suddenly seemed too small and intimate, the bed too large and overpowering.

"I think the timing's perfect," he said softly. "It occurred to me earlier that you're afraid of me. Afraid to let yourself go with me. I can't help wondering why."

"Five years is a long time," she said, fiddling with the top of her robe. "We've both changed. And everything."

"Yeah," he agreed, his eyes darkening suspiciously. "It's that 'everything' I want to talk about. You said there was no one else in your life, hasn't been anyone else. Does that mean you've abstained from sex for five whole years? Is that why you're so reluctant to be with me now?"

"I could ask you the same question," Jessica said. "Only, you don't remember, do you?"

His eyes were deep and probing as he searched her face. "I was never unfaithful to you."

Jessica knew the wave of relief flooding through her was ridiculous under the circumstances. She tried to fight it off, tried to think more rationally with her brain instead of her heart. "How can you be so sure? How can you say that when there are so many things you can't tell me about the past five years?"

"Because I am sure. Because I know, right here—" he touched his hand to his heart "—that there was never anyone but you. Can you tell me the same thing?"

She lifted her gaze to his. "Yes," she whispered. "I was never unfaithful to you, Pierce."

For just a moment, the darkness in his eyes lifted, and Jessica glimpsed an emotion so powerful, so intense, it took her breath away. "My God," he breathed, "I've been so afraid. I knew I had no right to ask, but I had to know. Jesse. . . ."

He pulled her into his arms so fast, Jessica felt as if the floor had given way beneath her. She grabbed his arms for support, letting him guide her back against the wall until he could press against her, his body hot and hard and insistent.

"It's been so long," he whispered. "We've been apart for so long. Sometimes I wonder how I survived at all without you."

"Because you had to," she said. "And so did I."

"Yes," he agreed, "but I don't think I can survive another night without making love to you. When I'm close to you like this, I can't stand not touching you. My God, I remember everything about you. How silky smooth your hair feels beneath my fingers."

As if to demonstrate to himself the truth of his words, he wove his hands through the dark cloud of her hair. "And your mouth . . ." He took a deep breath. "Your mouth is so damned sexy, sweetheart. I want to kiss you deep and hard every time I look at you." He rubbed a thumb across her lips, a prelude to what she really wanted. "We've been leading up to this all day. You know that, don't you?" he asked softly.

Jessica closed her eyes and leaned back against the wall, her breathing deep and uneven. He was quickly seducing her, with his hands and his mouth and his words, and she didn't know if she had the will to stop him this time, because she was remembering, too. She knew the feel of his hands against her flesh, the hardness of his body on hers. She knew what it was like, the exquisite thrill, the moment he plunged inside her. . . .

"I remember what it's like, seeing you lying on that bed, waiting for me." He slid his knuckles down her face, traced the line of her chin with one finger, then found the pulse point in her throat. His hand dipped lower. "You have the most beautiful breasts," he murmured. "So round and firm and just the perfect size for my hands. And my mouth," he added, watching her. His hands smoothed down her sides, barely skimming her breasts, but Jessica felt the sensitive peaks tingle and swell, aching for a deeper, more thorough touch.

"This is crazy," she breathed, trying to control the mounting sensations inside her.

"Insane," he agreed.

His hands were at her waist, pulling her toward him until he could lock his arms around her, holding her against him so tightly, Jessica had no doubt at all about his own state of arousal. Their mouths joined and he shot his tongue deep inside her, thrilling her with the urgency of his thrusts.

Jessica shifted, automatically adjusting her position to accommodate him. The feel of his erection caused something to gush inside her. Nerve endings quivered with sensation. Deep inside, she could feel her body start to clench and unclench, clench and unclench. Desperate now, she pressed herself against him, molded herself to him until only their clothing prevented penetration.

"Sweetheart," Pierce groaned, "let me get us to the bed."

He started to lift her, but Jessica pushed aside his hands. "No."

He hesitated. "Not the bed?"

Jessica shook her head, drinking in great gulps of air to try to calm her racing heart. "Not...this," she gasped. "Not sex. We can't."

His hands froze. "Why not?"

Jessica glanced away, her face flooding with color at the reality of the situation. He was her husband, for God's sake. No need to be embarrassed, but for some reason she suddenly felt unbearably shy. "Because I'm not...I'm not protected, that's why." Speaking her fears aloud effectively doused Jessica's passion. She retreated a few inches away from him, securing the belt of her robe. "I should have thought about it earlier, but I...I wasn't thinking at all."

Pierce just stared at her for a long, tense moment. He looked as if he couldn't quite believe what he was hearing. "You mean if we make love, you could get pregnant?"

"Surely you haven't forgotten the way that works," she said shakily. "Of course I could get pregnant."

Another pause. His gaze softened. "Would that be so bad?" he asked quietly. "We always wanted a big family."

"Yes, it would be bad," she practically shouted. "It would be horribly irresponsible of us. We can't bring another child into this world until we know...that is...until we're sure that...."

Pierce helped her out. "Until we're sure we'll stay together?"

Jessica ran a trembling hand through her hair. "Yes. It's the only sensible decision. The only mature one."

"Yeah," Pierce said, scrubbing his face with his hands. "But I'm not feeling too damned mature at the moment."

He brushed his lips against hers, an agonizingly brief contact, then he turned and strode out of the bedroom.

Chapter 11

"Max, I don't think you're going to have room for all those toys," Pierce said as he lifted a stack of T-shirts from one of Max's drawers and placed them inside the open suitcase.

Max struggled across the room, carrying a box of superhero figures. He eyed his suitcase warily, took out the stack of shirts Pierce had just carefully packed, then dumped the toys inside.

Pierce shook his head. "I think we're going to have to come up with a compromise here, or else your mother will have both our heads. How about just a few of those figures?"

Max shot him a glance. "How many is a few?"

"Five," Pierce said, then seeing Max's outraged look, quickly bargained. "Okay, ten. But we have to make room for your clean clothes somehow."

"How about we leave out my toothbrush?" Max suggested helpfully, digging under the pile of toys to find it. "I probably won't need it, anyway. I'm just going to be gone until Saturday."

Pierce smothered a grimace. "Well, a toothbrush doesn't take up all that much space, and the McReynoldses would probably appreciate it if you could somehow find the time to use it."

"Okay," Max agreed reluctantly. "Then what else can I leave behind? I need this stuff, Dad."

"How about Freddy?" Pierce pulled the bedraggled bear from Max's suitcase and held it up.

Max bit his lip, eyeing the stuffed toy longingly. "What if he gets lonely for me while I'm gone?"

"Remember what you told your mother last night? Freddy can think about you every night before he goes to sleep. And just to make doubly sure he doesn't get lonely, you can think about him, too. How's that?"

Max considered the suggestion. "That could work, I guess. Will you ... think about me, too?"

"You bet."

"And will you keep Mom from getting too lonely for me?"

Pierce smiled. "I'll sure do my best."

Max looked up at his father, his eyes wide and dark and solemn. "Can I tell you a secret? Promise you won't tell?"

Pierce crossed his heart with his finger.

Max nodded, satisfied. "I used to hear Mom crying sometimes at night when she thought I was asleep. I think she was lonely for you."

Pierce closed his eyes for a moment, feeling a wave of guilt wash over him. "I'm going to try to make sure that your mother never has a reason to cry again. That's a promise, Max."

Max grinned. "You always keep your promises, don't you, Dad?"

"Yes," Pierce agreed grimly, remembering the oath to the agency he'd taken years ago. "I always do."

Max took Freddy from Pierce and sat down on the edge of the bed, cradling the bear in his arms. He was silent for a moment, then he looked up at Pierce, his gaze serious. "If someone told you their secret, it wouldn't be right to tell someone else about it, would it?"

"Not usually," Pierce said. "But it would depend on what the secret was. There are times when you should. For instance, if the secret was one that might cause harm to someone else, then you'd have to tell. Or there are secrets like the one you just told me about your mother. You thought that was something I needed to know. Is there something else you want to tell me, Max?"

Max shook his head. "I promised I wouldn't tell, and I want to be like you. I want to always keep my promises."

This conversation was making Pierce feel uneasy. "Is this promise going to cause harm to someone if you don't tell? Is it dangerous?"

Max shook his head. "No. It's just about a dumb game me and my friend play."

Pierce let out a relieved breath. "Well, if it's a promise you made to a friend, and there's no harm to anyone else, then I guess I'd have to agree. I guess you'd need to keep your friend's secret. Otherwise he might not think he could trust you. But if you ever do need to talk to me about anything, I'm here, son."

"I'm here, too, Dad, if you ever need to talk to me," Max said soberly.

"Thanks, Max. I'll remember that."

A little while later, Max was all packed up, and he and Pierce and Jessica stood out in the front yard as Frank McReynolds loaded the rest of their gear into the back of the van.

Jessica bent down and gave Max one last hug. "Now you call me whenever you get a chance," she instructed.

"There won't be no phone in the woods, Mom," Max admonished her, but his arms clung to her neck a little longer than usual.

"Don't worry, Jessica. We'll call," Sharon assured her. "Ready to hit the road, Max?"

He nodded, pressing his face against Jessica's one last time. Then he climbed into the van, and Jessica felt the beginnings of tears as she watched him and Allie hopping up and down in excitement. Pierce's arm came around her, and automatically the loneliness began to ease. Jessica laid her head against his shoulder, and his arm tightened around her.

Amid a barrage of goodbyes and be goods and have funs, the van slowly backed out of the driveway and lumbered down the street. Jessica and Pierce stood on the sidewalk, still waving as the van turned the corner and drove out of sight.

"So," she said, taking a deep breath and letting it out.

"So," he said, watching her carefully.

Jessica self-consciously wiped the back of her fingers across the moisture on her face. "You must think I'm pretty silly, getting this upset over a camping trip. It's just ... he's never been away from me before. I always took him with me when I traveled."

Pierce lifted a finger to trace the path of a new tear sliding down her cheek. "I don't think you're silly at all. I miss him, too."

She gazed up at him. "You do? Already? I mean, you understand," she finished softly. He nodded, and for the first time Jessica spoke what was in her heart. "I'm glad you're here, Pierce."

"I'm glad I'm here, too." They smiled at one another to mark the beginning of a new understanding, and then he said, "What we need is a diversion."

"A...diversion?"

He kept his arm around her shoulders as they turned toward the house. "To take our minds off missing our son. How about dinner out tonight? Just you and me. Kind of like the old days. Except better. I'd love to take this new, independent career woman out on the town," he teased as they walked up the porch steps. "Of course, since you're working and I'm not, you may have to pick up the tab."

Jessica tucked her hair behind her ears as they stopped on the front porch and turned toward one another. A breeze drifted through the trees, stirring the scent of honeysuckle in the early morning air. Memories teased the fringes of Jessica's mind, and she wasn't sure if they were good or bad ones. "The shop is still yours, Pierce. You still own it."

He shook his head and smiled. "The shop is *ours,* Jesse. You've made it every bit as much yours as it ever was mine. Maybe more so." He paused, then said, "There could be a place for both of us, though."

In silent consent, they sat down on the porch swing and rocked slowly back and forth. It seemed like such an innocent thing to do, uncomplicated and normal, but Jessica knew that something important was happening between them. Something that had been building for days.

She considered his suggestion as the movement of the swing lulled her senses. She was surprised to find that she didn't resent Pierce's proposal. Not in the least. "You could be right," she said. "I would like to be able to spend some time with Max. I've missed so much, it seems."

"Not nearly as much as I have," Pierce said. "But we have the rest of our lives to make up for it. Why don't we start tonight? It could be a new beginning for us, Jesse."

He stopped the movement of the swing as he turned to her expectantly. Jessica could hear the hammering of her heart in the early morning stillness and wondered if he could, too.

"I'm not sure I'm ready," she murmured, avoiding his gaze.

Pierce started the swing again. "We'll start with dinner," he said easily. "We won't plan on anything beyond that."

He rested his head against the back of the swing and his eyes closed. He looked completely relaxed and unhurried, but Jessica knew his calmness was a facade. They were both thinking ahead to after dinner, to returning home where they would be alone tonight, with no interruptions.

"How about dinner tonight, Jessica?"

Jessica put the final touches to the jewelry display in the glass case before looking up. Brandon had come in unexpectedly this morning. She'd thought he was still in Amsterdam. Or Caracas. Where *had* he told her he was going last week?

She closed the case and glanced up. "I'm afraid I can't tonight. I've already made plans." At the thought of the promised evening with Pierce, her stomach began to flutter in anticipation. She caught herself smiling.

So did Brandon. Something flickered across his features before he tempered his expression, but Jessica felt the stirrings of an uneasiness she didn't quite understand.

"Do these plans include your ex-husband?"

"He isn't my ex-husband," she clarified. "Pierce and I are still married."

"I would have thought that situation only a temporary technicality," he said, leaning against the counter as he regarded her steadily. "After all, the man's been gone for five years. What can you possibly have in common with him now?"

Jessica thought about the way Pierce had touched her in the pool last night, and her face warmed at the memory. She brushed an invisible spot of dust from the Tiffany lamp on the counter. "You mean aside from our son? I don't know what we may or may not still have in common," she acknowledged. "Maybe that's why I want to have dinner with him tonight."

"I hope you know what you're doing." His voice was soft and concerned, but there was still something in his eyes, a hardness she had never noticed before. "I'd hate to see you get hurt," he added.

"I have no intention of getting hurt," Jessica said, but in truth she had no idea whether she was doing the right thing or not. All she knew for sure was that the feelings between her and Pierce were much too strong to ignore. God knows she'd tried. But she couldn't fight them any longer. Didn't want to.

"What did you bring me from your trip?" she said lightly, trying to return their conversation to business matters.

Brandon grinned. "Something irresistible. Something you can't possibly say no to."

"Well, let's see it," Jessica said, then caught her breath at the gold and jade earrings he withdrew from his pocket. They were the exact shade of green as the dress she planned to wear tonight. For Pierce.

The band played "Unforgettable."

Jessica remembered vividly that one detail, but on looking back later, so much about the evening with Pierce was only a hazy memory, a shimmering impression of a night destined to change her life.

She remembered that she wore her green dress and the jade earrings, and Pierce was dressed in a raw silk sport coat, a white shirt that looked irresistibly soft and inviting, and dark pleated trousers that fitted him so well she was certain they must be new. Jessica remembered thinking that he was dressed the way he used to, the casual elegance masking the soul of a man who dared to take risks, who had once thrived on living on the edge.

She remembered that the rustic, wooded setting of the restaurant Pierce had chosen made it seem as if they were miles from anywhere, and the candlelight flickering on the table made his eyes seem even darker, more mysterious.

She remembered that they danced. Close. Like lovers. And she remembered that later they strolled outside in the restaurant's garden, and that Pierce kissed her beneath a full moon.

But what Jessica always remembered most about that night was the anticipation that, like a drug, lulled her into an almost dreamlike state of lethargy, where everything looked beautiful and romantic, and where anything seemed possible.

Even love.

The house looked dark and deserted when they pulled up into the driveway, but Jessica had left a lamp on in the living room and another one on in her bedroom. The soft glow from the upstairs window drew her gaze for a moment as Pierce wrapped his arm around her and guided her in through the back door.

She stumbled once in the darkness, and he caught her against him, his hands finding her waist and holding her for a moment longer than was necessary. Jessica gazed up at him in the darkness, unable to read his eyes or his expression, but she somehow knew that he was feeling that same sense of expectation, that trace of recklessness that had been teasing them both all evening.

"Shall we say our good-nights down here, Jesse?" he murmured softly.

His hand skimmed her bare arm. His touch was electric. And Jessica wanted more.

She curled her fingers around his lapels, pulling him toward her for the kiss she had been craving all evening. Not the light, romantic kiss he'd given her in the garden, but a deep, soul-shattering kiss that would leave not one iota of doubt in either of their minds as to how the evening would end.

"I'd rather say good morning," she said daringly, feathering her lips against his.

Pierce let out a long breath, pulled her against him and trailed his hands up and down her back. "Do you know how good it feels to hold you? God, you can't possibly know."

"Oh, but I do," she said. "I've waited so long for you. For this night."

"Sweetheart," he breathed and captured her lips with his. He touched his tongue to hers, and Jessica felt the sensation all the way to her toes.

"Let's go upstairs," he said, taking her hand.

Jessica was floating again. She was barely aware of the stairs beneath her feet or the doors that opened at the slightest touch, but suddenly they were in her bedroom and she was in his arms again, and the king-size bed—their bed—was beckoning to them both.

Pierce swung one of the jade earrings with his fingertip. "Beautiful," he whispered. "Just like you."

"Brandon brought them to me today," she said. "I couldn't resist. I—I'd hoped you'd like them."

"I love them, but since Chambers brought them to you, we'll remove them first," he said teasingly, reaching to undo the backs. He tossed the earrings on her dresser, then reached for the zipper of her dress.

Suddenly shy, Jessica said, "Let me... I'll just be a minute." She scooped up her robe and sailed past him into the bathroom. She closed the door and leaned against it, fanning her face with her hand.

No turning back now, Jessica, she warned herself. You better make darn sure this is what you want. Away from Pierce she felt the doubts begin to sneak back in. The glow from the evening— from the wine and from his kiss—fizzled in the harsh glare of the bathroom light. She hadn't made love in five years, and Jessica had never felt very confident about her abilities to please him, even all those years ago.

What if she did something stupid? What if she did something that would embarrass both her and Pierce and make him wish he'd never come back? Or worse, what if he didn't like the way she looked anymore? She wasn't as thin as she used to be, she thought, gazing down at her figure. Pierce had always treated her like a china doll, but Jessica had lost that fragile look a long time ago.

But when she glanced at her reflection in the mirror, saw the glow in her eyes, the color in her cheeks, the slightly swollen line of her lips from his kisses, she knew suddenly that, no matter what the night held for them, no matter what revelations came to light, this was exactly what she wanted. For the first time in five years she felt like a woman again. Pierce had not only returned from the dead but he'd also brought her back into the world of the living.

Quickly she removed her dress and stockings and underwear, and belted the robe around her. She brushed her teeth, ran a comb through her hair, and spritzed her favorite perfume on all the pulse points she could think of. Then she opened the door and went out to join her husband.

Pierce saw the doubt and uncertainty in her eyes immediately. He watched her cross the room and stand for a second too long beside the bed before she curled up beside him. She looked so young with her long, dark hair fanned out across the pillow and her gray eyes wide and shadowed with apprehension and maybe just a hint of fear. She seemed sweet and vulnerable tonight, and so fragile that he wondered if he even dared touch her.

So he just looked at her for an agonizing moment, telling himself that he could make her happy. He could be the man she'd always thought he was. Tonight he had a lot to prove, not just to her, but to himself.

Would she still want him? When she saw what he looked like now, would she still find him attractive? Or would she be turned off by what the past five years had done to him?

She was waiting for him to make the first move, Pierce realized. She was gazing over at him, and he felt a surge of tenderness well inside him. She was looking at him the way she used to look at him.

He took his cue immediately.

"We can do away with this, can't we?" he asked, undoing the belt of her robe. Jessica raised herself up as he slipped the fabric off her shoulders and down her arms, and then it was gone.

The last barrier between them.

She slid beneath the covers and Pierce reached across her to turn out the light.

"You don't have to," she whispered shyly.

"It's best," he said in a tone Jessica couldn't quite decipher. Then he said, "Come here, sweetheart," and she stopped trying to analyze anything.

His kisses and caresses quickly returned her to that floating, dreamlike state of euphoria. Jessica had never felt so relaxed. So free from responsibility.

"We don't have a thing to worry about tonight," he said, echoing her thoughts. "It's just you and me, Jesse. The way it used to be. I'll take care of you, you know. I'll take care of everything."

Jessica knew what he was talking about. She'd seen the box of condoms sitting on the nightstand when she'd come back into the room. "I thought you said you weren't planning anything beyond dinner," she murmured, closing her eyes as his hand played along her side, riding over her hip, then lingering on her thigh.

"Do you mind?" he asked, tracing her lips lightly with his fingertips.

"No," she said, and meant it. "Sometimes it's nice to be taken care of." Jessica was amazed at herself for admitting it, but it was true. Tonight she needed to be able to rely on someone other than herself. She needed to be able to trust again. She needed Pierce.

Jessica sighed, and Pierce wrapped her even more tightly in his arms.

It was so easy, after all, she discovered. So easy to let go of the doubts and fears and frustrations. So easy to let him back into her life and back into her heart. Jessica caught his face between her hands and kissed him deeply.

Instantly Pierce responded to her need. He kissed her in return, tenderly at first and then with a growing demand that left them both breathless and aching. His head moved downward, leaving a trail of hot, wet kisses as he searched for, then found first one breast and then the other. He moistened the sensitive peak with his tongue, then took it into his mouth, drawing a long, shuddering breath from Jessica. She plunged her hands into his hair and held him close.

The darkness of the room only heightened her senses. Jessica could barely see Pierce's face, but she didn't need to see him. She could feel him, feel every inch of his long, hard body as he lay against her, touching her so intimately she thought she might die from the thrill of it all.

It was never this way before.

Jessica didn't want to think about that, didn't want to make comparisons with the way it used to be, but dear God, it *was* different. It *was* better. She guided him to the places that screamed for attention, and Pierce eagerly complied. She whispered his name over and over in the darkness, entreaties that came from her heart, her very soul, and Pierce answered her.

"I'm right here, Jesse," he whispered.

He took his time with her, kissing her all over, touching her in places that made her moan softly into the darkness. Pierce had only one thought and that was to please Jesse. For the moment, he put his own needs aside and tried to concentrate on making her want him as badly as he wanted her.

But it had been so long. So very long. Five years he'd spent without her. Even though he couldn't remember the passage of time, Pierce somehow felt the unbearable loneliness of every one of those years now, the desperation and despair of the long separation.

The intense emotions rushing through him made him want to hurry the consummation, to lay claim to his wife once again, to experience that heart-pounding thrill the moment he entered her.

But not yet, he thought. Not until she was ready for him. This night belonged to her.

He felt her hand on his. Unexpectedly she changed the rhythm of his touch, and Pierce heard her breath catch in her throat. It elated him to know that she could take such pleasure in their lovemaking now, that she could unasham-

edly let him know what she wanted, what brought her
pleasure.

It was never like this before.

Don't think about that, he admonished himself. It had
always been wonderful with Jesse, but Pierce had never been
quite sure of his ability to please her. She'd always been so
shy about voicing her needs, about showing him what
brought her the greatest enjoyment.

But not now. God, it *was* better between them now. So
much better. *He* was better, Pierce realized, and he knew
why. Because pleasing Jessica was so much more important—and so much more thrilling—than taking his own
satisfaction.

He heard her breath quicken, felt the muscles in her legs
tense and knew that she was almost there. He slid down in
bed and let his mouth replace his hand. The explosion was
almost immediate. Jessica's back arched and her hands
grasped his shoulders as she cried out. The convulsions
lasted an impossibly long time, and Pierce thought his own
body would explode just watching her. Before the shudders
quieted, he reached for the box on the nightstand, dealt with
the necessities, then moved over her and eased inside.

Jessica's heart was still pounding from the aftershock of
the powerful climax when she felt Pierce enter her. She
tensed. It was difficult at first. After all this time, the passage was almost too snug, but Pierce took his time, easing
in little by little, whispering to her how much he wanted her.

"It's been so long," she whispered a little desperately.
"I'm sorry it's so...tight."

Pierce shuddered above her. "God, I'm not. It's like our
wedding night, remember?"

The memory made Jessica smile. Made her want to experience again that closeness with Pierce, a man who had
been her husband and her lover and her friend. It could be

that way again, she thought. It could be that way again, only better.

His movements inside her were slow and undemanding, so Jessica began to relax. And as soon as she relaxed, the pleasure began to build all over again. She shifted her thighs until she was able to draw his full length inside her, and Pierce stilled for a moment, letting her body adjust to his.

It was Jessica who moved against him. It was Jessica who set the rhythm, moving her hips slowly at first, then faster and harder, taking him in so deeply Pierce knew he would come apart any second now.

"God, you're good," he groaned, matching her frenzied rhythm. "So damned good."

In the end it was Pierce who took charge. No longer able to sustain the motion, Jessica collapsed back on the bed, breathing deeply as the sensations rapidly began to build and build in the lower part of her body. Pierce plunged inside her, time after time, until the release ripped through her, shattering the last vestige of her control.

Holding him close, Jessica felt Pierce's shudders, his last deep thrusts, and knew with a sense of contentment that she had pleased him. Almost as much as he had pleased her. She felt like laughing and crying all at the same time.

After a moment, he started to roll off her, but Jessica clasped him tightly. "Don't leave," she whispered, feeling the emotions well up inside her. "Not yet."

Pierce touched the tear at the corner of her eye. "Did I hurt you? Oh, God, Jesse, I didn't mean to."

"You didn't. It's just...." Her voice trailed off and her eyes closed. "It was so wonderful being close to you again, but it was...so different this time. So intense. I've never felt this way before."

Pierce smiled. "So you noticed that, too." He rolled to his side, but he kept his arms around her, kept their bodies connected as he pulled her more snugly into his embrace. They lay face-to-face. Heart to heart. And Jessica couldn't imagine being anywhere else at that moment.

"Why do you think it's so different now?" she asked, laying her head against his shoulder.

His hand lazily traced her back. "I imagine it's because of what you keep telling me. We've both changed."

"That much?"

He grinned. "It would seem so. You've grown up, become very mature and independent. You know what you want and you weren't afraid to let *me* know."

Jessica covered her face with her hands. Now that the passion had subsided, she felt a little embarrassed by her behavior. "You must think I'm terrible," she said.

Pierce pulled her hands away from her face and kissed her soundly. "I think you're wonderful," he said. "But you're not the only one who's changed, sweetheart. I think I've grown up, too. I've learned that life is more than just living on the edge. More than just one momentary thrill after another. My family is the most important thing in the world to me now, and I want to be here for you for as long as you'll have me. Because I love you, Jesse. More than anything."

Jessica felt another tear slip down her face. She reached up and brought his mouth close to hers. "Please don't leave me," she whispered, just before their lips touched.

"Never again," he vowed.

Chapter 12

He was gone when Jessica awakened. She bolted upright in bed.

"Pierce?"

"I'm right here, Jesse," came his soft reply.

It was still dark, but a soft glow illuminated the room as if dawn hovered just on the horizon. Pierce was sitting in the wing chair near the window, and he'd turned on a lamp, angling the shade so that the light fell away from the bed. Jessica saw that he'd been looking through the stack of photo albums she kept in the bookcase near her dresser.

"Can't you sleep?" she asked, shoving the hair back from her face.

"I have a lot on my mind, I guess."

His head was bent over the pictures, and his expression was shadowed, but even from across the room, Jessica sensed that something was wrong. She reached for her robe and slipped it on as she got out of bed. She crossed the floor and knelt beside the chair, then gazed down at the pictures in the album spread open on his lap. By the looks of the pile beside his chair, he'd already been through most of them.

Jessica knew what they contained. They were a catalog of Max's life from the day he was born. His first tooth, his first step, his first day of school. Jessica had been meticulous about chronicling in photographs the five years Pierce had been away. She wondered now if it was because she'd always known somehow that he'd come back to her.

"That was the day Max started kindergarten," Jessica said softly, smiling at the image of her son's solemn little face as he waved to her from the school-bus steps. The camera had captured the tears glistening on his cheeks, and Jessica remembered that she'd had a hard time fighting back her own tears as she'd watched the bus drive away. She'd felt as if she'd lost a very precious part of herself that day.

"I've missed so much," Pierce said. His own eyes were shining as he looked up and met her gaze. "I've lost so much more than just memories, Jesse, and no matter what happens, I'll never get those years back. They're gone forever."

Jessica didn't know what to say. Something unleashed inside. She felt the last of her anger and resentment melt away as she gazed into Pierce's tormented eyes. She knew, without knowing how she knew, that he hadn't left her and Max all those years ago because he'd wanted to. He'd left because he had to. Because no other choice had been given to him.

She mourned his loss now, just as she had mourned hers the day he'd disappeared.

She reached up and smoothed back the lock of dark hair that had fallen across his brow. "I don't know how I would deal with a loss like yours," she said softly. "I can't imagine how it would feel to have missed all those years of Max's life."

"And yours," he said, gazing at her with dark, haunted eyes. "You can't know how deeply I regret losing those five years of our marriage, Jesse. Years that we can never get back. Sometimes I wonder...."

"What?"

He took her hand and squeezed it. "Sometimes I wonder if things will ever work out for us. I want them to. You don't know how badly, but sometimes I can't help thinking that we may never be able to find what we once had."

"Maybe not all of it," she said. "Some of it *is* gone forever." Jessica felt something of the loss she'd experienced the day Max had started to school. Something precious had been lost to her forever. But in a way, she and Max had grown closer after that day. She'd enjoyed immensely this new phase of his life, taken great pride in his accomplishments at school.

Her hero worship and youthful adulation for the kind of man Pierce had been was gone forever because the girl she'd been was gone. She was a woman now, and like her son, she didn't need a hero anymore. Didn't need someone to protect her from the cruelties of the world. She'd proven that she could do that for herself.

What she needed now was just a man. Someone to love her for better or worse. Jessica took a deep breath. She mourned the loss of her youth for just a moment, then she let it go. Maybe it was time she and Pierce moved into a new, more mature phase of their lives.

He was staring down at the pictures again, his expression deeply saddened, and Jessica's heart ached for him.

"Let it go," she whispered. "Let it go, love. You and Max have years and years ahead of you. You won't miss any more of his life, Pierce. I promise you."

"And what about your life, Jesse?"

Jessica didn't answer him. Instead she drew their linked hands up to her mouth and kissed each of his scarred knuckles. "It can never be the same for us again," she said softly. "I'm not the same woman you married, and you're not the same man who left here five years ago. But I do love you, Pierce. Maybe more than I ever did."

Pierce closed his eyes as if overcome by his emotions. "You don't know how I've wanted to hear you say that. I've seen the woman you've become, Jesse. I've seen the way you've raised our son. I admire and respect you more than anyone I've ever known. And if you don't need me anymore, well, that's okay." He set the album aside and stood, drawing her to her feet. "Because you see, sweetheart, I do need you. I need you desperately."

It was so easy to hold him, to offer him the comfort of her arms as he'd done so often for her in the past. For a long while they stood in the glow of the lamp, their arms around each other as they each grieved in their own way for what would never be again.

Jessica wasn't sure when things began to change, but suddenly their embrace tightened. Their bodies shifted and fitted together more intimately. She felt Pierce's lips in her hair and then at her ear and she turned her head just slightly, so their mouths were only a breath away.

"Oh, God," Pierce whispered, holding her close.

Then he kissed her, and Jessica felt the past crumble around them.

He unfastened her robe and slid it off her shoulders, then lifted her and carried her to the bed. Jessica kept her arms around him, pulling him down with her as she lay back against the pillows.

Their kisses became hot and greedy with anticipation. They knew what to expect from each other now, knew exactly how to give each other the greatest pleasure, and Jessica couldn't wait for that exquisite moment of fulfillment. She reveled now in the physical side of their love where once she had been too inhibited to fully enjoy it.

Pierce pulled away from her for a moment. "I'll turn off the light," he said.

"No, don't," she said, reaching for him again.

"But, Jesse—"

"I want to see you," she insisted. She sat up in bed and then knelt before him, still a little shy in her nakedness, but the look in Pierce's eyes made her awkwardness vanish. She let him look at her for as long as he wanted, and then, when he reached for her, she went gladly into his arms.

In the lamp glow, she could see the scar down the side of his face, and Jessica lifted her lips to kiss it. Pierce flinched beneath her touch, but he didn't move away. He remained still under her scrutiny, letting her get to know his body again as he'd done with hers.

Jessica's lips skimmed down the side of his face, tracing the length of the scar, then moved to his neck and across his shoulders. She shifted around him so that she was kneeling behind him. She bent and kissed the back of his neck as her hands caressed his arms and shoulders, and then moved to his back.

Her hands froze when she felt the mass of scars.

Pierce tensed but didn't move. He sat with his head slightly bowed as if waiting for her retreat.

Even in the soft light, the scars were horrible, worse than anything Jessica could ever imagine. The thin red ridges crisscrossed over the entire surface of his back, leaving very little skin that was unmarked. The horror of what he had gone through rose in Jessica until she thought for a moment she might be sick, not from the scars but from the suffering he'd endured and the pain she'd caused him when he returned home. It was almost too much to bear.

But no matter how badly she felt, Jessica knew she could do nothing to make him think she was rejecting him again. Far from it. If possible, she loved him even more. He'd survived incredible torment just to find his way back to her. She put her arms around him and held him close, her cheek against his scarred flesh.

Pierce felt her tears against his back, and it tore him up to realize what the sight of his scars must have done to her. He turned until he was able to take her in his arms and pull her into his lap. She clung to him, crying as he'd never seen her cry before.

Pierce didn't know quite what to do, so he simply held her as the sobs racked her body and her tears streamed down his chest.

"Jesse, Jesse," he soothed, putting his cheek against hers. "It's okay. It's all in the past, remember? We have to let it go, sweetheart."

"I'm sorry," she whispered over and over. "I'm so sorry."

Pierce held her even more tightly. "You have nothing to be sorry about. None of this is your fault."

"But it is, don't you see?" The sobs made her speak haltingly, brokenly. "You came back home...and after everything you'd been through...I made you think you weren't welcome here. I made you think...this wasn't your home anymore. That...Max and I...didn't want you or need you or...love you."

"Well, what were you supposed to do? I'd been gone five years without a word, and then I just showed up one day, expecting everything to be as I'd left it. I don't blame you for not welcoming me with open arms. You were right not to trust me, Jesse," he said, closing his eyes. There was a crushing weight inside Pierce's chest and he knew why. Because he still wasn't telling her the whole truth.

Maybe he should, Pierce thought. Maybe he should forget the oath he'd made to the agency years ago and clear his conscience right here and now with Jesse. He owed his allegiance to her now. She and Max were his only concern, but the need for complete secrecy had been too long ingrained in his makeup. He knew the life-or-death importance of discretion, and he couldn't be sure that any revelation he made now might not somehow jeopardize Jessica and Max's safety.

So he said nothing.

And he let Jessica give him her love, knowing that when she found out the whole truth, there would be hell to pay for this night that had brought them closer than they had ever been before.

Jessica lifted her tearstained face to his. "Make love to me, Pierce," she whispered. "Please. I need you so."

"Oh, Jesse—"

Her fingertip silenced his words. "Don't say anything," she begged. "We've said too much already. Just hold me. Stay with me."

"Yes," he whispered. "For as long as you'll have me."

Their lovemaking was more frenzied this time, more desperate and hurried as if they had suddenly realized just how long they'd been separated. Or as if they were new lovers, discovering passion for the first time.

He didn't lay her back on the bed as Jessica expected, but made her stand before him so that he could worship her body with his eyes and his hands and his lips. Jessica trembled as his mouth unerringly found the place she'd guided him to earlier. Her hands tangled in his hair as a wave of sensations raced through her. Jessica fought for breath, fought for balance as Pierce brought her in an astonishingly short time to another shattering climax.

She collapsed against him, and he caught her, then kissed her, deep and hard and thorough, his tongue thrusting in and out, in and out, in a teasing preview of what was to come.

This time it was Jessica who reached for the box on the nightstand, Jessica who dealt with the necessities, Jessica who made it a thrilling prelude to their lovemaking.

Pierce lifted her and settled her on his lap as she wrapped her legs around him. He lifted her hips, then let her slide slowly down on him, and Jessica thought she had never felt anything so wonderfully complete as the moment she felt him inside her.

They kissed, their tongues keeping pace with the frantic rhythm of their bodies.

They embraced, their bodies melding together so tightly that two heartbeats became one.

They whispered, their promises and demands and soft cries stirring the deep silence of night.

And they loved as if there were no tomorrows and no yesterdays, no past and no future, but only now and only them. Because nothing else mattered.

When it was all over, when the shudders of release had been spent, they fell back against the bed, still clinging to each other, still whispering to each other their promises and demands and soft words of love.

Pierce perched on the edge of Jessica's desk and watched her through the open door to the shop. She and a customer were talking animatedly about a silver spoon collection which had just arrived earlier in the week via Brandon Chambers.

At the thought of the buyer, Pierce scowled. He didn't care what Jessica thought of the man, he still didn't trust him, but so far he hadn't been able to justify his suspicions. Even Jay had said the man appeared to be on the up-and-up. But, of course, Jay Greene would be inclined to trust anyone that Pierce didn't.

Pierce moved back around the desk and sat down facing the computer monitor, but his mind wasn't on the figures he'd pulled up on the screen. He was thinking about the animosity he and his brother-in-law had always shared.

Pierce had never been quite sure why the two of them had taken such an instant dislike to one another, but from the moment Jessica had introduced them, Pierce had known that Jay didn't trust him. He'd often wondered if Jessica's brother had somehow found out about his secret life, if Jay's animosity was indeed genuine concern for his sister.

Or was it something else? Something more personally motivated?

Pierce couldn't imagine what. The agency was top secret with very limited access, even among the highest echelon of the United States government. As a special naval attaché assigned to the office of the Joint Chiefs of Staff in the Pentagon, Jay enjoyed top-priority security clearance, but that still would not have privileged him with knowledge of the agency.

Unless he'd stumbled onto something by accident that he shouldn't have, Pierce thought, his frown deepening. Perhaps it was time he had another talk with his brother-in-law.

Pierce scanned the sales figures in the columns on the screen, and he whistled softly under his breath. Jessica had done an incredible job with the shop. Her accomplishments never ceased to impress him, but as he studied the entries more closely, a pattern emerged that began to bother him. Her largest sales, her highest percentages of profit came on the resale of items Brandon Chambers had sold to her.

Pierce backdated the journal entries, going back first a year, then two, three, four, until he reached the figures for the months following his disappearance. That's when the resale of items Jessica had bought from Chambers first began to appear in her records. The evidence seemed to place Chambers on the scene just shortly after Pierce had left it. At best, it was a worrisome coincidence, but Pierce didn't believe in coincidences.

Jessica finished with the customer in the showroom and then came into the office. Standing behind Pierce, she wrapped her arms around his neck and kissed him on the cheek, making it difficult to concentrate on Brandon Chambers, Jay Greene or anyone else besides her.

Pierce smiled. The past few days with Jesse had been incredible. They'd spent almost every waking moment together, but Max would be home tomorrow, and in spite of how much Pierce would miss the closeness he and Jessica had shared, he couldn't wait to see his son again.

"I miss Max," Jessica said, echoing his thoughts. They'd been doing that a lot lately, it seemed. It pleased Pierce to know that they were once again becoming attuned to each other's thoughts and moods.

"He'll be home tomorrow," Pierce said, turning his chair around to draw Jessica onto his lap. "So we'd better make the most of tonight."

She struggled a little, then gave up and settled against him. "What if a customer comes in?" she protested weakly.

Pierce kissed her soundly. "We'll hear them first."

"Maybe *you* will," she murmured, nuzzling his neck with eager lips. When she was with Pierce, she couldn't seem to concentrate on anything but him.

And now that he had her undivided attention, Jessica realized that something was wrong. She saw that distant look in his eyes that she remembered from the past. He'd had that look the day he'd disappeared. Panic welled inside her as she sat up on his lap and stared at him. "What's wrong?"

"What makes you think something is wrong?"

"Because I can tell by that look in your eyes. Pierce, you aren't having second thoughts? About . . . us, I mean?"

His dark eyes seemed to melt as he met her gaze. "No, sweetheart. How I feel about you and Max is the one thing I am certain of. I've been thinking about something Dr. Prescott said," he admitted. Gently he lifted her from his lap, then got up, walked over to the window and stared out. Jessica had the distinct impression that it wasn't the street outside that held his attention. It was the turmoil going on inside him.

Her heart began to pound even harder.

He turned and stared at her, his expression shuttered. Jessica had no idea what he was thinking. Until he spoke.

"I think you and Dr. Prescott were right, Jesse. I think it's time I see someone. A psychiatrist."

Jessica's heart skipped a beat. "Why? I mean . . . why now?"

"Because until we both deal with the past, I'll be worried about our future," Pierce said.

"But we *have* dealt with the past. We've put it to rest."

Pierce let out a breath, shaking his head. "No, we haven't. Not really. We've merely swept it aside. But it's still there, waiting to tear us apart. And until I can tell you the whole truth about myself, you'll never really be able to trust me, to trust how I feel about you. And how you feel about me." He turned back to the window. "I've already made an appointment with Dr. Layton. He can see me within the hour."

A sick feeling formed in the pit of Jessica's stomach. "So soon?"

"The sooner the better," Pierce said. "Isn't that what you said, Jesse? Isn't this what you want?"

No! Jessica thought. Not anymore. She'd come to terms with the past. She'd accepted the fact that she might never know what had happened to Pierce. In fact, she didn't think she even wanted to know anymore.

Maybe they were better off not knowing. What if Pierce found out he'd lived another life during those five years and that there was someone else he wanted...besides her? What if he remembered he didn't love her anymore, didn't need her? Could she handle that? Jessica asked herself desperately. Could she?

"I've made up my mind," Pierce said, coming to stand before her. He took her hand and held it tightly in his. "It's the right thing to do, Jesse. It's the only thing I can do."

"But I'm so afraid," she said, and stepped into his arms.

"I know," he whispered, his lips against her hair. "I am, too," he said.

He was being followed.

Pierce felt the familiar sensation the moment he walked out of the shop. Jessica's Audi was parked at the curb, and as he strode across the sidewalk toward it, he gazed around, trying to locate the invisible eyes.

He unlocked the door, climbed in and started the engine. As he eased the Audi into the light traffic on Washington, Pierce glanced in the rearview mirror. Half a block down, a dark green sedan pulled into the traffic behind him. Pierce smiled grimly, satisfied that his instincts had been correct. He was being followed—but by whom? Someone from the agency?

Or someone with a more dastardly agenda in mind?

Pierce decided there was only one way to find out. Swerving his car into the center lane, he tromped the accelerator, and the Audi careered past two cars. Up ahead, a traffic light turned yellow. Pierce didn't slow down. He sped through the intersection, then checked the mirror again.

Two cars behind him swished through on yellow. The sedan should have been caught by the red light, but instead, the driver ran the light, barely missing a blue Mazda turning left from the intersecting street. Pierce remembered that somewhere around here an alley cut through from Washington to Jefferson Avenue, the next street over. A restaurant located next to the alley had changed names, and Pierce almost missed it, but at the last second, he recognized it. Cutting the car sharply to the right, he headed down the alley, praying it wouldn't be blocked this time of day by delivery trucks.

The Audi bumped along the broken pavement and forced to slow his speed, Pierce cursed under his breath. A quick glance in the mirror told him the green sedan hadn't been able to follow him. At least, not yet.

The Audi emerged on Jefferson, and Pierce shot across the street toward a parking garage. He pulled into a space facing the alley and sat with the engine idling.

Several minutes passed and still no sedan. Had he lost it? Surely not. Not unless the driver was a rank amateur, in which case that would eliminate anyone from the agency. Evasive driving techniques, as well as surveillance, were all a part of the training.

Maybe the agency was slipping, Pierce decided, after several more minutes had gone by. Or maybe his imagination was simply getting the better of him. Whatever the case, the green sedan was nowhere in sight.

Pierce shifted into reverse and started to back out of the parking space just as a car squealed to a halt directly behind him. Instinctively he dived for the floorboard an instant before the sound of a gunshot blasted through the parking garage. The back window of the Audi shattered into a million jagged pieces.

Trapped, Pierce reached for the door handle, opened the door and crawled out. The parking garage was half-empty, with very little cover. He scanned the area, deciding the best course of action, but before he could make a move, he heard the unmistakable sound of a pistol being cocked not five feet from him.

"No sudden moves," a voice behind him ordered.

Slowly Pierce got to his feet and turned.

The sun shone through the open side of the garage, backlighting the man standing a few feet away and making him seem no more than a faceless shadow. A mirage. Pierce squinted, trying to put a face on the silhouette.

"Who are you?" he asked.

The man laughed softly, a familiar, eerie sound that set Pierce's heart to pounding. He knew him.

"Welcome home, Kincaid."

A memory flashed through Pierce's mind, but before he could explore it, a splitting pain crashed through the back of his skull. Pierce registered the blow as he fell to his knees. He heard the man say, "You hit him too hard, you idiot."

Pierce put up a hand and felt the blood. Then he pitched forward as his world suddenly faded to black.

Chapter 13

Jessica glanced at the clock on the kitchen stove. It was after six, and she hadn't heard from Pierce since he'd left the shop earlier that day. His appointment was at five, and if it ran an hour, he would have left Dr. Layton's office by now. Jessica wondered if he would call her before coming home, prepare her for what he had learned.

But as the minutes slipped past and the phone remained silent, she grew more and more anxious.

By seven o'clock, she had worked herself up into a real panic. She even phoned Dr. Layton's office, but only got a recording with a pleasant female voice chiming off the office hours and advising callers that Dr. Layton only saw referral clients. Jessica glanced at the clock again as she hung up the phone. Even allowing for traffic, Pierce should have been home by now.

It was foolish to worry, she knew. He was a grown man, and he'd been gone for the past five years. She'd thought he was dead. Worrying because he was late for dinner seemed so ridiculous by comparison. But still, she couldn't imagine why he hadn't gotten home yet unless...

Don't say it, she scolded herself. Don't even think it.

But a sly little voice had already insinuated itself into the back of her mind. It whispered to her now like an icy wind in the dead of winter.

Pierce isn't here yet because he isn't coming back at all.

Jessica closed her eyes and leaned against the sink. Not a second time, she prayed. Please, not a second time.

Pierce woke up with a splitting headache. He gazed around the small cell-like room as a host of memories surged through him. He groaned, wanting to fade away the pain, but he knew if he did that, he'd never remember what happened to him all those years ago. He'd never be able to be back with Jessica completely.

He sat up on the cot and tentatively felt the lump on his head, then winced. Someone had really done a job on him. He remembered the gunshot, the man standing silhouetted in front of him, the pain, then nothing. Everything since then was a complete blank. How long had he been out, anyway? Jessica must be going out of her mind with worry—

His anxious thoughts broke off as the door opened and a man stepped through. They eyed each other warily, and Pierce thought the man looked somehow familiar. He was tall, perhaps six-two, and athletically built. His hair was brown and his appearance, apart from a thick brown mustache, was nondescript. Not ordinary precisely, but in no way memorable. He was exactly the kind of man the agency liked to recruit.

Pierce's gaze narrowed on him. "Who are you?" he demanded.

"My name's Walker."

"The man on the phone?"

Walker smiled and his mustache tilted at the corners. "One and the same. It's an honor to meet you, Kincaid. Your reputation precedes you."

"But you said we'd met in the Caribbean," Pierce said grimly. "And then at the café, the day I got back. I thought there was something suspicious-looking about you."

Walker inclined his head in acknowledgment. "I'd take that as an insult from anyone else." He took a few steps into the room, but his eyes never left Pierce. "Rumor has it, you used to be the best in the business. Until you turned, that is."

Pierce stared at him in shock as he fought a wave of nausea. His head hurt like a son of a bitch. "What the hell are you talking about?" he demanded.

"Five years ago you sold information to the leader of a two-bit Caribbean country that's hardly more than a blemish on the world map. We were looking to oust the generalissimo and install our own user-friendly dictator. You sold Valencio our game plan, and then he turned on you."

Pierce shook his head, unable to believe what he was hearing. "I worked on that case for over three years," he said. "We found out a double agent was on Valencio's payroll, someone selling him military information that could have jeopardized our whole peace plan in that region. It was my job to track down the traitor, to flush him out into the open."

Walker's mustache flicked. "A convenient assignment, considering you were the double agent. But, of course, you didn't count on your buddy, Valencio, double-crossing you, did you? He and his Cuban buddies got what they wanted, then threw you in prison for the better part of five years. We negotiated your release a few months ago."

"A few months ago? I've only been back a few days. What happened? Where've I been?"

Walker shrugged. "We don't know for sure. There was an explosion on board the boat bringing you in. You disappeared in the confusion, and we lost track of you until a few days ago when you showed up back here. We've been following you ever since you came through customs in Miami using a fake passport."

Pierce shook his head, unable to grasp all that he was being told. He got up and walked over to the window. They were on the ground floor, but metal bars on the outside of the window nixed any thoughts of escape. He turned back to Walker.

"Where am I now?"

"Langley, Virginia. Your old stomping grounds."

"Am I to assume I'm under arrest then?"

Walker's eyes were cold, hard, mercenary. The eyes of a trained professional. He said calmly, "That's what usually happens to a traitor, isn't it?"

Pierce's voice was just as cold. Just as steady. And just as deadly. "I'm not a traitor, you bastard."

Walker smiled. "Try telling that to the powers-that-be."

"Give me the chance and I will."

Walker shook his head. "Not yet. Not until we have a little more proof."

"Proof of what?"

Walker slanted him a look. "Of your innocence, Kincaid."

"My innocence? Are you saying you believe me?" At Walker's nod, Pierce's anger erupted. "Then what the hell was all that garbage about my being a traitor? Why am I here? What's going on?"

"I'm telling you what happened five years ago, before your disappearance," Walker said grimly. "That's what you wanted, isn't it? Why you were planning to see a shrink today?"

"How the he—the phone's tapped," Pierce said in disgust, shoving his hand through his hair. "I should have known."

"Don't be so hard on yourself. You've been out of circulation for years. No wonder you're a little rusty on the draw."

There was something troubling about Walker's voice, his attitude. Pierce watched him carefully.

"The double agent you were after got wise to you," Walker said. "He sold you out. He arranged an exchange of information with Valencio to make you look guilty. When the information turned out bogus, Valencio's henchmen, with the help of the Cubans, came looking for you. They nabbed you, took you back to their little island hideaway and worked you over good, trying to get the real information out of you. When that didn't work, they threw you in prison, hoping to use you as a bargaining tool at some later date."

"Wait a minute," Pierce said. "Are you saying that the agency bought the double cross? They thought I'd turned?"

"The verdict's still out."

Pierce muttered an oath he was surprised he still remembered. "Is that why I'm here?"

Walker propped one foot on the cot and folded his arms over his leg. "You aren't being detained by the agency, Kincaid. You're being detained by me."

Pierce gingerly felt the bump on the back of his head. "Detained? Is that what you call it these days?"

Walker ignored the sarcasm. "I had you brought in because I didn't want you seeing a shrink. The agency went to a lot of time and expense, programming the fade-to-black trigger in you. A shrink could undo it without realizing it."

"Fade to black," Pierce said slowly. "A programmed response? I was trained to forget, wasn't I?"

"That's probably at least part of it," Walker agreed. "The rest we can only guess, but we haven't much time for speculation. There are those in the agency who believe you're guilty of treason, Kincaid, but I'm not one of them. I know the real double agent is still out there somewhere, and you're the only man alive who can identify him."

Pierce was across the room in two strides. He grabbed Walker by the lapels. "You said there was no danger, damn you. You said Max and Jessica were safe from this."

Walker looked Pierce right in the eye. "They are, as long as he knows where to find you."

Pierce shoved him aside and turned away in disgust. "This whole thing makes me sick," he said. "I can't believe I was ever a part of it."

"You were the best," Walker said again. "You never hesitated to do what had to be done. Don't hesitate now, Kincaid. We have the perfect opportunity to catch him, to flush him out into the open. Sooner or later, he'll make a move on you, and when he does, we'll get him. After all this time, we'll finally nail that bastard."

"And I'm just supposed to sit tight and let you use my family as bait?" Pierce retorted coldly. "No deal, Walker."

"Unfortunately you're not in any position to bargain. It's in your wife's and son's best interests for you to cooperate with us. As long as he knows where to find *you*, he has no reason to harm *them*. If you were to up and disappear again, he might try using them to get to you. Besides, you're the best protection they've got right now. The only thing you can do is exactly what you've been doing."

"Which is nothing, damn you."

"You know as well as I do that a good portion of an agent's life is spent watching and waiting." Walker drew a

SIG-Sauer semiautomatic from his jacket pocket and laid it on the small wooden table beside the cot. He turned to Pierce and smiled, but there was no warmth in his eyes. Just an ice-cold resolve. Pierce wondered if he was seeing a reflection of himself five years ago. It was a thought that gave him no pleasure.

"Welcome back to the action, Kincaid. It's in our blood, you know. Men like you and me, we thrive on danger. We'd wither and die without it." Walker crossed the floor to the door and opened it, then glanced back. "By the way, the door was never locked. You were free to go at any time."

"You son of a bitch," Pierce muttered. Like five years ago, he was left with no choice. He picked up the SIG-Sauer and followed Walker out the door.

The house was quiet except for the ticking of the grandfather clock in the foyer. Jessica noted almost every minute that went by. She stood glued to the living-room window, where she had a clear view of the street. Every few seconds, she would whip her head around to look at the phone, willing it to ring, then turn back to the window to stare out into the darkness.

A misty rain had started to fall, and the streetlights reflected in wavering beams across the pavement, reminding her of how she had always hated rainy nights. They made her think of all the cold, lonely nights she'd spent in the orphanage, and all the cold, lonely nights she'd spent during the past five years. They reminded her of the night Pierce hadn't come back to her....

She touched her reflection in the window with the tip of her finger as a wave of remembered loneliness washed over her. How would she stand it this time? How would she cope if Pierce had walked out on her a second time?

Shivering, she started to turn away from the window, but the sound of a car engine drew her gaze back to the street. A late model, dark-colored sedan drove slowly past the house. Under the streetlight, she could just make out the dark green color, but the windows were tinted and against the wet night, completely opaque. The car turned right at the next street, and fighting down a bitter swell of disappointment, Jessica watched the taillights disappear.

When the telephone finally rang at eight-thirty, she nearly jumped out of her skin. She dashed to the phone and jerked it up. "Pierce?"

The only sound was static crackling across the line as if the call was coming from a car phone or a pay phone, perhaps. No one said anything, but just like the call a few nights ago, she knew someone was there. The back of her neck prickled with warning.

"Hello? Who is this?"

Still nothing. Jessica clung to the phone, listening intently. The caller remained silent for a moment, then the line clicked dead. Jessica cradled the receiver, her fingers trembling. It was just another hang-up call, she told herself. No need to worry.

But whether it was the fault of the rainy night or her worrying about Pierce, Jessica couldn't be sure, but suddenly she experienced an unprecedented sense of unease, an almost overwhelming premonition of danger. She imagined Pierce lying somewhere, hurt, bleeding, not knowing who or where he was. Not knowing how to get back home to her.

The house, quiet before, now seemed abnormally silent. Jessica didn't like the feeling of being frightened in her own home, but she couldn't shake the notion that something was wrong. She had the chilling sensation that the house was being watched. That *she* was being watched. But by whom? And why?

And where in God's name was Pierce?

She'd feel better if he were here. His presence had such a calming affect on her, a steadying influence—

Jessica stopped, realizing what she was thinking. Was she, like Max, already starting to rely too heavily on Pierce? It was a disconcerting thought. Jessica had long ago come to the conclusion that she could count on no one but herself, so why tonight, of all nights, did she feel she needed Pierce's protection?

Driven by a fear she didn't understand, Jessica dialed the number of the campsite that Sharon had left the first night when she and Max had called Jessica. Sharon had told her that in case of an emergency, the old couple who ran the park would be able to reach them. Jessica knew it was probably too late to be calling just because of a bad feeling she had, but she couldn't help it. She had to make sure her son was safe.

To her relief, the old woman who answered the phone was incredibly understanding. She knew just where the McReynoldses were camped, she assured Jessica. She'd get in her truck and go down there right now to make sure everything was okay. It was no bother at all. She had children and grandchildren of her own. It would take her a while to get there, though, so Jessica shouldn't worry if she didn't hear back right away.

Jessica hung up the phone and sat down in the chair beside it, waiting for it to ring again. Thirty minutes later, Sharon called her back. "Max is fine, Jessica," Sharon said for the third time. Jessica heard the exasperation in her friend's voice, but she couldn't help asking again.

"Are you sure?"

"Yes, yes, yes. He and Allie are already tucked in for the night. He was sleeping like a log when I checked him before I left."

Jessica let out a long breath. "I'm really sorry, Sharon. But I just had this feeling . . . I just knew Max was in some sort of trouble—"

"Look, it's okay. I'd probably be the same way if I were away from Allie. But we'll be home tomorrow, okay? And then you can stop worrying."

"Okay," Jessica agreed. "I'll see you tomorrow."

Satisfied that her imagination had been running away with her, Jessica turned to leave the room, then jumped violently when she saw a shadow in the doorway.

Her hand flew to her heart as she stifled the scream that erupted in her throat.

Chapter 14

He'd been so silent, Jessica hadn't heard a sound. It was terrifying to realize how vulnerable she was in her own home. The shadows in the hall made him look mysterious and dangerous, emphasizing rather than hiding the scar that twisted his brow.

Jessica put a hand to her heart. She could feel it pounding against her chest, so hard and so loud she wondered if Pierce could hear it, too.

"I didn't hear you come in," she said lamely. "You startled me."

"Sorry." The dark gaze held hers for the longest time. The uneasy feeling grew even stronger inside Jessica.

She said, "Do you know what time it is? I was so worried, Pierce."

He slanted her a dark glance as he stepped into the room. "Worried that I wasn't coming back? Maybe I shouldn't have," he said.

Jessica's heart skipped a beat. Had she heard him correctly? "What do you mean?" she asked fearfully. "Did you...did you learn something...disturbing?"

"You could say that." His tone was flat and seemingly devoid of emotion. Jessica wanted to scream at his calmness. He walked over to the window and stared out, much as she'd done earlier.

"Is that all you have to say?" she said angrily. "I was worried half out of my mind tonight. I thought for sure something had happened to you, Pierce. That you'd been in an accident or— or something. Don't you think I'm entitled to an explanation?"

At last he turned from the window and faced her. His dark gaze held hers until Jessica began to tremble with dread. He said, still in that toneless voice, "It's past time you had an explanation, Jessica. I'm going to tell you everything. I should have done it a long time ago."

"Then you...know?"

"I know more than I've told you. I've always known."

Jessica reached out blindly for a chair, felt it with her hand, then backed into it. She sat down, sensing somehow that what Pierce was about to say would change everything between them, everything they had worked so hard to rebuild.

Pierce turned back to the window, as if he could no longer face her. He said, "It all started when I was a senior at Georgetown. My parents had died the year before, and I'd inherited The Lost Attic from them. I wasn't much interested in running an antique shop until one day when a man approached me on campus. He had a proposition for me, a job offer of sorts. It seemed my reputation for recklessness, along with my prelaw and political science courses, had drawn some attention from a government agency that I'd never even heard of before."

Jessica sat in stunned disbelief as she listened to Pierce's revelations about his secret life as an agent, how he'd used The Lost Attic to ferry information to and from foreign countries, and how his true identity became his deep cover.

When he'd finished, Jessica gazed at him for a moment, trying to absorb it all, then slowly she felt a red haze of anger taking hold of her. She got up and walked toward him, her back ramrod straight, her eyes dry.

"And what was I?" she asked coldly. "How did I fit into all this? Was I part of your cover? Did you think you needed a wife to complete the picture? Answer me, damn you!"

For the first time since he'd begun his story, Pierce let his gaze meet hers. Something flickered in his eyes. Something that looked almost like pity. Then he said, "Yes. You were part of the cover," and Jessica's world came crashing down.

"Oh, my God." Her hand flew to her mouth as she started to back away from him. It was a nightmare come true, hearing him confirm her deepest, darkest suspicions. "I knew it," she said. "Somehow I always knew it. I always wondered how someone like you could want someone like me. Oh, God." A wave of humiliation swept over her. Jessica turned, shoving her hands through her hair. "How could I not have seen it? How could I not have known?"

"It's not what you think, Jesse." Pierce reached for her, but Jessica flung his hand away.

"Don't touch me," she screamed. "Don't you dare touch me again." She faced him, her anger blazing, but suddenly the tears started to flow down her face. She collapsed back into the chair, staring up at him. "How could you do this to me? How could you do it to your son? All these years—they've been nothing more than a lie. You never cared about us, did you?"

"I loved you more than anything," Pierce said. "I never stopped loving you. Please, Jesse, just hear me out."

"I've heard about all I can stomach," she said, wiping her face with the back of her hand. She stood and faced him. "I want you out of here. Now. Tonight. I never want to see you again."

"Don't say that. I love you—"

"What does a liar know about love?" she demanded. "You used me. You used your son. I don't even know you. I never did. And right now, I can't stand the sight of you."

"All right, that's enough," Pierce said, his tone hardening. He turned away rubbing his face, then spun back around to face her. "I can understand how you feel, and I won't force my presence on you any longer than I have to. But what you don't seem to understand, Jessica, is that right now neither of us has a choice in the matter. I can't leave you until this whole mess is cleaned up. Until the traitor is caught, I have to stay here and protect you and Max."

"*Protect* us?" Jessica asked sarcastically. "You're the one who put us in danger in the first place. If anything happens to Max because of you, so help me, Pierce, I'll never forgive you."

"Then that makes two of us," he said grimly.

Jessica wept until there were no more tears left to cry. Pierce hadn't married her because he loved her but because he needed a wife, someone to complete his cover. And poor unsuspecting Jessica had fitted the bill perfectly. He'd completely swept her off her feet. She'd adored him. She'd never done anything or asked any questions that might have jeopardized their relationship. She had blindly accepted everything he'd told her because she'd been so pathetically needy.

But she knew. Deep down she'd always known that someone like Pierce could never really love someone like her.

When the phone rang at one in the morning, Jessica had only been asleep for a few minutes. Exhausted from the endless tears and the self-recriminations, it took her a moment to get her bearings.

She eased up in bed and reached for the phone but barely had time to say hello before Sharon's frantic voice ripped her world apart again.

"I'm sorry, Jessica. Oh, God, I'm so sorry."

Jessica's heart slammed against her chest. She fought for breath and lost, making it impossible to speak. She clung to the phone, terrified. "Wh—"

"What happened?" Pierce demanded, his voice strong and clear and in control. Jessica realized dimly that he must have answered the phone the same time as she had.

Sharon's voice babbled across the line. "He woke up Allie in the middle of the night and told her that he and a friend had to help his dad. It was a secret mission, he said, and he couldn't tell anyone. He made Allie promise not to say anything to us, but after Max had left, she got scared and came and woke me up. I don't know what to do. Frank's out looking for him right now—"

"Have you called the authorities?" Pierce asked.

"I've got a call in to the sheriff's office at the nearest town, but no one answered and they don't have 911 service out here. What should I do, Jessica? Oh, God, this is all my fault," Sharon sobbed.

"It isn't your fault," Jessica managed to say. It was Pierce's fault.

Pierce said, "I'm coming up there right away. Just sit tight, Sharon. The local authorities won't be of any help in this matter, anyway. I'll take care of it."

"All right," Sharon said. "But please hurry. When I think of that poor little thing out in the woods wandering around in the dark..."

Dear God, Jessica thought. She'd been thinking the same thing. She'd had the same image since the moment she'd heard Sharon's voice. Her baby. Her poor baby.

Let him be safe, she prayed, as she hung up the phone and ran out of the room. She hurried down the hallway to the stairs. Pierce met her at the bottom. He didn't waste time with apologies. She had to give him that.

"I'll find him," he said. "Everything will be all right."

"You don't know that. Oh, God...." Jessica covered her face with her hands and wept.

Pierce grabbed her shoulders and shook her. "You have to be strong, Jessica. For Max. I'm leaving right now, but I want you to call the man I told you about—Walker. Have him meet me at the campsite."

Jessica shook her head, ignoring the tears streaming down her face. "I'm coming with you," she said.

"Jesse, it's too dangerous—"

"Don't," she warned. "Don't you try to talk me out of it. I don't need you to protect me anymore, and I won't be left behind this time."

Pierce took only a second to decide. "All right," he agreed. "Go get dressed and let's get started."

Within minutes, they were on the road heading for the campsite, which was a little less than an hour's drive from Edgewood. Pierce hoped to hell that the house was being watched as Walker had said and that Walker's men would follow him and Jessica. He had no idea what scenario they might be stepping into. All he knew was that he had to get his son back. He had to get to Max.

Jessica sat in the seat beside him, her face turned toward the window. She hadn't spoken two words to him since they'd left the house, but he knew from the drawn look on her face what she was thinking. This was all his fault.

Pierce concentrated on the road, his thoughts grim as the Audi ate up the remaining miles to the campsite. Thank God Walker had had the presence of mind to have the back glass repaired while Pierce had been out, he thought. Otherwise, precious minutes could have been lost procuring another vehicle. As it was, the seconds seemed to be ticking away too quickly, the miles passing too slowly.

Jessica felt numb. The same little prayer kept playing over and over in her mind.

Please let him be all right. Please let Max be all right.

It was like looking at the photo albums the other night. Bits and pieces of her son's life kept flashing through her mind. She saw his smile, his eyes, his mischievous grin, and her arms ached to hold him again.

Please let him be all right.

She felt Pierce's hand close over hers for a moment before returning to the wheel. Jessica looked at him, and their eyes met in the darkness.

"He'll be all right," Pierce said.

"How can you be so sure? That man has him, Pierce. He's using him to get you. What happens when he no longer needs Max?" What happens when he finds you? Jessica wanted to cry.

"I won't let anything happen to our son, Jesse. You have my word."

For what little that's worth.

Neither of them said it, but the unspoken words hung in the air between them.

Jessica turned again to the window and stared out at the flying darkness.

After a moment, Pierce said, "I'd like to tell you why I joined the agency, Jesse. I'd like you to know what my life was like."

Jessica looked at him in surprise. "You never wanted to talk about your past with me before."

Pierce shrugged. "Maybe I should have. Maybe I should have talked about a lot of things that I didn't. I know it won't change anything, but I'd like to make you understand at least why I did what I did."

When she didn't object, Pierce tapped his finger on the steering wheel a few times as if figuring out where to start. "My mother was forty-three when I was born, and my father was forty-nine. They were college professors who'd always dreamed of owning an antique shop. So one day they just up and left their teaching positions and opened The Lost Attic. It was a dream come true for them, and then I came along."

Jessica saw his jaw harden, but his gaze never left the road.

"I was the old cliché, a middle-aged accident. They never wanted me, and they never pretended otherwise. If they ever noticed me at all, it was when I got in their way. They both loved to travel, and they didn't stop just because they had a child at home. I was left with housekeepers and baby-sitters and anyone else who would take me in. I was never wanted and I was never needed and I damn sure was never loved," he said.

"Maybe they just didn't know how to show it," Jessica said softly, moved in spite of herself. An image of a lonely little boy started to form in her mind, but it wasn't Max she saw. It was Pierce.

"By the time I was eleven, I was getting into trouble at school. Nothing serious, just some stupid pranks to get attention. My parents were... annoyed. They disciplined me and then forgot me again. By the time I was fifteen, I was working a full eight hours after school, first at a grocery store, then at a gas station, then at various other jobs that turned up. When I was sixteen, I bought my first car and paid cash for it. My parents didn't even ask me where I got the money. They didn't care, because by then they hardly ever saw me anymore. We all carried on with our separate lives, and everyone was happy.''

Everyone except you, Jessica thought, the ice around her heart starting to melt in spite of herself. She gazed at Pierce's profile, amazed at how little she knew about the man she had married. In so many ways he was still a stranger to her, but during the past few days, Jessica felt she'd gotten to know him better than she had in all the years they'd been married.

"Where did the agency fit into all this?" Jessica asked quietly.

"As I said, they approached me after my parents' deaths. You know what they said to me, Jessica? They said, 'We need someone like you, Pierce. You're exactly the kind of man we're looking for.'" He gave Jessica a wry smile. "Can you imagine? After all those years, someone was actually telling me that I was needed. That my life could mean something to someone. They didn't even have to ask me twice. I joined the agency, spent two years of grueling training and ended up right back at The Lost Attic."

"And then you met me."

"And then I met you." He slanted her a glance. "The agency had been telling me for several months that they thought my cover might be becoming suspect. They were the ones who suggested I think about getting married, starting a family."

The heaviness inside her was almost unbearable. Jessica wondered just how much more she could take. "So you agreed," she said, feeling the anger grow inside her again.

"No, I didn't," Pierce said. "Because by that time I'd already met and fallen in love with you, and I told them there was no way I would ever put your life in danger just for the sake of my cover. I told them I wanted out. I was through. I wanted to marry you and lead a normal life.''

Jessica swallowed. Her hands were trembling, so she folded them in her lap. ''Then what happened?'' she whispered, almost afraid to hear any more.

''It wasn't as easy to quit as I'd hoped. About the same time you started working at the shop, I got involved in this case. The players were already in place. The agency made me see that the whole plan would have been jeopardized if I'd tendered my resignation. They needed me, they said. No one else could manage the job. And so I stayed. And one year turned into two, then three, and then...well, you know the rest,'' he finished, lifting his hands from the wheel in a gesture of frustration.

''You put their needs before mine,'' Jessica said, stung by his revelations. Earlier tonight, she'd thought she couldn't be hurt anymore, but she'd been wrong.

''It wasn't like that,'' Pierce said quietly, helplessly. ''It wasn't a conscious choice I made. I did what I thought was right. If I had to do it over again, well, it doesn't matter, does it? We can't turn back the clock, can we, Jesse?''

''No,'' she whispered. ''We can never go back.''

No matter how much one might wish it.

Chapter 15

Sharon was standing in front of the cabin, watching for them when they drove up. She came rushing out to meet them and threw her arms around Jessica as soon as she climbed out of the car.

"Did Frank find him?" Jessica asked quickly. "Is Max here?"

Sharon shook her head. "Frank got back just a little while ago. He couldn't find any sign of Max, but he's going out to look again, and Jessica, I...I called Jay. I hope you don't mind, but I just thought..." She trailed off as she glanced at Pierce. She didn't say anything else, but her message was loud and clear. She didn't trust Pierce to find Max. She didn't trust him period.

Jessica registered a faint prickle of resentment somewhere inside her. She said sharply, "Is he here yet?"

"No. At least, he hasn't come to the cabin. Shouldn't we call the state police or something?"

Pierce said, "I want to talk to Allie."

Sharon looked as if she was about to protest, but behind her, Frank's calm voice cut through the darkness. "Come on in, Pierce. I think that's a good idea."

As it turned out, Allie wasn't much help. She could vaguely recall the direction Max had gone off in, but not much more than that. When Jessica asked her about Max's friend, she pursed her little lips together and refused to say more.

"Allie," Sharon said, "please tell Jessica and Pierce everything you know."

The little girl looked doubtful, then nodded. "His friend came and got him."

Jessica's heart slammed against her chest, making her feel momentarily faint. She had to sit down on a nearby chair. Pierce said softly, "What friend, Allie?"

"Max's new friend. The one he played secret mission with."

A memory flashed through Jessica's mind. "You mean the little boy who moved in next door to Mrs. Taylor?"

Allie shook her head. "He wasn't little. He was like you," she said, pointing to Pierce.

"You mean he was an adult?" Pierce asked.

She nodded. "He said he was going to take Max up the mountains to a cabin. He said you were waiting for them up there. He said you needed Max to come get you. I watched them walk down the path until I couldn't see them no more. Then I went and got Mommy." Allie turned her big liquid eyes up to Sharon. "Am I in trouble?" she asked, her voice trembling.

Sharon hugged her daughter closely, making Jessica's arms seem even more empty. "No, darling," Sharon whispered, "you aren't in trouble."

Jessica put her hand to her mouth, stifling the sobs. "This is all my fault," she said. She turned her terrified eyes on Pierce. "He told me about this secret mission game days ago, but I didn't know ... I didn't think ... Oh, God. What are we going to do?"

"We're going to find him," Pierce said steadily. With his hands on her arms, he lifted Jessica until they were both standing face-to-face. He gazed deep into her eyes. "Listen to me," he said. "I'm going to go out there right now. I'm going to find that cabin and I'm going to find Max and bring him back to you. What I want you to do is stay here and wait for Jay. He'll know what to do."

"Please," she begged, "please don't leave me here."

"It's the only way," he said. He bent and brushed his lips across hers, and for just a second or two, Jessica clung to him. Then he turned, motioned for Frank to follow him, and the two men walked outside.

Jessica fought the urge to run after him, to make him take her with him. This time she knew he was right. This was his element. He knew what to do, and she'd only get in his way. She had to trust him to bring back her son.

She ran to the door and threw it open just as Frank was stepping back inside. Jessica brushed past him and ran outside. The first thing she saw was the gun in Pierce's hand. The metal glinted in the moonlight, as dark and deadly as Pierce's eyes.

They stared at one another for a moment, then Jessica whispered into the darkness, "Be careful. Please be careful."

And then he was gone, swallowed up by the deep shadows in the woods surrounding the cabin.

The moon had risen, and the path was easy to follow. There was a chance, of course, that they hadn't kept to the trail, but Pierce didn't think that likely. The whole point was to reel him in. He hadn't let on to Jessica, but she'd been right earlier. Once the traitor had Pierce, he had no reason to let Max go. He wouldn't. Not if the boy could identify him.

Pierce knew the game, knew how it was played, but he'd never had stakes this high before. It was harder to keep a cool head when he thought about his son, alone, frightened, needing him. But Pierce knew what he had to do. He'd promised Jessica he'd bring Max back to her, and he had every intention of keeping that promise.

He emerged from the woods onto the bank of a small lake. Moonlight silvered the water, making it look like a giant mirror in a darkened room. Keeping to the deep shadows of the woods, Pierce canned the area. He left the path and circled the lake, coming up behind a small cabin perched at the edge of the water.

It was a trap. Pierce knew that. There was only one way in and out of the cabin, but he also realized there was no other choice open to him. He watched the darkened cabin for several minutes, then crouching, he headed across the clearing, scaled the front porch railing, and kicked open the door.

Moonlight flooded inside what appeared to be an empty room. And then, just as he was about to leave, he heard a small voice whisper from the shadows, "Daddy? Is that you?"

Pierce resisted the temptation to run to his son. He flattened himself against the wall, his gaze roaming the cabin. His every sense screamed danger. He knew he and Max were being watched. He knew somewhere out in the darkness, a killer waited for him to make a move.

"I'm here, son," he said softly. "Where are you?"

"Over here. I can't move." He heard Max struggle and whimper. Pierce slid along the wall, following the sound.

Max was curled up in a corner, his arms and legs bound with rope. When Pierce knelt and touched the little boy's face, he felt the wetness of tears on his fingertips.

"It's okay, son," he whispered. "I'm here now. Everything's going to be okay." With his pocketknife he slit the ropes, and the second they were severed, he gathered Max into his arms and held him close.

"I knew you'd come," Max whispered over and over. "I knew you'd come."

Pierce held his son for only a moment longer, then he said, "We have to get out of here, Max."

Max gazed at him with wide dark eyes. "That man—he's not my friend, is he?"

"No."

"He just pretended to be. He brought me here so he could hurt you, didn't he?"

"He's going to try," Pierce said. He picked up his gun from the floor and saw Max's eyes widen even more. "We're not going to let him, though, are we, Max? You and I are going to get out of here, but I need you to do exactly as I say. Okay?"

Max nodded, his eyes still on the gun.

"Okay," Pierce said, standing, "I want you to stay behind me. There's a piece of railing broken on the side of the porch. It's hard to see in the dark, but you'll find it if you look. When I give you the word, I want you to crawl through that opening and run toward the woods. Run as fast as you can, Max. Do you remember where the path is? Do you think you can find it in the dark? Good. You find the path and you stay on it until you get all the way back to the campsite. Your mother will be waiting for you there."

"But what about you?" Max asked, his voice trembling in spite of his brave front.

"I'll be all right. I'm sending you on a real secret mission, son. Think you can handle it?"

Max nodded, lifting his chin. Right then, he looked the spitting image of Jessica. Pierce wanted nothing more than to haul his son into his arms again, hold him so tightly to

protect him from the outside world. But he couldn't afford
the time. He had to think with his head and not his heart.
He had to be just as cunning and ruthless as the enemy who
waited for them beyond the front door.

"Let's go," he said.

They edged toward the door. Caution was useless because Pierce knew they were being watched, their every
move monitored. Keeping Max behind him, he moved out
on the front porch.

He hesitated just a fraction of a second, his eyes scan-
ning the immediate area around them. Then he said, "Now,
Max!" and the moment the little boy took off for the side
of the porch, Pierce dived toward the steps, hoping to draw
the fire. A bullet splintered the wood beside him as he rolled
to a crouch in the shadows of the steps. Another bullet
whizzed overhead. Out of the corner of his eyes, he saw Max
slip into the woods. Another shot rang out, and Max fell to
the ground.

Pierce's heart stopped. Had he been hit? Dear God—

Suddenly a burning wave of rage swept over him. Oblivious to the danger, he stood and walked out of the shadows. "Let him go, you bastard," he yelled. "This is between
you and me."

He heard a laugh, the same laugh that had tormented him
for years, and then a voice he recognized said, "Throw
down your weapon and we'll talk."

Pierce gazed at the woods where he'd seen Max fall. Was
that a movement he detected? Was his son all right? Pierce
knew that all he could do for Max now was to buy him some
time. He tossed his gun to the dirt a few feet from him. After a moment or two, a figure materialized out of the shadowy woods. Pierce's enemy, his nemesis, the man who had
sent him to hell five years ago, slowly walked out of the
darkness toward him.

"You," Pierce said in disgust. "I should have known."

Chapter 16

The man who called himself Walker laughed again. "As I said earlier, you shouldn't be so hard on yourself, Kincaid. You've been out of circulation for too many years." Moonlight glinted off the gold eagle he wore at his throat, and suddenly Pierce remembered. A bird soaring against the sunlight. It had been Walker's medallion he'd seen that day.

"Why didn't you just kill me earlier?" Pierce asked, appraising his options.

Walker laughed again, the same laugh Pierce had heard in his prison years ago. "The agency's been following you for weeks. I couldn't take you out without bringing suspicion on me. I had to get you away from all those eyes, Kincaid. You know the game."

"Yes, I know," Pierce agreed grimly, inching forward.

There was a snapping sound from the woods as if someone had trod on a twig. Max! He was alive!

Pierce saw Walker's head turn just a fraction as if he was thinking the same thing. Pierce fought his own elation, knowing that he might not have another chance. He lunged toward Walker, and Walker fired. But he'd been thrown off guard, and the shot just missed. Then Pierce was on him. He rammed into Walker as hard as he could, and the momentum carried them both stumbling backward into the dirt. The gun went flying from Walker's hand, and both men saw it land in a bed of pine needles not three feet away.

Simultaneously they rushed for it, but a bullet kicked up the dirt mere inches from the weapon. It took Pierce a second to register the fact that someone else was on the scene. Someone else with a gun.

"Hold it," the disembodied voice ordered, as Walker whirled around. Brandon Chambers came out of the woods, his gun leveled first at Walker, then at Pierce. "Nobody make a move," he said.

"Chambers," Walker said in relief. He started toward the man, but Brandon lifted the gun, and Walker halted. He said in an excited undertone, "We've got him this time. He tried to kill me. He knew I was the one man who could put the finger on him."

Brandon's gaze swept over Pierce with icy disdain. "I've waited a long time for this night, Kincaid."

"Who the hell are you?" Pierce demanded.

"I'm with the agency, deep cover," he said. "I was assigned to your case the day you disappeared. I've been waiting for the day you returned."

"So you could kill me?" Pierce asked coldly. "I ought to kill *you* for using my wife the way you have."

"Using her?" Brandon shook his head. "You've got it all wrong. We were helping her, making sure she and your son were provided for."

"Somehow I don't think she'd be too grateful if she knew that," Pierce said.

"This is ridiculous," Walker said. "Let's take him in. Let me get my gun, Chambers." He reached for his gun, and another bullet hit the dirt. He glared up at Chambers. "What the hell are you doing?" In one lightning move, he reached down, scooped up the weapon and spun, leveling it at Pierce. "You're going down this time."

It happened so fast, Pierce had no time to react. He felt the pain rip through his shoulder before he heard the report of the gun. He stumbled backward as someone—a woman—screamed. Then another shot rang out, and dimly he saw Walker pitch forward into the dirt. Pierce struggled to remain on his feet, but the pain was excruciating. Don't fade to black, he thought. Not yet. Not until he could find out everything he needed to know.

Chambers holstered his gun. "Dammit! I told you to let me handle this!"

Pierce looked around in amazement as Jessica came running out of the woods, followed more slowly by Jay, who carried the proverbial smoking gun.

"You were too slow to suit my taste," Jay said, tossing his own gun in the dirt at Chambers's feet. "I told you I don't like taking orders from a civilian, especially not some damn spook from Langley."

Chambers muttered a curse. "You military stiffs are all the same."

Jessica took one look at the blood flowing from Pierce's shoulder, and her face turned white. He thought for a moment she might faint, but Jessica was stronger than that. She'd had to be.

"Oh, my God," she said. "How badly are you hurt?"

"I'm all right," Pierce said. "Jessica—"

Jessica looked around frantically. "Where's Max? Pierce, where's Max?" she demanded.

"He ran into the woods," Pierce said. "Jessica, stay here while I go find him."

Her eyes widened as she realized what he was saying. She turned and started running blindly toward the woods. "Max! Baby, where are you? Please, Max. Answer me."

Pierce guided her in the right direction. He was at her side when they saw Max. He was lying still on the ground, his little face buried in his arms. He didn't make a sound, didn't move a muscle, and Pierce's heart stopped beating. Dear God, no, he prayed. Not Max. Not my boy.

Jessica screamed, "Max! Max!" Pierce tried to hold her back, but Jessica tore loose from his grasp. She ran to Max and flung herself on the ground beside him. "Max! Answer me, baby! Please be all right!"

"Mom? Is that you?"

Pierce thought for a moment he was hearing things. That his prayer was making him see things. Max lifted his head and peered up at Jessica, and then Pierce heard her laughing and crying at the same time as she pulled their son into her arms.

"Did I do it right, Dad?" Max asked, struggling out of Jessica's embrace. "I ran as fast as I could, but when I heard the gun, it scared me and I fell down. I pretended to be dead. That's what Superman told Lois Lane to do once. Was that okay?"

Pierce dropped to his knees beside them. His shoulder was throbbing, he felt sick to his stomach, and he was pretty sure he was going to pass out at any minute. But he had never felt so damned good in all his life.

"You did just fine, son," he said. "I'm proud of you."

Max beamed, then saw the blood on Pierce's arm. "Oh, wow," he said reverently. "Are you all right?" When Pierce nodded, Max said, "I bet you'll have another neat scar, huh, Dad?"

"I hope not, son," Pierce said, gazing at Jessica's tear-stained face. "I think I've got a few too many as it is."

Max turned back to Jessica. She couldn't seem to keep her eyes off him. Her fingers fluttered up to touch his cheek as if she was reassuring herself he was really all right.

"Can we go home now?" Max asked.

Jessica nodded. "Yes. We'll go in a minute or two."

"Is Dad coming with us?"

Jessica's gaze met Pierce's for just a split second, then she looked away. Pierce felt a sinking sensation in the bottom of his stomach.

Jessica said, "Why don't you go tell Uncle Jay what an excellent job you did here tonight? I know he'll be impressed."

"Yeah," Max agreed, grinning proudly. He turned and shot past Jessica and Pierce, and when he had gone, the silence around them seemed deafening.

Pierce waited for Jessica to speak. She remained kneeling on the ground, her eyes lowered.

"Jesse?"

She still wouldn't look at him. She twisted her hands together, giving away her nervousness. "Jay tried to keep me from coming up here with them, but I couldn't stay away. I had to be here...in case you needed me. But you didn't need me, did you, Pierce? You've never really needed me."

Pierce closed his eyes for a moment. The pain in his arm was nothing compared to the torment in his heart. "That's not true, Jesse. I do need you."

"As part of your cover," she said scornfully. "As part of your lie."

"No, sweetheart. As my wife. That part of my life is over. I couldn't go back if I wanted to. I don't even know the person I was back then."

A flicker of something that looked like hope passed through Jessica's eyes, then she lowered them. She shook her head. "I don't want you to come home with Max and me tonight, Pierce."

Pierce felt as if he'd taken another bullet, this one in the gut. "Why?" was all he said.

Jessica closed her eyes and took a deep breath. "You know why. Do you know what went through my mind when I saw Max lying on the ground just now? I thought he was dead. I thought our son was dead, and that you were responsible."

"I know," Pierce said softly. "I was thinking the same thing."

"But you're used to this sort of thing," Jessica said, reluctantly meeting his gaze. The look in her eyes tore Pierce up inside. She was closing him out of her life again, this time for good. "I can't live like this, Pierce. I can't. God knows when I'll even be able to sleep again, much less let Max out of my sight. It's too much happening too soon. I need some time to sort it all out. I need some space."

"How much time?"

Jessica shook her head, her expression resolute. "I don't know."

"You gave me a month," Pierce reminded her grimly. "You said thirty days."

"In that case, my timing is perfect," Jessica said with tears glistening in her eyes. "Because your thirty days ended today."

And so, just like that, it was over. Pierce had been debriefed in Langley, and slowly but surely all the pieces of the puzzle began coming together. Most of what Walker had told him was true, but what Walker hadn't known was that for some time Brandon Chambers had been on to him. He just couldn't prove his suspicions. It was Chambers who finally negotiated Pierce's release, but after the explosion aboard the boat—arranged by Walker, they suspected— Pierce had disappeared again.

When he'd turned up in Miami, Chambers had traced the passport he was using to a man—a doctor—living on a small island in the Caribbean. Evidently Pierce had washed up on shore after the explosion, near death, and when he'd finally regained consciousness, his memory was gone.

For months, as Pierce recovered physically, snatches of his memory began returning. He dreamed about Jessica and the life he'd had with her in Edgewood. As the anniversary of the day he'd disappeared approached, Pierce experienced an almost overwhelming sense of urgency. He knew there was somewhere he had to be, someone he had to protect.

Dr. Morales helped him forge a passport and gave him money to return to the States. From Miami, guided by his inner compulsion, Pierce managed to find his way back to Virginia, to Edgewood, and finally to the grocery store where he'd been headed five years ago. And then everything had clicked back into place for him. Everything except for the five years he'd been imprisoned.

Pierce remembered it all now. All the horrors, the despair, the intense longing for Jesse, for the son he had never seen. Everything Jessica had suffered for so many years, Pierce suffered now. He understood more than ever what she had gone through, and why she felt she had to protect herself from him. Pierce didn't blame her one damn bit. He'd put her through hell, and just because he'd suffered too, it didn't make what he'd done to her acceptable. But the facts didn't make her rejection any easier to take.

He was in Langley at CIA headquarters for three days, and at the end of that time, he walked out a free man. He'd tendered his resignation, the lies were over, and now it was time to start building a new life for himself. Pierce took a deep, cleansing breath.

But first there was something he had to do. Another part of his past he had to put to rest.

* * *

Jay Greene eyed Pierce's outstretched hand warily. He was wearing his uniform, and his attitude was very stiff and unyielding. Pierce wondered briefly if their antagonism toward one another had been the natural distrust that often sprang up between the military and civilians.

"You don't owe me anything," he said gruffly, but he accepted Pierce's handshake, anyway.

"You saved my life," Pierce said.

"You'd have done the same for me."

Their eyes met, and at that moment, Pierce realized that his brother-in-law was right. No matter how strong the animosity between them had always been, they were still family. Their love for Jessica bonded them together in spite of their feelings about each other.

"I always knew there was something suspicious about your activities," Jay admitted. "But I never could find out anything. That made me doubt you even more."

"You had good reason," Pierce said grimly.

"I only wanted what was best for my sister. I didn't want to see her hurt."

Pierce didn't blame Jay for the accusation in his tone. He said simply, "I've always loved her. That hasn't changed."

"Then what are you going to do about it?" Jay demanded.

"I don't know," Pierce said. "I don't know if there is anything I can do about it."

Jay scowled his disapproval. "That's what I've always disliked about you damned CIA spooks. You guys can't tell your butts from a hole in the ground. You couldn't make a decision—"

Pierce didn't wait to hear the rest. He just shook his head, grinned and walked off.

* * *

"When's Dad coming home?" Max asked again. Jessica had lost count of how many times she'd heard that question in the past week. She watched her son as he sat slumped in the lawn chair, idly dangling his legs. He scowled deeply. "It's boring around here without him."

Jessica had to agree. A week without Pierce and the house had taken on the atmosphere of a tomb. She couldn't even muster up enough strength to work on the game room upstairs, and even the downstairs wore an uncharacteristic clutter. It was funny, but suddenly she'd lost the desire for a neat and orderly existence. She took a strange sort of comfort in leaving the dishes in the sink a little too long or letting the beds go unmade all day.

She hadn't even bothered to comb her hair since she'd gotten up this morning, Jessica realized, blowing away the bangs from her forehead. Much less put on lipstick. There was no one around to see her, anyway, except Max, and he seemed to be suffering from the same lethargy that gripped her. They both missed Pierce.

So call him, Jessica told herself. Call him and tell him you've changed your mind. Tell him how empty you feel without him. Tell him you like the excitement he brings to your life. Tell him that you need him. Desperately.

But instead, Jessica sat on the terrace and did nothing. What could she do? She didn't even know how to get in touch with Pierce. He'd only called once in the past week and then only to talk to Max. He hadn't even asked to speak to her.

It took Jessica a long time to admit just how much that had hurt her. She'd told him that night in the woods that she needed time to sort out her feelings, but it had only taken her one night without Pierce to know that she wanted him back in her life. More than anything.

But he was gone now. And for all Jessica knew, he wasn't coming back.

She took a deep breath and tried to quell the fresh batch of tears brought on by that thought.

"What's that noise?" Max asked, stilling his legs. He sat up and listened. "It sounds like a dog!" he cried excitedly. Before Jessica could say a word, he shot past her like a bullet, rounded the corner of the house, and headed toward the front yard.

Jessica jumped up and hurried after him. She didn't like the idea of a strange dog hanging around the neighborhood. "Max, wait!" But he had already disappeared through the back gate, heading for the street.

Jessica ran through the gate and hurried around the house. Then she stopped at the sight that greeted her in the front yard. A shiny red 'Vette was parked in the driveway, and Max was down on his knees in the grass, laughing wildly as a puppy, a little black-and-white mutt, avidly licked his face.

Jessica's gaze went from Max and the dog to the man standing near the front porch steps, watching them. Pierce immediately got a defensive look on his face. "Now, I know what you're going to say, Jessica."

No, you don't, she thought. You have no idea.

"But I found him on the side of the road. Someone had dumped him, and he had nowhere to go. I guess I sort of felt a kinship with him," Pierce said apologetically. "I couldn't just leave him there."

"No, you couldn't," Jessica agreed, smiling.

"I've already taken him to the vet's. He's had his shots and everything. I thought maybe I could keep him at my place, and Max could visit him there whenever he wanted."

Jessica's heart stopped. *His* place?

"You've . . . found a place to live?" she asked. Her heart had started beating again at an awfully painful rate.

Pierce shrugged. "Not yet," he admitted. "But I'm sure I will."

"I know where there's a vacancy," Jessica said quickly, admiring her nerve.

Pierce gave her a strange glance. "Oh?" he asked noncommittally. "Is the rent reasonable?"

"Very. And there are lots of fringe benefits."

His jaw dropped, and Jessica almost laughed out loud. He took a step toward her. "Are you saying what I think you're saying?"

"Come home, Pierce," she whispered. "We need you so."

He closed the distance between them in no more than three strides. Jessica fell into his arms, and he held her close, kissing her eyelids and her nose and her mouth. Jessica's laughter mingled with her son's.

"I know I've made a lot of mistakes in the past," he said, his hand in her hair. "But, Jesse, I'll spend the rest of my life trying to make it up to you. I have my priorities straight now, sweetheart, and it feels good. It feels really good. My family is the most important thing in the world to me now."

"To me, too," she whispered. "Just don't ever leave me."

"Never again," he promised. "I'm here for as long as you'll have me."

She lifted her face for his kiss, and as their lips joined, sealing the vow, Jessica heard her son whooping with laughter.

"Hey, Mom," he yelled. "Krypto just went to the bathroom on my new shoe."

* * * * *

Dark secrets, dangerous desire...

Lovers
DARK AND DANGEROUS

Three spine-tingling tales from the dark side of love.

This October, enter the world of shadowy romance as Silhouette presents the third in their annual tradition of thrilling love stories and chilling story lines. Written by three of Silhouette's top names:

LINDSAY McKENNA
LEE KARR
RACHEL LEE

Haunting a store near you this October.

MILLION DOLLAR SWEEPSTAKES (III)

No purchase necessary. To enter, follow the directions published. Method of entry may vary. For eligibility, entries must be received no later than March 31, 1996. No liability is assumed for printing errors, lost, late or misdirected entries. Odds of winning are determined by the number of eligible entries distributed and received. Prizewinners will be determined no later than June 30, 1996.

Sweepstakes open to residents of the U.S. (except Puerto Rico), Canada, Europe and Taiwan who are 18 years of age or older. All applicable laws and regulations apply. Sweepstakes offer void wherever prohibited by law. Values of all prizes are in U.S. currency. This sweepstakes is presented by Torstar Corp., its subsidiaries and affiliates, in conjunction with book, merchandise and/or product offerings. For a copy of the Official Rules send a self-addressed, stamped envelope (WA residents need not affix return postage) to: MILLION DOLLAR SWEEPSTAKES (III) Rules, P.O. Box 4573, Blair, NE 68009, USA.

EXTRA BONUS PRIZE DRAWING

No purchase necessary. The Extra Bonus Prize will be awarded in a random drawing to be conducted no later than 5/30/96 from among all entries received. To qualify, entries must be received by 3/31/96 and comply with published directions. Drawing open to residents of the U.S. (except Puerto Rico), Canada, Europe and Taiwan who are 18 years of age or older. All applicable laws and regulations apply; offer void wherever prohibited by law. Odds of winning are dependent upon number of eligibile entries received. Prize is valued in U.S. currency. The offer is presented by Torstar Corp., its subsidiaries and affiliates in conjunction with book, merchandise and/or product offering. For a copy of the Official Rules governing this sweepstakes, send a self-addressed, stamped envelope (WA residents need not affix return postage) to: Extra Bonus Prize Drawing Rules, P.O. Box 4590, Blair, NE 68009, USA.

SWP-S994

MONTANA Mavericks

Stories that capture living and loving beneath the Big Sky, where legends live on...and the mystery is just beginning.

This October, discover more MONTANA MAVERICKS with

SLEEPING WITH THE ENEMY
by Myrna Temte

Seduced by his kiss, she almost forgot he was her enemy. *Almost.*

And don't miss a minute of the loving as the mystery continues with:

THE ONCE AND FUTURE WIFE
by Laurie Paige (November)
THE RANCHER TAKES A WIFE
by Jackie Merritt (December)
OUTLAW LOVERS
by Pat Warren (January)
and many more!

Wait, there's more! Win a trip to a Montana mountain resort. For details, look for this month's MONTANA MAVERICKS title at your favorite retail outlet.

Only from **V** *Silhouette*® where passion lives.

HE'S AN

AMERICAN HERO

They're back! Those amazing men whose heroic spirits inspire passion and pride in the hearts of women everywhere. And they're yours for the reading.

In October: NIGHT SMOKE by Nora Roberts— Rugged arson inspector Ryan Piasecki wasn't prepared for the blaze of desire that coolly beautiful Natalie Fletcher ignited in him. But he was more than ready to deal with the vengeful arsonist hot on Natalie's heels.

In November: CALLAGHAN'S WAY by Marie Ferrarella— Kirk Callaghan had returned home in search of peace, but he soon found himself playing surrogate dad to Rachel Reed's son—and playing for keeps with her heart.

In December: LOVING EVANGELINE by Linda Howard— Robert Cannon had vowed to destroy the thief who'd stolen classified information from his company. But when the trail led to beautiful Evie Shaw, Robert found both his resolve—and his heart—melting fast.

AMERICAN HEROES: Men who give all they've got for their country, their work—the women they love.

Only from

INTIMATE MOMENTS®

™ Silhouette®

IMHER010

Return to the classic plot lines you love, with

In October, Justine Davis delivers LEFT AT THE ALTAR, IM #596, her telling twist on the ever-popular "jilted" story line.

Sean Holt had never forgotten the pain and humiliation of being jilted five years ago. Yet runaway bride Aurora Sheridan had had her reasons—dangerous reasons that had just turned deadly.

And there will be more ROMANTIC TRADITIONS titles coming your way in the new year, starting in January 1995 with Beverly Barton's THE OUTCAST, a bad-boy book you won't want to miss. So come back to the classics—only in